call *it* what *you* want

call *it*
what
you want

BRIGID KEMMERER

BLOOMSBURY

NEW YORK LONDON OXFORD NEW DELHI SYDNEY

BLOOMSBURY YA
Bloomsbury Publishing Inc., part of Bloomsbury Publishing Plc
1385 Broadway, New York, NY 10018

BLOOMSBURY and the Diana logo are trademarks of Bloomsbury Publishing Plc

First published in the United States of America in June 2019
by Bloomsbury YA

Text copyright © 2019 by Brigid Kemmerer

Bloomsbury books may be purchased for business or promotional use. For information on
bulk purchases please contact Macmillan Corporate and Premium Sales Department at
specialmarkets@macmillan.com

Library of Congress Cataloging-in-Publication Data
Names: Kemmerer, Brigid, author.
Title: Call it what you want / by Brigid Kemmerer.
Description: New York : Bloomsbury, 2019.
Summary: Once-popular Rob and overachiever Maegan, both dealing with
serious family issues, quickly form a bond that is threatened when Rob confides
plans to repair damage his father caused.
Identifiers: LCCN 2018045398 (print) | LCCN 2018051477 (e-book)
ISBN 978-1-68119-809-5 (hardcover) • ISBN 978-1-68119-811-8 (e-book)
Subjects: | CYAC: Family problems—Fiction. | High schools—Fiction. | Schools—
Fiction. | Conduct of life—Fiction. | Embezzlement—Fiction. | Fathers and sons—
Fiction. | People with disabilities—Fiction. | Pregnancy—Fiction.
Classification: LCC PZ7.K3052 Cal 2019 (print) | LCC PZ7.K3052 (e-book) |
DDC [Fic]—dc23
LC record available at https://lccn.loc.gov/2018045398

Book design by Jeanette Levy
Typeset by Westchester Publishing Services
Printed and bound in the U.S.A. by Berryville Graphics Inc., Berryville, Virginia
2 4 6 8 10 9 7 5 3 1

To find out more about our authors and books visit
www.bloomsbury.com and sign up for our newsletters.

call *it*
what
you want

CHAPTER ONE

Rob

I eat breakfast with my father every morning.

Well, I eat. He sits in his wheelchair and stares in whichever direction Mom has pointed him. If I'm lucky, all his drool stays in his mouth. If he's lucky, the sunlight doesn't fall across his eyes.

Today, neither of us is very lucky.

I'm blasting alternative rock, the volume turned as loud as I can tolerate. He hated this music when he had the cognitive ability to care. I have no idea whether he can hear it now.

I like to imagine he can.

"Rob!" Mom bellows from upstairs, where she's getting ready for work. She never used to bellow.

She never used to have a job before, either.

It's been a great year.

"Rob!" she calls again.

I stare across the table at Robert Lachlan Sr. and shove a spoonful of cereal into my mouth. "You think she's talking to me or to you?"

A drop of saliva forms a circular mark on his shirt.

"What?" I yell back.

"Turn that down, please!"

"Okay."

I don't.

Until last spring, I never knew there was a right way and a wrong way to kill yourself. If you put a gun to your temple and pull the trigger, it's possible to survive.

It's also possible to miss and blow half your face off, but luckily Dad didn't do that. I'm not sure I could sit across the table from him if that had happened.

It's bad enough now. Especially knowing what he did *before* he tried to commit suicide. That's worse than all of it.

The suicide, I can kind of understand.

Mom says it's important for Dad to know I'm here. I'm not sure why. My presence isn't going to magically reconnect the neurons that will let him walk and talk and interact again.

If I could get my hands on a magic wand that would put him back together, I'd do it.

That sounds altruistic. I'm not. I'm selfish.

A year ago, we had everything.

Now we have nothing.

The living, breathing reason is sitting at the other end of the table.

I get up and turn off the music. "I'm leaving!" I call.

"Have a good day at school," Mom calls back.

Like that'll happen.

CHAPTER TWO

Maegan

My sister is throwing up in the bathroom. It's awesome.

I want to offer help, tissues or water or something, but I tried yesterday, and she snapped at me.

Mom says it's the hormones. Maybe she's right, though Samantha has never been someone people would call *nice*. If she's on your side, you're her best friend. If she's not, look out.

When Samantha left for college, half the cops at Dad's precinct threw her a party. It's not often that blue-collar kids go to an Ivy League school—on a full lacrosse scholarship, no less.

It's not often they come back pregnant, either.

There's a small, dark part of me that's glad I'm not the troublemaker, this time.

Another part of me squashes the thought and shoves it away. That's not fair to my sister. Unlike her, I've always been someone people call nice.

Well, until last spring, when people started calling me *cheater.*

The toilet flushes. Water runs. A minute later, Sam's door closes quietly.

Mom appears in my doorway. She's in a bathrobe, a towel wound high on her head. Her voice is soft. "Dad says he can drive you to school, if you're ready now."

"Almost."

"I'll let him know." She hesitates in the doorway. "Maegan . . . about your sister's condition—"

"You mean the baby?" I study my reflection in the mirror, wondering if the ponytail is a mistake. My fair skin looks pale and washed-out already. Besides, the first day of November has brought freezing temperatures, and my homeroom class has a cracked window.

She eases into the room and closes the door. "Yes. The baby."

I wonder if Samantha had hoped to keep the pregnancy a secret, even from our parents. She was already planning to come home this weekend, so her appearance wasn't unexpected. I just don't think she'd planned on walking in the door, hugging Mom, and then throwing up on her feet.

Even that might have been explainable, but then Sam burst into tears.

Mom's not an idiot.

Then again, Mom and Sam have always been close. Sam probably would have told her anyway. Just without the projectile vomiting. I reach for a colorful scarf. "What about it?"

"Your sister doesn't want anyone to know yet." Mom wrings her hands. "She's only ten weeks pregnant, so she's trying . . . she's trying to decide what to do." A pause. I wonder if my mother can't bring herself to say the word *abortion*. "I'm asking you to respect her wishes."

I pull on a denim jacket over my sweater. "I won't tell anyone."

"Maegan, your sister deserves your compassion."

"Mom. No one talks to me. Who would I tell?"

"Rachel?"

My best friend. I hesitate.

Mom's eyes almost fall out of her head. "*Maegan*. Did you tell her already?"

"No! No. Of course not."

"You know your father doesn't want gossip."

That makes me pause. I don't want to let Dad down. Well, I don't want to let him down *again*. "I won't say anything."

"Not to *anyone*, Maegan." Her gaze turns steely. "I need to know we can count on you."

I flinch. Dad honks the horn out front.

I grab my backpack. "I need to go."

"Be good!" she calls after me.

She says it every time I leave the house.

I used to say, "I always am," but that's not true anymore.

Instead, I say, "I'll try," and I let the door slam behind me.

CHAPTER THREE

Rob

The front entrance to Eagle Forge High School is packed with students. Bodies everywhere. They crowd the concrete quad out in front of the doors, they shove their way through the narrow foyer, they slam lockers and fill every available space until the last possible minute. Once upon a time, I would stride across the parking lot and those bodies would part like the Red Sea. Everyone knew me. Everyone wanted to be me.

Now? No one wants to be Rob Lachlan Jr.

Not even me.

I don't go in through the front. That's Connor Tunstall's turf now. He'll be leaning against the round concrete platform that holds the flagpole, telling a risqué story about whatever he did over the weekend. A Starbucks cup will be sitting next to him—a tall dirty chai—and it's overcast, so sunglasses will be hanging from a button hole of his vintage bomber jacket. He's got blond hair with a couple of random brown patches, as well as mismatched eyes: one blue, one brown. Around here, quirky looks could throw you to the bottom of the social pile or spit you out on top. His family's got serious money, so you can guess where Connor ended up. He plays lacrosse—even has a private coach—so he's built like someone you don't want to mess with.

God, I sound obsessed with him. I'm not.

He used to be my best friend.

Connor got the quad in the breakup, I guess. His dad got a legal settlement.

My dad got a subpoena—and later, a self-delivered bullet to the frontal lobe.

And here we are, eight months later.

I park in the side lot and walk halfway around the school with the bitter November wind eating through my parka, then slink in through the back entrance by the library. It's the very definition of "the long way," because my first class is near the front, but I don't mind the walk, and I certainly don't mind the solitude.

I have books to return anyway, so I peek through the windows along the wall. The librarian isn't there, so I slip through the doors. We're supposed to wait for someone to check the books in—some kind of accountability thing, I guess—but I always leave mine. I'd rather pay ten bucks for a paperback that goes missing than deal with Mr. London.

The air pressure seems to change in the library, as if even the books demand a special kind of quiet. I stride silently across the carpet and slide two hardcovers onto the gray Formica counter, then turn to slip away.

"Mr. Lachlan."

Damn.

I stop. Turn. Mr. London is coming out of the storeroom behind the counter. He's wiping his hands on a napkin, clearly still chewing whatever he was eating. He's lean and wiry and pushing sixty. He's wearing a black polo shirt with tiny colorful stitching along the edge of the sleeves, which doesn't do his sallow skin any favors.

"I'll check those in for you," he says, sliding the books toward his computer as if I weren't halfway to the door.

He doesn't meet my eyes.

I don't try to meet his. I don't actually know if his comment was a request for me to stay and wait while he pushes buttons on his keyboard or more of a dismissal, but in the span of time it takes me to think about it, I've already stood here too long.

Now it's awkward.

He scans the bar codes on the back of each book. They're high fantasy, and they hit the circulation desk with a *thunk* as he sets each one down. "What did you think of these?"

What does he want, a recommendation? *They were life changing. I stayed up all night reading.*

I actually did do that. My social life is nonexistent.

But then I realize his question was automatic. Every time we interact, it's as awkward for him as it is for me. He probably feels some kind of obligation to treat me with practiced courtesy, as if my family wouldn't simply rob him of his life savings; we'd go after his job, too.

I shrug and study a poster about Edgar Allan Poe. "They were fine."

"Just fine? Neal tore through them."

Neal is his husband. He's a retired teacher from somewhere else in the county. Mr. London was supposed to retire last year, too, but they trusted my dad with their retirement accounts.

Every cent was long gone before Dad got caught.

I clear my throat. "I've got to get to first period."

That's crap, and he knows it. The bell won't ring for another twenty minutes.

"Go ahead," he says. "These are in."

I bolt like I'm guilty of a crime. I can feel his eyes on my back as I go.

I wonder if it would be better if I had a reputation for hating my father. If I hadn't spent school holidays interning in his office. If he hadn't shown up for every lacrosse game, throwing his arm across my shoulders to crow about his boy's skills on the field.

Unfortunately, I didn't hate him. And afterward, I heard every whisper.

Did Rob know? He had to know.

I didn't know.

CHAPTER FOUR

Maegan

Dad drops me off in his police cruiser, as usual. I wish he'd do it around back, where kids won't see me climb out of the black-and-white sedan, but he thinks people won't mess with his little girl if they know her dad's a cop.

He's right. No one messes with me. No one really *talks* to me.

It has nothing to do with the fact that he's a cop.

It has everything to do with the fact that I got caught cheating on the SAT last year—and a hundred kids' scores were invalidated.

Dad reaches over to give my shoulder a squeeze. "Have a good day now, sweetheart." His voice is deep and rumbly. A good cop voice. "Text me if you need someone to pick you up, okay?"

"Okay." I lean over to kiss his cheek as his radio starts squawking codes. He smells like soap and menthol. "Love you, Daddy." But he's already reaching for his radio.

Then I'm out in the cold, and his cruiser is pulling away.

The first bell doesn't ring for another fifteen minutes, and it's cold as crap on the quad, but the concrete is still crowded with students who have no desire to start their school day early. Most of them are debasing themselves to Connor Tunstall, who's leaning against the flag stand, talking about some party over the weekend.

"Seriously," he's saying. "They couldn't even get the keg down the stairs between the two of them. I ended up carrying it myself."

"All by yourself?" his groupies chorus, fluttering around him. "Can you pick me up? I bet you can't pick me and Sarah up at the same time."

He grins at them. "Come here. Let's see."

Ugh. I would have no time for a guy like that. He and Rob Lachlan used to run the school, until Rob's dad got caught embezzling from his clients and tried to blow his head off. Now Connor's the only one sitting on the throne. I have no idea what happened to Rob. He's like a ghost now, flickering from class to class. We have AP Calculus together or I wouldn't know he went to school at all.

My best friend, Rachel, peels herself away from the fringe of the crowd and attaches herself to my side. She waits for me every morning, even though I've told her she doesn't have to. Most of the drama died down before school let out last year.

Back then, I could barely walk across the quad without getting spit on. You don't invalidate a hundred kids' SAT scores without a few repercussions.

Rachel is one of the few people who stuck by me after I got in trouble. It's hard to be part of the brainiac crowd when everyone thinks you cheated your way in. Rachel and I have been friends practically since birth, so I know she'll always have my back.

She links her arm through mine, though she's really too tall for it to be comfortable. Her dad's this hulking, blond, Nordic-looking cop, while her mom is a tiny, round, second-generation Mexican. So Rachel has light brown skin and curly dark hair, combined with a stocky build and broad shoulders, and a height that tops five foot eleven. She's taller than most of the guys in the junior class and prettier than most of the girls.

"Do you think Connor Tunstall stands in front of a mirror flexing every morning?" she says.

"Are you kidding? He probably takes a daily selfie."

She giggles and pulls at the front door. "How's Sam feeling?"

My heart freezes in my chest. Mom's warning is an echo in my head. "What?"

"You said she was sick Friday night."

Right. I did say that. Rachel and I were supposed to go to the movies, but then Sam walked in the door and threw up. "Oh. Yeah. She's fine. Food poisoning."

It sounds like I'm lying. I don't know if it's from being a cop's daughter or what, but I'm a terrible liar. That's why I folded when they accused me of cheating last April. Rachel's going to call me on it, and I'm going to dump the truth on her feet.

But she doesn't call me on it. She doesn't even give me a funny look, just accepts it at face value and tows me toward her locker.

Somehow that's worse.

Her boyfriend, Drew, is waiting when we get there. He's tall, with deep brown skin and eyes, and he's built like a linebacker, which makes sense since he plays football. His parents own an upscale restaurant at the edge of town, and they expect Drew to work most evenings, so between that and football, his grades sometimes pay the price.

I've known Drew since grade school, but he and Rachel have only been going out since midsummer, when he drunk dialed her to profess his love. I can think of more romantic overtures, but she didn't seem to mind. I personally think he's a little abrasive, but he's good to Rachel. She's been such a good friend to me that I want to be able to return the favor.

He grabs Rachel by the waist and gives her a sloppy kiss.

I sigh. Rachel giggles.

I can probably be a good friend without watching an exchange of fluids. "I need to get to math," I say breezily, turning away.

"Eyes on your own paper, okay?" Drew calls behind me. Then he cracks up.

Rachel hushes him, but it's too late.

I already heard.

CHAPTER FIVE

Rob

Time for calculus. Let the learning begin.

I'm actually pretty good at math. I'm good at most of my classes. When Dad was a bigwig—or, really, *pretending* to be a bigwig, if you want to split hairs—he insisted on it. You can't brag about your son being at the top of his class if he isn't actually there. I'm not number one or anything, but I'm in the top twenty-five. I used to be in the top fifty, but that was when I had a social life and money for lacrosse. Now I've got nothing to do, so it's late-night fantasy novels and homework.

There was a time when I would have mocked a kid like me.

What's Nelson doing at this party? Isn't he supposed to be at home waiting on his acceptance letter from Hogwarts?

The joke would have been on me. *Harry Potter* isn't too bad a read.

Sometimes I wish I'd gone to a private school. Not because I'm a snob—though I probably was, if I want to get technical. But no: when Dad got caught and our assets were frozen, I would have had to quit a private school. I would have been able to switch to a public school where no one knew me.

But also no. It's been public school all the way. Dad wanted people to know we were a part of the *community*. Not too good for public school, no sir.

Everyone can be a millionaire! You just have to invest wisely with good ol' Rob Lachlan Sr.

Seriously. He had commercials. There are fraud parodies all over YouTube.

It's probably a miracle we got to keep our house. That was titled in my mom's name alone, so it wasn't seized when everything else was. I don't know if Dad planned ahead or what, but we weren't out on the street.

Mom had to go back to work, though. They fought about that. Before he pulled the trigger.

I remember the arguments. She screamed that we had a $5,000 painting on the wall, but we didn't have money for groceries. The bank accounts were frozen. Their credit cards were frozen. He kept assuring her it would all blow over.

It's okay, Carolyn. It's fine. It's a misunderstanding. Please, honey. You'll see.

Oh yeah. We saw. In a spray of red all over the den wall.

So. Calculus.

Our teacher's name is Mrs. Quick. She's fine. Nothing special. Khakis and T-shirts, olive skin, straight brown hair, rectangular glasses. She might be thirty, she might be forty, I have no idea. She doesn't take any crap, but she doesn't give any, either. Some teachers have colorful classrooms with lots of flair and decoration, but hers is sparse, with mostly blank walls, except for a few bulletin boards sporting equations in black and white. Even her desk is neat and orderly, with papers kept in a locked drawer. The only hint of quirk or attitude lies in the clock over the white board: the numbers have been replaced with equations, like the square root of four in place of the two.

I like her class because everyone shuts up and works. I don't need to interact.

And then I realize she's saying, ". . . like you to find a partner for a group project that we'll be working on over the next two weeks. Some work will be done outside the classroom, so you'll need to be able to meet outside of school."

I quickly scan the room. Students are scrambling to change seats and partner up. Outside of my corner, there's a lot of giggling and fist bumping.

Maybe there's an odd number of kids in here, and I'll be able to do this independently.

No. Wait. Maybe Mrs. Quick would make me form a trio. That's worse.

I look out over the class again. Everyone seems to be settling into partners.

My breathing quickens. Like in the library, I've been sitting here too long spinning my wheels. I need to talk to Mrs. Quick. Maybe she'll take pity on me.

Maegan Day is already talking to her. I barely know Maegan, but she's the only other student not scrambling to pair up. She got into trouble for cheating on the SAT last year, but I don't know the details. I was buried too deeply in my own family's mess.

I know her dad, though. He was the first cop to question us when Mom called nine-one-one.

Mrs. Quick looks up. "Does everyone have a partner? Maegan needs a partner."

The room quiets. No one says anything. Including me.

I hear someone mutter, "Cheater's gonna cheat."

"I can do the project independently," Maegan says quickly. She sounds like this is what she's hoping for. We have that in common.

Mrs. Quick turns back to her. "I'd like this to be done in teams. Find a group and join them, please. Three will be fine."

That means she'll assign me to a group, too.

I clear my throat. "I need a partner."

I might as well be saying, *I need a colonoscopy.*

"Thank you, Rob," says Mrs. Quick. "Maegan, go ahead."

Maegan hesitates, then turns. She returns to her desk and sits down.

There is an empty desk beside me—because I sit in the farthest back corner of the room. My preferred spot unless a teacher assigns seats. Maegan could have grabbed her things and moved back here.

But there's an empty desk beside her, too, because the front row is rarely a favorite.

I don't want to move.

She doesn't want to move.

Mrs. Quick doesn't suffer fools. "Rob, please move beside Maegan so you can start the assignment together."

I shove my book into my backpack and shuffle to the front row.

CHAPTER SIX

Maegan

We've been sitting here for twenty minutes, listening to Mrs. Quick spell out the details of our assignment, and Rob Lachlan hasn't even looked at me. It's bad enough that teachers give me the side-eye. I don't need it from him, too.

Cheater's gonna cheat. I don't know who said it, but I wonder if it was him. He sure doesn't look happy to be my partner. His hair is kind of longish on top, and unkempt, hanging into his eyes like his mother needs to remind him to get a haircut. He won't make eye contact, and we've never been friends, so I have no idea what color his eyes are. A few freckles dust his pale cheeks, like the remnants of a summer tan that just won't let go. He's wearing a black, long-sleeved Under Armour shirt that clings to his frame.

His life might suck, and he might have been ejected from his social circles, but he's still a back-of-the-class jock.

And I'm still me.

Mrs. Quick is outlining our project, which actually sounds interesting—choosing objects to drop from different heights and trying to calculate their bounce and trajectory—but I keep covertly studying the boy next to me.

He's taking sparse notes. Keeping his eyes on his paper. Looking like he'd rather be anywhere else.

When the bell rings, he jams his things into his backpack. Still no acknowledgment that I'm his partner.

When I got caught cheating, people made this kind of broad assumption that I was going to turn into a total slacker. I didn't, but I wonder if that's the problem here.

"Hey," I say to him.

He jerks at the zipper. His head lifts a fraction of an inch. "Hey, what?"

"I really care about my grades. You can't slack off on this."

His hands go still. His voice turns lethally quiet, and I expect a dig, but instead, he says, "I have an A in this class. Figure out what you want me to do and I'll do it."

I follow him out. "Why didn't you answer Mrs. Quick when she asked about a partner?"

"What?"

I can barely hear him over the cacophony of students in the hallway, but I can't let this go. I need to head the other direction, toward Honors English, but I dog him through the pack of students. "When she asked if anyone still needed a partner, you didn't say anything."

"So what?"

I want to hear him say it. I want him to admit it. "You *knew* she was asking for me. If you don't want to be my partner, just say so."

"I don't want to be your partner."

I stop short in the hallway. He says it so . . . *evenly.* Without emotion. Without looking at me. Without even stopping. It's worse than a dismissive glance. This is a statement of fact.

I don't want to be your partner.

I feel like he's slugged me in the chest. I can't move. The worst part is that I asked for it. Literally.

While I'm standing there trying to recover, he slips between students and vanishes like a ghost.

At lunch, Rachel and I split a salad in the cafeteria. She and I don't have any morning classes together, so it's my first chance to whine about Rob Lachlan.

"Skip the project," she says to me. "Refuse to do it."

"Yeah, okay." I stab at the lettuce. "I *need* this grade. We don't all have a college fund waiting for us."

She jabs at a cherry tomato. "How is that my fault?"

"Nothing is your fault." I sigh, irritated, though I can't really parse out *why.* Maybe it's Drew's comments this morning; maybe it's Rob's. I probably shouldn't be taking it out on her, though.

"What are we talking about?" Drew swings a leg over the bench on Rachel's side of the table and drops down beside her. His tray is loaded with two burgers, a bowl of broccoli, a cup of yogurt, and two bags of chips.

She scoots closer to him until she can rest her head on his shoulder. Drew drops a kiss on the top of her head, then peels the lid off a yogurt and licks the bottom of it.

They're adorable. And disgusting.

Now that she's snuggled up against him, Rachel's sobered. "Maegan's been assigned to work with the class felon."

Drew shovels yogurt into his mouth and follows her gaze. "Rob Lachlan?"

"Yeah." She's staring into the far corner of the cafeteria, where Rob is sitting alone at a round table. He's eating a sandwich from a brown paper bag, a thick paperback cracked open on the table in front of him. He didn't strike me as a reader, but he didn't strike me as a guy who'd be carrying an A in AP Calculus, either. I actually always thought he was the kind of kid whose grades were boosted thanks to his parents' donations to the school—or maybe his prowess on the lacrosse field.

"His dad stole seven million dollars," I say. "Not him."

"That we know of," says Rachel.

She sounds callous, but about six tables over from Rob sits Owen Goettler, a kid whose single mom never had very much money at all, then lost what little she had left to Rob's father. He's got smooth, cream-colored skin that's blemish-free, which might be enviable if not for the lank brown hair that hangs to his collar. Owen is eating a plain cheese sandwich—what they give to the kids who can't afford lunch. His entire house could probably fit in Rob's living room.

Rob doesn't have a plate of delicacies in front of him, but he has more than a slice of cheese between two pieces of bread. I feel like they should be forced to switch. Not just food. All of it.

"Just because they couldn't prove it doesn't mean he wasn't in on it," agrees Drew.

Her voice drops. "His dad tried to kill himself."

Drew grunts. "To stay out of prison."

"Didn't your dad interrogate him about the suicide? Or his mom?" Rachel screws up her face. "Or . . . something?"

I go still. I'd forgotten that. Dad doesn't bring a lot of work to the family dinner table, but he does unload on Mom. They're not quiet. Sometimes I eavesdrop.

He did question Rob about the suicide.

That poor kid, he said that night. *He didn't deserve to find that.*

My family is a wasp's nest of tension right now, but finding out your sister is pregnant isn't anywhere close to finding your father after he tried to shoot himself.

I pull a notebook from my backpack and tear a sheet free. Then I write down my name and number and fold it up.

"What are you doing?" says Rachel.

"I'm giving him my number so we can work out a time to do the project." I sigh. "It doesn't matter what he did or what his dad did. I feel like half the teachers in this school are waiting for me to screw up again. It'll be fine. It's math."

Rob doesn't look up when I approach. His eyes stay locked on his book, though there's no way he can't see me standing in front of the table.

I'm tempted to fling the piece of paper at him.

I don't. I slide it next to his book. "Here's my number," I say. "Text me when you want to meet. We can go to your house if you want—"

"I don't." He starts crumpling up his trash and shoving it in the brown paper bag. "We can go to yours."

My house features a surly sister who pukes 24-7. No, thank you. "I don't want to go to my house, either."

"Fine. Whatever." He finally looks at me, his eyes full of

censure, as if I'm the one being difficult. He stuffs the paper with my number on it into his backpack. "We can go to Wegmans and drop stuff from the second floor. I don't care."

He's so hostile. I hesitate, replaying our entire interaction as if I'm somehow missing something. "Look—I know—I know I got into some trouble last spring, but I'm not a cheater. I really do want a good grade. If you have an issue with me, ask Mrs. Quick if you can trade." I pause. "Or I will."

He stands and slings his backpack over his shoulder. His voice is low and rough. "I don't have an issue with you. If you want to trade partners, go ahead."

I'm either losing my mind or this is the slickest gaslighting ever. "After class, you literally said you don't want to be my partner."

He hesitates. His eyes flick upward. He's replaying his words. Then he shakes his head. "I didn't mean you."

"You—what—"

"I didn't mean *you*. I meant I don't want to be partners with anyone."

I'm not sure what to say to that.

Rob must decide I'm done talking. He steps away from the table and tosses his trash into the wastebasket. "So, if you want a new partner, go for it."

I open my mouth. Close it.

And once again, he disappears before I have a clue what I want to say.

CHAPTER SEVEN

Rob

A year ago, I'd buy whatever I wanted for lunch. I didn't even have to carry cash: I had an automatically reloading account, so I could buy anything the cafeteria offered without even thinking about it.

Today, I'm debating whether I want to waste a dollar twenty-five on a bottle of water, or if I should risk the germ-infested water fountain for the rest of the day. There's a five-dollar bill in my wallet, but those don't grow on trees anymore, and I hate taking money from Mom. I hate spending money where anyone can see me. Whether I earn it myself or get it from my mother, I always wonder if people are thinking I'm spending stolen cash.

I mean, I *was*. Once. For so long. I didn't know it, but I was doing it.

But today, I forgot to pack a drink with my lunch, and I'm thirsty.

I grab a bottle from the case by the registers and shuffle into the line. I pull my phone out of my backpack and play a brainless game so I don't need to make eye contact with anyone.

We move in tiny increments, shifting forward with each beep of the register.

"Oh, hey, Rob. Want me to get that for you?"

I know the voice. I snap my head up.

Somehow I've ended up behind Connor. So much for trying to keep my head down.

You'd think his offer was genuine. Warm, even.

It's not. He's being an asshole.

"No," I say flatly. I have no problem meeting his eyes. His father is the one who turned mine in. Hard to have good memories of your best friend's dad when you know he's part of the reason your own dad needs to be fed through a tube.

Connor pulls a twenty out of his wallet. His expression is even, and his voice gives away nothing. "You sure? I've got plenty."

He wants to goad me into a fight. It's tempting, especially because adrenaline is pumping through me. I could put my hands against his chest and give him a good shove. Send him to the ground. Grapple it out. Draw some blood. It would be nice to put all this anger *somewhere*. Especially since Connor has been begging for it.

But there's another part of me that doesn't want to hurt him. There's a part of me that wants his words to be real.

No. It's worse than that. There's a part of me that *misses* him.

I hate that part of me.

When we were fourteen, we had these dirt bikes, and we'd go tearing through the back woods of Herald Harbor. The area gets a lot of rain, and it was always muddy. Once we misjudged a stream crossing, and Connor's wheels got stuck in the mud. He went flying. Sprained his ankle and broke his arm. Compound fracture. The bone came right through the skin. It was the most horrifying thing I've ever seen.

Well. Until last February.

But *then*, it was. He threw up all over himself. Couldn't stop crying and puking.

My cell phone wouldn't find a signal. I remember Connor digging his fingers into my forearm until his nails broke the skin. He was pale and shaking. "Please don't leave me here, Rob. Please don't leave me."

I didn't leave him. I dragged him half a mile until we got a signal.

I thought about that moment a lot after I found my father. After the cops and paramedics were gone, and my house smelled like blood and vomit. How I called Connor, knowing his family hated my family but having no one else to talk to.

He didn't answer the phone.

I left a sobbing message on his voice mail.

He never called me back.

Now he's standing in front of me, giving me a hard time about a stupid bottle of water, while his tray is packed with food.

Maybe I don't miss him at all.

I make my eyes hard. "I've got it."

"Okay, if you're sure." He smirks and turns away, shoving his wallet into his back pocket.

He must not have tucked the cash in all the way, because a ten-dollar bill catches on the edge of his pocket and flutters to the ground, landing right in front of the toe of my sneaker.

I stare at the cash. I wonder if this is a trap. A trick. I don't want to pick it up. If I pick it up, I'm going to have to give it back to him, because I don't want someone to see me snatch it from the ground and shove it in my pocket.

Did you see Rob Lachlan steal ten bucks in the cafeteria? So typical.

Yeah, that's all I need. I've already got Maegan Day on my case because I didn't throw confetti about our assigned partnership.

I grab the money from the ground and twist it between my fingers, then pay for my bottle of water with my own money. Once I have change, I go after Connor.

"Hey," I call. "Connor."

He's made it to the table with our old crowd, but I don't look at any of them. He sets his tray down and turns to look at me, his expression slightly wary, as if he's worried he pushed too far, and I might throw a punch.

A small, dark part of me likes that.

"What?" he says.

"You dropped this." I hold out the money.

He glances at it, then back at my face. The table behind him is quiet. Watching this interaction.

The symbolism isn't lost on me, either.

The moment breaks. His eyes darken. "Keep it," he says flippantly. "Use it to pay your legal bills."

Then he turns away and drops onto the bench at his table. I'm dismissed. None of them are looking at me now.

My fist closes around the money. Hell if I'm going to stand here and demand the chance to return it to him. I wish I hadn't bought the water. I wish I hadn't gotten in line. I wish I didn't have three dollars and seventy-five cents left to get through the week.

I wish I didn't want so desperately to keep this money.

I wish for a lot of things.

None of them come true.

My face burns as I turn away. I head for the far side of the cafeteria. Maegan and her friends are gone. The double doors over here don't lead anywhere I need to be, but I'm not likely to run into anyone I know.

Owen Goettler is still sitting at a table by himself. His mother is one of the dozens of people suing my family. He's pulling his cheese sandwich into minuscule pieces. Trying to make it last, I guess. He's never said a word to me. I've never said a word to him.

I drop the ten dollars in front of him. "Here," I say. "Buy some real food."

Then, before I can hear his response, and before I can change my mind, I blow through the doors of the cafeteria into the empty corridor beyond.

CHAPTER EIGHT

Maegan

When I get home from school, Samantha is in the backyard, a blue lacrosse stick in her hands, flinging balls against the rebounder in the back corner. Her motion is effortlessly fluid, the ball making a clean arc as it sails into the elastic, then springing back to land in the net of her stick. She comes at it from all angles, but no matter where she shoots from, the ball finds its way back to her.

I stand at the sliding back door and watch for a while. She's got a knit cap over her blond hair, the ends pooling in the neck of her royal blue Duke sweatshirt. She's a year older than me, and I remember standing just like this, years ago, watching her practice late into the night, trying to make varsity in her freshman year of high school.

She made varsity. She made it all the way. She was the family star. No matter how hard I tried, I couldn't keep up.

I wonder if she'll lose her scholarship. Keeping that college money is contingent on her *playing*. It's not like they'll give her a pass for the spring tournaments. Might look kind of awkward to have a fully pregnant athlete sprinting across the field.

Watching my sister with a lacrosse stick reminds me of Rob Lachlan. Dad always says that kids aren't responsible for the crimes of their parents—but if he picks up a teenager for committing a crime, he also says it's not hard to see where they learned it. Rob's father stole millions from other families in town. Even if Rob didn't know about it, his father had to have some kind of entitled disregard for everyone else, to be able to steal from people—some people who truly had nothing to lose. That kind of attitude would have to bleed down to his son, right?

I think of his voice when he said, *I don't want to be partners with anyone.*

Disregard? Or something else? I can't tell.

I sigh and unlatch the back door. Samantha doesn't turn. The ball keeps flying to the rebounder and back.

"You look like you're feeling better," I offer.

She says nothing. The ball continues arcing back and forth.

I wonder if I should be feeling badly for Samantha, too. But like Rob, she doesn't make it easy. She's been so snappish since she got home.

Then again, so have I.

"Want me to practice with you?" I'm not as good as she is, but I can play well enough to give her more variety than a stretch of elastic on a frame.

"I don't really want company right now."

Her voice is sharp, with an edge of something I can't figure out. Despite everything that happened between us, she's still my sister. "Are you okay?"

She doesn't answer.

I edge off the steps of the porch and into the crunching leaves of the backyard. "Sam?"

Still nothing. When I reach her side, I see that tears have dried in streaks through her makeup.

My sister rarely cries. She dislocated her shoulder once, and she was barking orders at the paramedics from where she lay on the lacrosse field.

A sudden chill sweeps over me. Mom's voice from this morning, when she said my sister was still trying to decide what to do about the baby.

Did she go get an abortion? Without waiting for anyone to go with her? Mom and Dad are still at work, for god's sake. I've only been gone for six hours.

But that would be so much like Samantha. She would make a decision and execute the plan without any input from anyone else.

"What happened?" I say softly.

"I told you I don't want company," she says. "But I guess no one cares what I want."

"Sam. Do you—do you want me to call Mom?"

"No. God, no." She swipes at her face. But then she says, "David blocked me."

David. So it's got nothing to do with the baby at all. "Who's David?" But as I'm saying the words, I realize I'm being stupid. "Oh. *Oh.*"

Sam glances at me. "Yeah." Another swipe of her cheeks. "He's the father."

I swallow. "He blocked you?"

"Everywhere." The ball flies at the net with a sudden

viciousness. "I can't call him. I can't text him. I'm completely blocked on social media. Blocked."

I have so many questions. "Does he—does he know?"

The ball sails into her net and she stops throwing to look at me with absolute disdain. "Yeah, Maegan. He knows. Come on."

I take a step back. Swallow. "So—did you break up?"

"I don't know. I don't know what's happening." Her voice cracks. "I didn't—I don't know what to do."

"With David?" I hesitate. I know so little of my sister's life lately. She doesn't tell me anything anymore. "Or with the baby?"

"I don't know what to do about any of it." She drops the stick and presses her fingers into her eyes.

"Are you sure you don't want me to get Mom?"

"No." She reacts with surprising venom. "I can't talk to her right now. And Dad—Dad is so disappointed . . ."

I don't know what to do. We used to do everything together. When Samantha first got her driver's license, she'd take me places all the time. The movies. For ice cream. To dinner, where we'd pretend to be adults, having a nice evening out, scraping together stray dollars from our wallets to pay.

We haven't done anything like that in ages. Even Sam distanced herself from me, as if my misdeeds could somehow rub off on her.

My sister is crying full out now, her face in her hands.

I take a breath. "Do you want to go to dinner?"

She slides her hands down. "Really?"

For the first time since she got home on Friday, she sounds vulnerable. Samantha, a girl who's so fierce on the lacrosse field that she earned the nickname "the Jackal."

Rachel and I used to call her "the Dog," but Samantha doesn't need to know that.

"Yeah," I say to her blotchy, tear-streaked face. I reach out and give her arm a squeeze. "Really."

Taco Taco used to be our favorite place when we were kids, but I haven't been here in years. In my memories, the restaurant is large and loud and full of laughter. A place of warmth and love. Walking in the door today, it seems small and cramped, with broken painted tiles on the wall and torn vinyl seats. The warm sense of family is gone, and I wonder if it wasn't part of the restaurant at all, but something we brought with us.

Then again, it's barely five o'clock. The place is nearly empty.

Our server is a boy named Craig. He's cute in the way baby chicks are cute: fluffy and bouncy. He even has orange-blond hair that sticks up from his head in tufts. I'd think it was a dye job, but a tracing of reddish-orange stubble along his jaw tells me it's probably real.

His sky blue eyes keep drifting to Samantha. Shocking.

She's deliberately oblivious. "I'll have the skinny enchiladas," she says, then yawns and hands him the menu. "And a Diet Coke." She never makes eye contact.

"I'll have the chicken flautas." I make sure to look at him, and I appreciate that he's not too busy macking on my sister to meet my gaze. "And a Sprite." I hand over my own menu.

"I'll have those right out," he says.

Samantha rubs her face, then places her hands on the table.

"It's so nice to get out of the house and go somewhere no one knows me."

"I'm pretty sure Craig wants to know you."

Her nose wrinkles. "Who's Craig?"

Typical. "Our waiter."

"Oh. Yeah. I think we graduated together. Whatever." She pulls the elastic out of her hair, and a spill of gold cascades down over her shoulder. She shakes it out.

Craig is standing by the soda machine, and he stares so long that Diet Coke pours over his hand. He swears and moves to wipe it up.

I snort. "Sure looks like *whatever.*"

That wrinkle on her nose turns into a full-on frown. "What are you even talking about?"

Maybe she really is oblivious. "Never mind."

Craig arrives with our drinks and silently unloads them.

My sister barely glances at him.

"Thank you," I say pointedly.

She sips her soda. He walks away.

"You're being kind of rude," I whisper to her.

"I'm pregnant. I'm allowed."

I wonder how often she's going to trot *that* out over the next nine months.

I sip at my Sprite and consider the way I found her crying. I keep my voice low. "So, was David your boyfriend?"

Her expression goes still, and any attitude melts out of her eyes, leaving only sorrow. "I thought he was." A pause. "I thought . . ."

She breaks off and swallows. Her eyes grow misty again.

I want to put my hand over hers, but I'm worried she'd snatch it away. "You thought what?"

"I thought he might one day be more." She sniffs and uses her drink napkin to dab at her eyes. "I fell hard, I guess. I'm so stupid."

"You're not stupid, Sam—"

"I am. I should have stayed focused. I told myself *no boys.* And then I met him and that all went out the window. I can't play like this. Even if I can finish the year in school, they'll never renew my scholarship." She wipes at her eyes again. "I signed a code of conduct. It specifically references impropriety."

I flick my eyes toward the swinging doors that lead to the restaurant kitchen, but Craig is nowhere to be seen now. Regardless, I keep my voice low. "You're allowed to have sex, Samantha."

Her face twists like she's going to burst into tears again, but she catches it and takes a long breath. I've never seen my sister like this, broken and vulnerable. The quiet stretches until I'm not sure whether I'm supposed to say something or she is.

"Were you dating him a long time?" I ask quietly, though I know it couldn't have been *too* long, because she left for college in mid-August.

"Almost three months." Another dab with the napkin.

"Why do you think he blocked you?"

"Why do you think?" she snaps. "Because he doesn't want anything to do with this baby." A long breath. "He says it isn't his. But it is. It has to be."

"He's the only one?"

She wipes at her eyes again. "He's the only one. Ever."

I stop my eyes from growing wide. We used to talk boys, back when we were close, when we'd hide in her room after Mom called for us to turn our lights out. Sam is so fierce and outgoing that I always thought she had half a dozen guys strung around her little finger.

"I worked so hard, you know?" she says. "In high school? I could have had any guy I wanted. I turned them all down. I wanted to be the best. And I was." She presses her fingertips into her eyes and sighs. "And here I threw it all away anyway."

She takes a breath and looks at me over her fingertips. "What would you do?"

I go still. I don't think my sister has ever asked for my opinion. On anything. Even before. Samantha knows what she wants and she goes after it.

Her hands lower from her face. "You don't know either, do you?"

"No," I whisper.

Craig reappears with our food, and Samantha goes silent. He must pick up on the tension, because he unloads the plates silently and slips away. The food is steaming hot, the air full of cilantro.

I push my food around my plate. "Do you want to use my phone to call him?"

Samantha snaps her head up. "What?"

"Well. I mean. I'm not blocked."

She stabs at her food and eats a bite. "That's kind of devious."

I'm not sure if that's an insult. It kind of sounds like one. "That's me," I say flatly. "Nothing but trouble."

She either ignores my sarcasm or she doesn't pick up on it. She holds out a hand to gesture. "Here. Give it to me."

I do. "You're going to call now? In the restaurant?"

"No. I'm going to check his Instagram."

I can't tell if she's serious. But when I lean over, I see she's tapping on the app for Instagram, typing in his name. *@DavidLitMan*

LitMan. Is that a marijuana reference? Or something else?

Samantha stabs her fingers at the phone.

Then she stops. Her face goes pale.

She slams it down on the table and bursts into tears. She's quiet about it, but her shoulders are shaking, her elbows pressed into her abdomen.

I pick up my phone.

The top photo is a man and a woman. Kissing in front of the sun. Streaks of light span the photo. Their eyes are closed. The man has dark hair and a thin beard. The caption reads, *I love you more every day.*

The woman is not Samantha.

"He has a girlfriend," I whisper.

"A wife," she says.

I almost choke on my breath. *A wife.*

Holy crap. "Does Mom know?"

"No!" My sister's eyes turn fierce again, somehow made more threatening by the tears hanging suspended on her lashes. "And you're not going to tell her."

There's been too much in the last hour. My brain can't process all this. "Sure. Okay."

Married.

I don't even know what to do with that. We both sit there breathing, inhaling the steam from our dinner.

Eventually, Samantha picks up her fork and digs in, so I do

the same. We eat in silence for a while, and eventually the tension gives way.

"How old is he?" I ask.

Her voice is nasally from all the crying, but she keeps her voice as low as mine. "Twenty-nine."

I almost choke on my food. Samantha is eighteen, so she's legal, I guess, but that's . . . that's a *man*. A married man.

Then she adds, "He's my literature professor."

DavidLitMan.

Samantha shovels food into her mouth. "Stop staring at me like that." Her voice breaks again. "I know, okay? I was so stupid."

"Samantha." My hand lifts. I want to touch her. To hug her. To help her.

I wish she would tell Mom. But now I understand why she hasn't.

"Stop judging me," she says. "You're not the only one who can screw up, okay?" She's crying again.

I flinch. "I'm not judging you."

"Of course you are. I'm judging mys—" She stops short. Her hand slaps over her mouth.

She jumps up. Runs for the restroom. I can hear her throwing up before the door swings closed.

I stare after her. She's right. I am judging her.

I'm also pitying her.

CHAPTER NINE

Rob

Dinner is breaded chicken over linguini and cream sauce. It sounds fancy, and it is, but Mom was always a good cook. It's not like they can sue away her culinary skills. It's not organic cream and free-range chicken anymore, but it still tastes good.

Dad sits at the other end of the table and gets his through a tube. He used to obsess over how well his Vitamix made kale smoothies. He'd probably love that it's doing triple duty on all his meals now.

"Anything happen at school today?" Mom says to me.

I think of Maegan and her judgmental eyes. I think of how badly I wanted to punch Connor in the back of the head. I think of Owen Goettler and his million-piece cheese sandwich.

I stab a slice of chicken. "No. Anything happen at work?" My voice isn't surly. Mom's the only person who doesn't treat me like a walking felony.

"One of the senior partners asked if I know how to file alphabetically." She makes a scoffing noise.

My fork goes still. I glance up. She's sitting across from me, which means Dad is at the end of the table, a zombie in my peripheral vision. I can never decide if that's better or worse than sitting directly across from him. I always want to do a double take.

"The guy was asking if you know the alphabet?"

"Yes."

I snort. "Prick."

She smiles. "My words exactly. Well. My *word*."

Once upon a time, she might have criticized my using that word. Not too harshly—Mom has always said that words are words, and it's more about *how* we use them—but she would have made a comment about it. Especially at the dinner table. In front of my father.

She certainly wouldn't have used a word like that herself.

When Dad pulled the trigger, it completely toppled our family dynamics.

I spin pasta on my fork.

"Come on," she says. "Talk to me. At least my own son knows I know the alphabet."

"I've heard you can read, too," I say.

"Sometimes I have to look up the big words." She's kidding. Mom has her master's in business management. It's ridiculous that she's stuck temping, but it's a tough balance being able to take care of Dad and still put in a full day's work.

I rifle through my memories of the day. I don't want to talk about any of it.

"Do you ever see Connor anymore?" she says, her tone musing. "I'd hoped his parents would leave you boys out of it all, but—"

"I don't want to talk about Connor." I stab another piece of chicken.

A blanket of quiet tension drifts over the table, and we eat through it, our weird sentry watching over us from the end of the table.

I wonder if he'd notice if I put a literal blanket over his head.

Suddenly, I can't eat anymore. I put my fork down. "I have homework."

"Rob." Mom's voice is quiet.

"What?" I keep my eyes on my plate.

"I'm worried about you." A pause. "I'd really like it if you'd see someone."

"We can't afford it." I stand up, taking my plate with me.

"There's a counseling center on—"

"No." I push through the swinging door into the kitchen, then scrape my half-eaten meal into the trash can.

When it first happened, I went to a psychologist. The woman wanted me to draw pictures and talk about how they made me feel. I told her they made me feel like I was in kindergarten, and I got the hell out of there.

I haven't gone back.

Mom pushes through the swinging door. "Would you please talk to me?"

"I am talking to you."

"Rob."

I hate that I have the same name as him. I hate it.

But what are my options? Bob? Bert? No.

I start to place my plate in the sink, but then think better of it and rinse it to put in the dishwasher. "School is fine," I tell her.

"Connor is fine." I grab one of the pans from the stove and run it under hot water. "I just want to finish the year and get out of there."

The water runs hot, almost too hot to bear, but I thrust my hands into it and scrub hard. The air behind me is so quiet that I think Mom has left the kitchen.

Her hands settle on my shoulders, and I jump. Suds fly.

"You were such an outgoing kid," she says. "It's not good for you to lock yourself in your bedroom all the time."

I duck and swipe suds off my cheek with my shoulder. "It's fine."

"It's not fine." She pauses. "You shouldn't be carrying all this—"

"You shouldn't, either."

"Please, Rob."

It's the *please* that gets me. Mom never asks me for much. I try not to ask *her* for much. We're trapped in this private hell together, so we try to take it easy on each other.

I drop the pan in the sink and snag a dish towel, then turn around to look down at her. She's six inches shorter than me, and I can see every gray hair along the edge of her forehead.

She wouldn't like me pointing that out. I know from experience.

The gray doesn't matter, though. When I was a little boy, I always thought she was beautiful, and I still think so, even now. Soft cheeks. Warm eyes. Kind hands. Connor's mom is always hard. Pointed joints. Severe makeup. Stiff hairspray and rigid styles. Mom wears loose dresses, her hair long and wavy. Workout videos in the living room have replaced a personal trainer at the gym, but she stays active.

I can't remember the last time I ran a mile.

"Tell me what you want," I say, my voice low. "I'll do it."

"I want you to start going to the free counseling center on Mountain Road. Once a week."

I roll my eyes. "Mom—"

"Didn't you just say I could tell you what I want and you'd do it?"

"Fine." I try not to sound surly. I fail.

"And I want you to get out of the house and get some exercise. Three days a week."

"It's thirty degrees outside."

She pokes me in the chest. "So run fast."

I smile.

She doesn't smile back. "We'll get through this," she says quietly. "Okay?"

I take a breath. "Okay."

From the dining room, my father begins making noise. It sounds like a persistent humming, but there's no mistaking the element of panic in it. Something is frightening him. Or causing him pain. Or something we won't even be able to identify.

Mom and I burst through the door.

The smell hits us both at once.

I don't know if he recognizes that we're here, but he doesn't stop the noise. He won't stop until he's cleaned up.

Early on, Mom once lost her patience and started screaming at him. "Shut up! Shut up! Shut up!" I thought she was losing her mind. I thought she'd hurt him. I wrestled her away from him, and she burst into tears and sobbed all over me.

He didn't stop humming then, either. She was clutching me,

sobbing into my shoulder, and behind her, Dad was sitting in a pool of his own crap, groaning incoherently.

I didn't know what to do. I wanted to run.

I probably would have, if she hadn't been hanging on to me so tightly.

When Mom finally got herself together, her breath was shaking. She didn't look at me. Dad was still humming, a sound that was growing into a keening panic.

She didn't look at him, either. She walked out of the house and slammed the door.

I couldn't leave him there like that. I cleaned him up the best I could.

It was my seventeenth birthday.

Now, I'm used to it.

I sigh. "I'll get the stuff," I say.

In a weird way, homework is a relief. My bedroom windows are dark and cold, reflecting my studious self bent over a physics textbook. Dad's in bed, his clothes are in the laundry, and Mom is downstairs falling asleep in front of the television. The house is silent.

Too silent.

I'm jittery, thinking about what I've agreed to do for my mother. When I went to the art therapist, I remember telling her about finding my father, and she kind of paled and said, "Wow. I'm not really sure what to say."

If a professional doesn't know what to say, I sure don't.

I haven't talked to anyone else about it. Everyone knows I found him. They don't need the details. I'm perfectly content to keep those locked up in a corner of my brain, collecting dust.

Except . . . those memories aren't content to stay locked up. They come out when it's quiet. When I'm stressed. When I'm lonely.

Like right now.

Do you ever see Connor anymore?

I keep thinking about the ten dollars in the cafeteria. The expression on his face when I tried to give it back. How, for one flickering moment, he thought I was going to hurt him.

I dragged your ass a mile through the woods, I want to say to him. *You couldn't pick up the phone when my dad almost died?*

My phone is sitting on the desk beside me. Dark and silent, much like the house.

The only person who ever texts me is my mother. And she's downstairs.

I wonder what Connor would do if I texted him.

I don't even know what I'd say.

I don't know what *he'd* say.

Knowing him, it would be a smartass response.

Or more likely, no response at all.

I can't focus on this homework. My brain is spinning out like a top gone wild. I don't want to talk to anyone, yet I'm also desperate for someone to talk to. But who wants to hear about a wild evening spent changing your father's overflowing diaper? No one.

I shove my physics book into my backpack. I'll be up at the crack of dawn anyway, so I can do it then. I yank free *An Ember in the Ashes*, my latest fantasy read.

A piece of notebook paper was stuck to the book, and it flutters to the ground. I snatch it off the carpeting.

Maegan Day's phone number.

Without thought, I type her number into my phone.

ROB: Did you ask Mrs. Quick for a new partner?

Her response appears almost immediately.

MAEGAN: Who is this?
ROB: Are you trying to avoid multiple partners? Who do you think?

No answer comes back.

Maybe I was kind of a jerk. I'm not exactly swimming in remorse about it.

Okay, maybe I am. A little.

ROB: It's Rob
MAEGAN: The attitude gave it away
ROB: So did you ask for a new partner or not?
MAEGAN: Not
ROB: OK

Nothing. Though I haven't given her much to respond to.

I don't really know why I texted her. No, I do. Desperation. The need to send words into the world and get a response.

But I don't know her. It's not like I can spark a conversation. We're from opposite ends of a spectrum. Or we used to be. I skidded straight off the end of the spectrum last spring, and I've spent the last eight months drifting.

But she's the only other person in my message list.

MAEGAN

MOM

Before, it was just Mom.

This is so depressing.

ROB: When do you want to meet?

MAEGAN: Anytime

ROB: Wegmans in 30?

MAEGAN: 30 minutes? It's after 10

ROB: They're open til midnight

She says nothing.

I wait. And wait.

ROB: You said anytime. Sorry. So when do you want to meet?

Nothing. I sigh and pick up my book.

We'll get through this.

Mom means well, but I feel like we've been trapped here for all eternity. *Through* implies an ending point. Dad won't get better. He won't die either, not for a while anyway.

She should have said, "We'll *survive* this."

That's not a relief, either. Is survival the best we can hope for? Isn't that what Dad's doing? Maybe he's the lucky one in this scenario. He barely knows what's going on.

Lucky. I consider the mess I helped my mother clean up after dinner. And to think he wanted to put a gun to his head *before*.

But at least he doesn't know. Only we do.

Without warning, my chest tightens. My eyes burn.

Hell, no. I am not crying over this. And why? Because some girl I don't care about didn't want to meet at Wegmans to measure drop distances? I'm so pathetic.

I sniff it back. Clear my throat.

My phone chimes.

MAEGAN: I need time to get dressed. See you at 11.

CHAPTER TEN

Maegan

Mom is asleep, but Dad is up, watching *SportsCenter*. There's only one thing that would get my father to let me borrow Mom's car at eleven at night without too many questions: tampons. Even still, he says, "Can't you borrow some from your sister?"

That almost throws me, but then he catches himself and grunts, his dark eyes returning to the screen. "Right. I forgot. Go ahead."

I don't know if he thinks all her feminine supplies evaporated the instant her egg was fertilized, but whatever. It gets me out of the house. I tell him I only like the brand they sell at Walgreens, because he won't ask for details, and that will give me an hour before he expects me home.

The car is dark and cold, but I don't bother waiting for it to warm up. I shiver and shift into drive.

I'm not usually up this late, but I have too many secrets rattling around in my head. I wish Samantha hadn't confided in me. This is too big. Too much. It was a relief to avoid the dinner table, until

I realized I was going to have to lock myself in my room to avoid blurting out all this information to my mother.

I've even been avoiding Rachel. Every time I look at my phone screen, my fingers itch to type out the whole story.

My poor sister. That man's poor wife. My poor family. What about her scholarship? What about her education? Will this ruin her life? Will it ruin his? What will happen to the baby?

At the center of it all is Samantha. Is she a victim? An accomplice? Am I supposed to pity her or resent her? Somehow I don't have enough information, but at the same time I have too damn much.

These thoughts were rattling around my brain so hard that when my phone chimed, I nearly burst through the drywall.

Then it was Rob Lachlan—and he was as much of a jerk as he was at school.

But at least it gave my brain something new to think about.

Rob sits on a bench in front of the store, breath leaving his mouth in long streams that make it look like he's smoking. His dark hair drifts across his forehead, fluttering into his eyes in the wind. His hands are buried deep in his pockets, his eyes fixed somewhere in the distance, maybe even on the stars overhead.

No backpack. Figures.

When I approach, he stands up. His eyes are dark and inscrutable. "I'm surprised you came."

I can't read anything into his voice. I have to stop myself from saying the exact same thing. A part of me worried this would be some kind of prank.

I realize he's still waiting for an answer.

"You were right." I suck a shivering breath between my teeth. "I did say *anytime*."

He says nothing. He doesn't move. He looks a little . . . scattered. My eyes narrow a fraction. I wonder if I've misread this entirely. "Are you high or something?"

His entire demeanor darkens. Standing turns into looming. He glares down at me. "Did you ask if I'm *high*?"

"You're just standing there! You don't even have a backpack! I'm trying to figure out why you wanted to meet at eleven o'clock. You sure don't look ready to do homework."

He takes a long breath, then looks away and runs a hand through his hair. "That's great. Thanks a lot, Maegan." He turns and heads for the front of the store.

I have no idea whether he expects me to follow or if this is a dismissal.

I storm after him. The store's sliding doors *swish* open like they're in a hurry to get out of his way. He strides toward the staircase that leads to the upstairs café seating area, then takes the steps at a jog, two at a time.

It takes me a minute to catch up to him, and when I do, I realize he's at a table that's covered in notebooks and textbooks. He's in the process of packing them all up.

Into the same backpack he had this morning in calculus.

"Wait." I haven't pieced this all together in my head yet, but I've assembled enough to know I've read this all wrong. "Wait."

His angry eyes flick up to meet mine. "You said you wouldn't get here until eleven. I couldn't keep sitting around the house, so I headed over. It's dark outside, and I didn't want you to have to park and walk in alone, so five minutes ago I went down to wait on the bench." A vicious yank at the zipper on his bag. "Or maybe I'm high and wasting your time. Who can tell?" He grabs his bag and walks away.

Not only was he ready to work, he was being *chivalrous*.

I go after him. "Please. Rob. Wait. Stop. I'm sorry."

"Forget it." He doesn't stop. "Ask Quick for someone else. It doesn't matter."

"Would you stop? Please?"

He doesn't. He takes the steps going down nearly as fast as he went up. This time, I try to keep up with him.

He practically leaps off the bottom step to stride toward the store entrance.

I attempt the same thing and my foot goes out from under me. I grab at the railing to steady myself, but my bag goes skidding across the floor and I land in a heap at the bottom of the stairwell.

I swear like a sailor. The last step is digging into my back in a way I'm sure I deserve.

I make enough noise that he stops and turns. "Did you just fall down the stairs?"

"No, it's an illusion. I did it all with mirrors." Thank god it's winter and I'm wearing jeans.

By the time I'm standing, Rob is holding my bag out for me.

"Thanks." I'm humiliated for so many different reasons that I can barely look at him.

I force myself to look up. Rob's eyes are as dark as they were when we were standing in the parking lot, but now his are shining a bit, his mouth a thin line.

My dad has this thing he does when my sister or I get

emotional. He'll put a hand on our shoulder and kind of turn us away, then say, "Take a minute." He means for it to be reassuring, for us to get ourselves together before facing him. As if we need that minute to preserve our dignity. I'm sure it's a cop thing, something he learned for when a crime was too much to bear, but he couldn't break down in front of his officers.

He had to do it last spring, when I stood shaking in the principal's office, wondering if cheating on the SATs was going to ruin my life.

It didn't, but it's never felt right to be on the receiving end of that momentary dismissal. I've never been able to put my finger on why, until this moment, when Rob's rich-kid-jock facade slips a notch and I see a glimmer of vulnerability underneath.

"I'm sorry," I say. "Maybe . . . we can start over."

His eyes search my face. "Fine." He puts out a hand like a businessman. "Rob Lachlan. Non-slacker."

"Maegan Day." I shake his hand. Most boys at school shake hands with the passivity of a trained cocker spaniel, but Rob's fingers close around mine securely. I can feel the strength in his grip. I have to swallow. "Overly judgmental."

His eyes flinch a little, and he lets go. "It's not all your fault. I'm not easy to get along with lately."

I glance at the coffee bar beside the staircase. "Want to get some coffee?"

He hesitates. "Okay."

At the counter, I order a white chocolate mocha and pay for myself. Dad hates overpriced coffee drinks, but Mom loves them, so I slap down five dollars without thinking about it. Then I step aside and watch Rob survey the menu board on the wall.

After a moment he says, "I'll have a small coffee."

It costs him a dollar. There are three ones in his wallet. No credit cards that I can see. I don't know why this feels significant, but it does.

Maybe because he slips out a dollar like he's extracting a kidney from his abdomen.

My heart kicks with adrenaline, but I'm not sure which kind.

"It's on me," I say quickly, jerking my wallet back out of my backpack. "I owe you, after what I said."

He goes still. His fingers tighten on the currency. "You don't have to do that."

The cashier glances between us. We both have a dollar in hand.

I thrust mine forward. "Here."

After a moment, Rob shoves his back in his wallet. His jaw is set. He says nothing.

The girl hands him a cup to fill from one of the dozen carafes lining the wall, and he turns away. He chooses the Christmas blend—Snickerdoodle—and pours two inches of cream into the top of it, then dumps in a ton of sugar. Every motion is slow and controlled.

"Miss? Your drink . . . ?"

I turn and realize the barista has been trying to get my attention.

Rob is waiting when I turn, cup in hand.

"Do you want to go back upstairs?" I say.

"I'm not sure I trust you on stairs with a hot drink."

His voice is low, and it takes me a second to realize he's making a joke.

Before I can react, he says, "We can sit down here. It doesn't matter."

So we sit in the nook under the stairs. There are two armchairs with a low table between them. We drop into them.

Tension continues to hang between us, but it's a different tension from before. It's not antagonistic anymore, more like we've both been scraped a bit raw, and our wounds are more exposed to the air.

Once we're seated, he doesn't touch his backpack. His hands wrap around his coffee cup, and he sits there inhaling the steam.

I couldn't keep sitting around the house.

"You don't really want to work on math, do you?" I say quietly.

His gaze doesn't lift. "No." That seems to spur him into action, though, because he tugs at the zipper of his backpack. "But we can."

"No! No. It's fine." I hesitate. "I really don't have a lot of time anyway. I kind of had to sneak out of the house."

That startles him. His eyes finally meet mine. "You snuck out of the house to meet me?"

When he says it like that, it sounds like a tryst. Like I'm crushing on him. I remember Connor Tunstall's dismissive glance at the front of the school, and my cheeks burn. "No! I mean—yes. I mean—I snuck out of the house to do *calculus*."

Yeah, that's better. Go me.

He's looking at me like I need a psych evaluation. "You really didn't have to come out."

"It's fine. I was up." I pause. "I snuck out because I didn't want a lot of questions. My dad's weird about us being out late. He's a cop."

A breath of time passes, and then Rob says, "I know who your father is."

Oh. Right. I knew that. And I know *why* I knew it.

Rob's voice turns dry again, but there's no real humor in it. "I'm sure you know who mine is, too." He takes a sip of his coffee.

I bite at my lip. "Yeah."

This is so awkward. I have no idea how we're going to do a whole project together. I said we don't need to work on it, but now I wish I could pull out my textbook.

Between dinner with Samantha and coffee with Rob, my evening has been one long stretch of weird revelations, bad judgment calls, and awkward silences.

"Why didn't you want to be at home?" I ask him, trying to imagine what his home life must be like. I know he doesn't have any siblings, so it would have to just be him and his mom, right? I wonder if he gets along with her. I can't build an idea of what kind of woman would be married to someone who stole millions of dollars. I can't imagine what kind of mother she would be. Everything my brain conjures is some kind of cartoon caricature of a buxom woman in a bikini swimming in a jacuzzi filled with diamonds, cackling while sipping from a glass of champagne.

Rob's expression tightens. "Rough night with my dad." A pause. "Trust me, you don't want details."

Wait.

"With your dad? But—but your dad—" I jerk my words to a stop.

Rob's eyes bore into mine now. "Tried to kill himself? I know. I was there." A pause. "He missed."

"I know." I choke like I'm swallowing my tongue and stumble

over my words. "I mean—I thought—I thought he was in a nursing home. Or something."

He looks back at his coffee again. Takes a sip. "He's not."

I had no idea. *No idea.*

I wonder if anyone else knows. I never see Rob talk to anyone anymore, so maybe it's a really well-kept secret that's not a secret at all. It's not like the Lachlan family is a constant source of gossip—not anymore, anyway—but I feel like this is a detail that's escaped most people's notice.

I want to ask what happened tonight. At the same time, I'm afraid to wade into waters where I'm not welcome.

That veil of tension still hangs between us.

"Why were you so eager to get out of the house?" Rob asks me.

I hesitate. "What?"

"Well, I know you don't have the highest opinion of me." He says this as if it's not a surprise. "What were you sneaking away from?"

"There's—" I swallow. I should play it cool, like I sneak out all the time. He'd probably believe it. The only problem with that is that I'm not actually a rebel. Not at all. "There's a lot going on with my sister. She's home from school for a few days."

"Oh." He nods and takes another sip of coffee, but then his eyes light with interest and he focuses back on me. "Wait, didn't your sister sign for some big lacrosse scholarship?"

"Duke," I say hollowly. "Full ride."

He smiles and whistles through his teeth. "Nice. Connor and I thought we might have a shot at money from a Division I school, but then . . ." His voice trails off. The light in his eyes dies. It's like watching a plane crash. He shrugs. "Well."

"You don't play lacrosse anymore?"

His eyes settle on mine, and his expression is tense, like he thinks I'm messing with him. But I'm not, and he must see that, because his face smooths over. "No. I don't."

"Why not?"

He runs a hand across the back of his neck. "You writing a book?"

"What?" Then I get it, and I suck back into my chair. "No. I'm sorry."

For the first time, his voice finds an edge. "You want to talk about whatever's going on with your sister?"

"No."

He lifts one shoulder in that half shrug again. "Well then."

I can't decide if I'm irritated or not. "You want to sit here in silence and drink our coffee?"

"Yeah, I kind of do."

I'm startled by his answer—but he doesn't say it with any attitude. Like in the school hallway or the cafeteria, it's a genuine response to my question. Rob's a straight shooter.

"Okay," I say.

He sinks back in his chair and sips at his coffee. The fluorescent lights overhead are almost too bright for this time of night, but in this nook under the staircase, it's not too bad. This could be a quaint little coffeeshop, not a café carved into the side of a mega-supermarket.

After a moment, I sink into my own. I turn his comments over in my head.

Connor and I thought we might have a shot at money.

Then his voice fell off a cliff. He doesn't hang out with Connor anymore. Rob's regular absence from the quad is proof enough of that. I wonder what the history is there.

I watch him surreptitiously, from under my eyelashes, while sipping my coffee. His angled cheekbones are shadowed beneath the staircase, and even stationary, he carries himself like an athlete. Like he's very aware of the space he takes up in the world.

Rachel will never believe this moment. Rob Lachlan flies under the radar for the most part, but he used to be a bit of a walking legend. I'm shocked to hear he doesn't play lacrosse anymore. I don't follow sports much beyond Samantha's teams and stats, but I remember seeing his name at the top of the rosters when I'd look for hers. He was an attacker, like she is.

I consider the way Samantha was standing out back, throwing shots at the rebounder.

I wonder if he misses it.

I inhale to ask him.

Just as I do, he crumples the now-empty cup in his hand and pushes to his feet. "Thanks," he says. "It's been a long time since I did that."

I stare up at him, unsure what that means. "Anytime."

"Tomorrow night?"

I really need to stop saying *anytime*. "Um. Okay."

"We can meet earlier so you don't have to sneak out. Seven?"

"Sure."

He hoists his backpack onto his shoulder, then hesitates. "You want me to walk you to your car? Or are you going to hang out for a while?"

Where does all this chivalry come from? It must be his mother. I can't imagine a man stealing from half the people in the community taking the time to teach his son to walk a girl to her car.

Or maybe he would. Maybe that's all part of the illusion. Maybe that's how he got away with it for so long.

Flustered, I say, "No. It's fine. I'm fine. I need—I said I'd pick something up."

"See you tomorrow." He turns on his heel and walks out.

CHAPTER ELEVEN

Rob

I go for a run at five a.m. It's so dark that I feel invisible. My lungs burn with cold, and it's been long enough since I last hit the pavement that I'm hating it. Especially since I didn't go to sleep until after midnight.

I push through anyway.

You can always push a little harder, Robby. My father's words throb in my head. *If there's something you want, you have to be able to push past whatever is stopping you.*

He didn't seem to have much trouble pushing past his morals. If he ever had any to begin with.

Music pours into my headphones, and the air tastes like snow. Each time my feet slap the asphalt, it's like a smack, reminding me of what a freak I was last night.

Are you high or something?

Did I look that out of it? *Do* I?

I liked that Maegan was willing to sit in the quiet. It took me by surprise, because she didn't strike me as the type. It was nice to sit with someone who doesn't share my DNA and doesn't want to rag on me about my father's misdeeds. It was nice to *go* somewhere. To *do* something.

My life has collapsed to the point where a ninety-nine-cent cup of coffee with a stranger is meaningful.

This run is killing me. Damn, it's cold. My calves are burning. I push my legs forward.

She surprised me when she thought Dad was in a nursing home. I wonder if a lot of people think that. I wonder if *everyone* thinks that.

Not like it matters. The only thing worse than all the accusatory glances would be pitiful ones.

A whistle sounds in my ears, loud over the music. My running app. I can walk now. Thirty minutes, done. I ran three miles. My legs are going to hate me tomorrow. They'll probably hate me later this morning when I help Mom heave Dad out of bed.

Suddenly, I wish I had another thirty minutes of running in me. I wish I could keep running forever. Away from here.

I can't. And I can't leave my mother.

I turn the music down and head for home.

At school, I reach Mrs. Quick's classroom before Maegan does. Before most of the class does, really. No one ever holds me up in the hallway, so I have nothing to distract me on the way to the classroom. When I walk through the door, most of the seats are empty.

The ones in the back.

And the ones in the front.

I stand there, deliberating.

"Forget where you sit?" Maegan asks from behind me.

My defenses snap into place like a vault door swinging closed. Now I've lost my chance to choose. I don't look at her. "No."

She moves past me, toward the desks. To my surprise, she walks beyond the front row and heads all the way to the back. Right beside the chair I used yesterday.

Like an idiot, I stand there staring at her.

We've also garnered the attention of the three other kids who've already taken their seats.

Maegan's cheeks turn faintly pink. "You moved up front yesterday. Seemed fair."

Okay. I force my feet to move. I shuffle down the aisle and drop into my regular seat. No one ever sits back here. Other kids are filing in to fill the room now, but we're alone in this corner. It's weird to have company, especially first thing in the morning.

It never used to be weird.

She's pulling her things out of her backpack, and she hasn't really looked at me. She wears glasses, and her hair is piled into one of those loose ponytail buns, with strands escaping to frame her face. A thin gray scarf with random pink threads winds around her neck.

I never really noticed before, but she's very pretty. In an understated way.

Her head swivels to look at me. "Okay. What?"

I jump. "What?"

"You're staring at me."

I jerk my eyes back to my desk. I was staring. It's like I've lost any grip on social conventions.

But then I turn back to look at her. "Sorry. I was surprised. That you wanted to sit back here."

Maegan shrugs. "Like I said. Seemed fair. Maybe we can swap on and off."

Mrs. Quick comes into the room, and everyone shuts up to pay attention.

Except me. I can't pay attention to anything at all.

I'm too stuck on the fact that, for the first time in months, someone treated me like *me*, and not like the son of my father.

It has to mean something. I feel like I'm missing something important.

But we don't work on our group activity at all. We barely exchange three words.

When the bell rings, she disappears into the hallway, as much of a mystery as she was before.

By lunch, isolation is back with full force. I only share one class with Maegan. There's a part of me that wants to trail after her like a beaten dog looking for a pat on the head, but there's a bigger part of me that tells the first part to sit down and shut up. I remembered my bottle of water this morning, so I cling to my usual table in the back part of the cafeteria. I have a roast beef sandwich, an orange, a bag of grapes, and a plastic bag of pretzels.

And a big empty table. Today's novel hits the plastic surface with a *thunk*. I'm close to the end. I'm going to need to swing by the library again.

I've read three pages before I realize someone is standing in front of me.

My eyes lift. It's Owen Goettler. He's got a full tray—and when I say *full*, I mean there's enough food for six people. Oranges and bananas and bags of chips and pretzels, along with boxes of dry cereal and granola bars.

Something about his stance seems confrontational. I want to ask if he's asking for donations, because it kind of looks like he is, but considering what I know of him, that feels immeasurably cruel.

I can't believe I threw that ten-dollar bill at him. In retrospect, that was probably cruel, too. Dismissive.

I put a finger in my book and close the cover. "What's up?"

"If I keep this stuff, are you going to screw over my mother?"

I stiffen. "I don't even know your mother."

"Yeah you do."

I don't, actually, but that's not a hill I'm going to die on. "Well, I'm not going to screw her over. Do what you want. Enjoy your six bags of Goldfish." I flip my book open again.

He slams his tray down, then shoves the cover of my book closed. "Is there some weird thing about me taking something from you that's going to screw up the lawsuit? Because—"

"What the hell are you talking about?"

And then I realize his face is red. His hands are trembling at the edge of the tray. He's either ready to cry or ready to punch me in the face. "My mom said we have to be careful. So if you're trying to trip me up . . ."

I have to look away. "I'm not doing anything to you, Owen. The money wasn't even mine."

He jerks back. His hands let go of the tray.

I can hear the words almost before he says them. *You stole it?*

"I didn't steal it," I say, before he can speak. My voice is rough. "Connor Tunstall dropped it in the line, and he wouldn't take it back from me. It was floor money. I didn't want it. The end."

He stands there breathing. He doesn't touch the tray.

I flip my book open again and shuffle through the pages. This dickhead lost my page.

After a minute, he slides onto the bench across from me. He breaks open a banana.

I refuse to lift my eyes from the book, but I go still. "What are you doing?"

"Eating lunch." He bites off a chunk of banana. "What are you doing?"

"Reading." But now I can't focus on the words on the page.

He says nothing else, just continues eating his banana. He does it slowly, the way he eats a cheese sandwich. Tiny bites.

I have absolutely no idea what to do with this. It's weird. Invasive. I'm tempted to stand up and go find another table.

But then Connor Tunstall himself stops beside this one.

WTF is up with my day?

"Hey, Rob," he says, his voice full of mocking brightness. "Find a new friend?"

I don't look at him. "Go to hell."

Across from me, Owen continues to eat his banana with meticulous precision.

Connor leans down close to him. For an instant, I'm worried he's going to be a total shit to Owen, but I should know better.

"Don't trust anything he says. Rob knows how to run a con."

I keep my eyes on my book. The sword-wielding centurions on the page could have started a massive orgy, for all I know. The words have become a swirling mass of anger and regret.

Owen swallows the piece of banana he was chewing. "I'll keep my eyes open." I can't tell if his tone is sarcastic or genuine.

Not like it matters. I wish he hadn't sat down.

My jaw is so tight I'm seeing stars. "Go away, Connor."

"I'm looking out for a classmate. You understand, right?"

I shove up from the bench, and like yesterday, he flinches almost imperceptibly.

But then he laughs and turns away. "Careful, Lachlan. The last thing you need is a suspension."

It takes me a minute to sit back down. Owen is still picking at his banana. His bizarre collection of snacks sits on the tray beside him.

"So, you know how people say the opposite of love is hate?" he says.

I frown. This is the most surreal lunch period ever. "What?"

"My mom once said that's not true. She said the opposite of love is indifference. She said love and hate both require directing energy at someone. I think I'm seeing that in action."

I am so confused. "What the hell are you talking about?"

"That guy. Connor. He used to be your friend, right?"

"So?"

"It's not like you can turn that off. I mean, isn't that why divorced people hate each other?"

"I wasn't in *love* with him, I was—" I break off and make a frustrated sound. "Why are you even sitting here? What do you want?"

"I don't know." He shrugs. His face is no longer red. "I guess I was trying to figure out why you gave me the money."

I run a hand back through my hair and close my book. "I don't know."

"Yeah you do."

"God. Fine." I'm angry now, and most of it has nothing to do with Owen. "Because I felt bad. Is that what you want me to say? I felt bad that you have to eat a cheese sandwich every day."

He finishes his banana and balls up the peel. He tosses it at a trash can at least fifteen feet away—and to my surprise, he makes it.

He doesn't touch anything else on the tray. "Did you know what your dad was doing?"

After eight months, he's the first person to ever ask me that question in a direct manner.

"No," I say.

"Okay." He shrugs and starts shoving all the other snacks into his backpack.

That's it? I take a breath to demand more information, but then I let it out. I don't deserve more of an explanation. "Why did you just buy snacks?"

He zips up his bag but makes no move to leave the bench. "Because they'll last longer."

Oh. *Oh.*

And he only ate one banana. I want to ask why he didn't get his trusty cheese sandwich, but maybe they won't give him one if he shows up at the register with money.

I tear a strip of paper from my lunch bag, then set half my roast beef sandwich on it and push it across the table.

Owen hesitates, then says, "Thanks."

I shrug. He shrugs.

And then we eat, and we don't say anything else.

CHAPTER TWELVE

Maegan

Mom likes to whisper when she's talking about things you don't say in polite company. Samantha and I have known about sex since fifth grade, but Mom will still drop to a hushed voice when she mentions anything even close to it. You'd think that the wife of a cop wouldn't flinch from a word like *heroin* or *affair*, but when Mom wants to make a commentary about the drug problem in the community or our next-door neighbor's proclivities, she acts like she's shielding our precious ears.

Our supposed innocence doesn't stop her from *talking* about these things. It stops her from talking about them at a normal volume.

Tonight, at the dinner table, she's whispering the word *abortion*.

"I told you I don't want to talk about it yet," Samantha snaps. She grabs a piece of garlic bread from the pile on the table.

Dad clears his throat. He's only been home for twenty minutes, so he's still in his uniform. His low voice rumbles as he puts his hand over Mom's. "Maybe this isn't the time or place, Allison."

"She needs to make a decision," Mom hisses, as if our conversation is being recorded. "Her future is at stake."

"I'm not going to have the baby under the table in the next twenty minutes," Samantha says.

"You're already ten weeks pregnant, and I think you're being very cavalier about this." Mom points her fork at Samantha. "I think that's how you got into this situation. You always think you know best, but sometimes you don't."

Samantha takes a long sip of chocolate milk. The combination with spaghetti and meat sauce is enough to turn my stomach, but she said it's the only thing that calms hers. "I didn't hear you complaining when my cavalier attitude won me this scholarship."

"Oh, and what's going to happen to that scholarship if you decide to keep this baby? What's going to happen if you take a month to make a decision?"

"Are you telling me to get an abortion?" Samantha asks. "You want me to kill your grandchild?"

Mom pales a shade. She might have been okay with an abortion, but it's obvious the grandchild angle didn't occur to her. She swallows so hard I hear it. "Samantha. I'm asking you to look at your options. Have you talked to the athletic director?"

"No."

"Surely you aren't the first girl to get pregnant while on a scholarship."

"So I get rid of the baby or I get rid of my future." Samantha tears another piece of garlic bread in half. "Great."

"No one is telling you to get rid of the baby," Mom snaps. "But

I'm asking you to stop hiding in your room and deal with the problem you created."

"Yeah, I created it all by myself. The turkey baster was *so* sexy. You should try it, Mom. Might spice up your—"

"*Enough.*" My father's voice doesn't rise much. It doesn't have to. We both know when to shut up.

Silence falls like a woolen blanket.

"You're not going to talk to your mother that way," he says to Samantha. "Do you understand me?"

She shoves the second piece of bread into her mouth and doesn't look at him. Her cheeks are faintly pink.

I spin pasta on my fork and keep my eyes fixed on my plate. I would rather be anywhere than at this dinner table. Literally anywhere.

I'm meeting Rob at seven. Sixty minutes away.

I don't know if I can last that long.

"You keep refusing to talk about the boy," Dad says. "Can you share *his* feelings on the matter?"

The word *boy* throws me, because David isn't a boy at all. The spaghetti in my mouth turns to stone. I hate secrets. Especially the secrets of other people.

Samantha doesn't answer him. The silent tension in the room grows by leaps and bounds.

Mom sets down her silverware. Quietly. Then she smooths her napkin over her lap. When she speaks, her voice is softer. "Maybe we should talk to his parents about setting up a family meeting. Do they live near the university? We could meet somewhere in the middle."

Samantha takes a drink of milk.

I force down another forkful of spaghetti.

We've all been sitting here in silence for a while.

Finally, Samantha says, "He doesn't think it's his." Her voice is so quiet we can barely hear her over our breathing.

Beside me, my father's fingers curl into a fist. I'm not sure if he's mad at Samantha or this "boy," but either way, it's never good to be on the wrong side of my father's temper. "He what?"

"He doesn't think it's his." Samantha swallows. "He—"

"He what?" says our mother.

"Nothing."

My father's voice, usually a low, calming rumble, is lethally quiet. "Is it his?"

"Yes." Samantha's voice breaks. A tear snakes down her cheek.

"You're sure?"

"*Yes.*"

"Then I want his name and phone number. I'm going to call him myself. I'm not going to watch you go through this on your— Where are you going?"

Samantha has burst from her chair and bolted through the kitchen doorway.

A sob escapes her as she tears up the stairs. A moment later, a door slams.

My father sighs and twists his fork in his pasta. His voice is tight. "This is ridiculous. I want you to find out who this boy is, Allison. We pay for her phone. If she's not going to give us information, I'm going to figure it out on my own."

Then he points his fork at me. "Not a word to her about that, either. You hear me?"

I squeak and nod quickly.

He sighs, then reaches over and squeezes my forearm. "I'm sorry. I'm not mad at you. You always do the right thing."

But then he goes still, as if he's realized what he's said. He looks back at his food. I look back at mine.

The table falls silent for a while, broken only by the crunch of garlic bread. They haven't asked me one single thing since we sat down at the dinner table, and I am one hundred percent okay with that.

My phone chimes. Rachel.

> **RACHEL:** Drew is working and I'm bored. Want to see a movie?
>
> **MAEGAN:** Can't. Meeting Rob Lachlan to work on our project.
>
> **RACHEL:** Awkward
>
> **MAEGAN:** Tell me about it

But as soon as I send the message, I regret it. I replay our late-night meeting at Wegmans. It was definitely awkward—mostly because of me—but it was also sad.

He seems so lonely. I don't think I ever realized that. His eyes lit up when he mentioned lacrosse scholarships, but that light burned out so quickly when he remembered his current situation.

"Do you really want her to have an abortion?" Dad says softly.

"I don't know," says Mom. Her voice is thin and reedy. "I don't know what to do."

My chest is so tight it hurts. We aren't religious, and I've always considered myself pro-choice.

It's a lot easier to say that when the choice isn't staring you in the face.

"I don't like it," Dad says. Then he sighs. "I don't like the idea of her having a baby at nineteen, either."

"Even if they let her defer for a year," says Mom, "how is she going to keep up a sports scholarship while raising a baby?"

"There's always adoption," Dad says.

"Are you going to hand over our grandchild?" says Mom.

"Would you rather she kill it?"

I can't be here for this.

"Can I borrow your car?" I say to Mom.

She sniffs. "What, Maegan?"

"We have a group project in calculus, and we're meeting at Wegmans. Is that okay?"

She smiles at me, but her eyes are watery and distracted. Mentally, she's still fixated on my sister. "Oh. Yes. Of course. Go ahead."

Today, I'm the one with schoolbooks spread across a table in the upstairs eating area. I'm half an hour early, but I had to get out of there. I can't listen to the abortion debate in the middle of our kitchen. Every time someone says *kill it*, I want to throw up.

I need to think about calculus.

I can't think about calculus.

I try to imagine my vivacious, unpredictable sister giving up lacrosse and school to raise a baby. And what would she do for a job? She can't live with Mom and Dad forever. Besides, Mom and

Dad both work. Would the baby have to go to day care so Samantha could keep going to school? Could Mom and Dad afford that? I remember one of our teachers had a baby and came back for a week after maternity leave, then quit. She said she had to work a week to keep what they paid her during her maternity leave—but if she kept working, most of her salary would have to pay for day care. She didn't want to work so someone else could raise her daughter.

Then again, we were in day care when we were young, because Mom was a graphic designer, and she didn't want to give up her career. So it's not like a baby automatically closes the door for Samantha.

But Mom had Dad around to help pay expenses, so they were able to make it work. Samantha wouldn't have that. DavidLit-Man probably isn't going to write a rent check every month.

Would he pay child support? Would that cover rent?

I never realized this would be so complicated—and I'm not even the one making the decision.

I have a plan to go sit on the bench outside and wait for Rob, kind of an apology for jumping down his throat yesterday, but he surprises me by showing up at six forty.

He's startled to see me. He pulls ear buds out of his ears, then pulls his phone out of his pocket, checking the time. "Hey. I thought maybe I was late."

"No." I hesitate. "My house is a little weird now. I had to get out." I almost ask if he wants to get coffee or a soda or something, but it seemed to throw him last night. I don't say anything.

He drops his backpack on the floor beside a chair, then sits. "My house is weird, too." No further explanation—but maybe none is needed. He pulls out his textbook. "I was going to do the homework while I was waiting . . . or do you want to go right to the project?"

I want something other than fetal brain development to occupy my thoughts.

"Whatever," I say. "I haven't done the homework yet, either."

His eyes narrow slightly, like he's trying to figure me out. "Want to get it out of the way?"

"Sure."

I sit there and stare at my textbook. I can't make myself care about math when I can't stop thinking about my sister.

I wish I knew what *she* wanted to do.

I'm not going to have the baby under the table in the next twenty minutes.

It sounds like what she really wants to do is procrastinate. Or maybe I'm just channeling my mother.

"What's up?" Rob's quiet voice makes me jump.

"What?"

"You haven't written anything down."

I look down at my notebook. He's right. For some reason, that's a surprise. "Oh."

He sets down his pen. His voice affects a breathy falsetto. "I care about my grades. You can't slack off on this."

Checkmate. Hearing my own words recited back makes me sound like a real shrew. I blush and fold in on myself. "I'm sorry. You're right. I'll work."

"I'm messing with you. I haven't written anything down, either."

I look across. His notebook is equally blank. His expression seems to match how I feel.

"We have to do *something*," I say.

"Okay. I'll do the first problem and you do the second, and we can copy each other's."

I sit up straight. "You—wait. That's—that's cheating."

He hesitates, and I can almost hear the question before he asks it. *Why do you care about cheating on* homework *if you blew the whole SAT?*

But he doesn't ask. He says, "It's not a test. You can check my work and I'll check yours."

This feels like a decidedly gray area. I'm already on rocky ground. I don't know if I like it or not.

Rob shrugs and looks back at his paper. His expression is closed off again. "Forget it," he says quickly. "It doesn't matter. I can do them all."

He puts his pencil to the page.

I look at my own book. If I do four problems instead of eight, I'm still working. And he's right—by virtue of copying over his answers, I'll be working through the problem to make sure he solved it accurately. It's not like copying a research report or an English paper.

I bite my lip.

I write *2.* halfway down my page.

Then I do the second problem.

It takes a few minutes, not including the time I spent hesitating. When I finish and look up, Rob is watching me.

"What? I can break the rules once in a while."

His eyes hold mine. "I've heard that."

I don't flinch from his gaze, though I want to. "You were right. We can check each other's work when we copy over. What's the difference?"

"Agreed." He pauses. "Want to do three and four?"

"Sure." We work through the rest of the assignment. My thoughts are burning for a new reason, but I'm kind of glad for the change.

When I'm near the end of the eighth problem, Rob says, "What makes your house weird?"

I tense, but then he adds, "Is it because your dad's a cop?"

My pencil goes still on the paper. "What?"

My voice is sharper than I intended, mostly because I was thinking about my parents' arguing at the dinner table, not what's in front of me. Rob looks back at his notebook. "Sorry. I didn't mean to pry."

"No . . . it's fine. I don't understand the question."

"Is it weird, your dad being a policeman? Is he on your case all the time?"

I shrug and set down my pencil. "It's not weird. It's kind of all I've ever known." I pause, thinking of last spring, when Samantha learned about her full scholarship. How I walked into that testing room, thinking I'd never do anything that would measure up to my sister's success. "Dad expects a lot from us."

"I remember that feeling," says Rob, and I go still.

He looks away, as if he's said too much. I'm not sure what to say.

He clears his throat. "If your dad's not on your case, what is it?"

I hesitate. He's so forward. And I'm a terrible liar.

Rob tips his head back and stares up at the fluorescent lights before I can say anything. "God. I'm such a social reject. It's none of my business. I haven't talked to anyone in months, so it's like I forget how."

"It sounds lonely."

"You have no idea." He pauses, and he looks back at me before flipping a page in his notebook. "Now I sound pathetic. Most people probably think it's what I deserve."

I should say that I don't think that—but I don't know what to think of the boy sitting in front of me.

"Do *you* think that?" I ask.

"I don't know." He hesitates, then fiddles with the metal spiral of his notebook. "My dad used to say that hard work and dedication pay off. I used to believe that was true. I mean, it worked for him. And then it worked for me, too. I mean, I get good grades. I was great at lacrosse. But then . . . well. You know. And after it all unraveled, I started to wonder about all of it. Like, was I working harder than anyone else at lacrosse, or was I better because my parents had money to pay a private coach? Is that a weird form of cheating? I mean, *yes*, because it wasn't our money to spend. But beyond that . . . I don't know." He makes a disgusted sound, and his eyes meet mine. "Sorry. Like I said. Social reject."

"You're not a social reject." But he is. Literally. "Life at home must be really awful."

He shrugs a little, but his shoulders are tight. He picks up his pencil and spins it through his fingers. "Is your life at home awful?"

No? Yes? I have no idea how to answer his question. "It's not like yours, I'm sure."

"You said your sister's home sick. Is she still?"

I look at my paper. "Yeah."

The air between us thickens with unspoken words.

Then he says quietly, "Cancer?"

My pencil skips across the page. "What? No!"

He draws back. "Oh. Sorry. You seemed . . . upset." He runs a hand across the back of his neck. "What, is she knocked up or something?"

I can't speak. I literally feel the blood rush out of my face.

He must see it, because his eyes widen by about a thousand percent. "Holy shit. Really?"

I can barely breathe. I can't believe I gave it away. "Please don't tell anyone," I gasp.

"Who the hell would I tell?"

"I . . . please—" I feel like I'm hyperventilating. "Please."

"Chill out. I'm not going to say anything. But . . . wow." He frowns. "What's going to happen to her scholarship?"

"We don't know. She hasn't made a decision yet. No one knows." My throat is tight. My chest feels like it's going to cave in. He might be a social reject, but he knows everyone involved in lacrosse at Eagle Forge. All he'd have to do is mention this juicy bit of gossip to one person, and it could be all over. "Please, Rob. Don't say anything. My parents would kill me."

"I'm not going to tell anyone!" He flings his pencil at the table. "God, does everyone think I'm going to screw them over?"

My heart is in my throat. I push back in the chair, but he's already looking repentant.

His hands are up. He sighs. "I'm sorry. That's not about you." A pause. "But seriously. I won't tell anyone. I'm just trying to keep my head down and graduate."

My heart begins to slow. Of all people, he probably is the best person I could have told. He really does keep his head down.

A moment passes between us.

"Project?" he says.

I nod. "Project."

I pick up my pencil, and we get to work.

CHAPTER THIRTEEN

Rob

If I made a list of all the places I don't want to go right now, the library would top it.

I sneak in before the first bell on Wednesday, but of course Mr. London is right there at the desk. I can see him through the windows. My book technically isn't due until next week, but if I don't return it and find a new one, I'm going to be stuck staring at my lunch later.

I need to get over myself. Maegan told me her sister is struggling with a decision that will affect the rest of her life. I'm standing here debating whether I have the courage to face a librarian.

My father would be so proud.

That thought alone is enough to spur me through the door. I stop at the desk and slide my book onto the Formica surface. I don't make eye contact with Mr. London. I don't even say anything.

So brave. I want to punch myself in the stomach.

"Finished already!" Mr. London is reacting like I swept through the doors with unbridled enthusiasm, and a small, dark part of me wonders if he's mocking me. "What did you think of this one?"

"It was fine." I'm lying. It's a five-hundred-page fantasy, and I finished it in two days. It was phenomenal.

"We got the sequel in yesterday. Just finished putting it into the system." He pauses. "If you're interested." He slides *A Torch Against the Night* across the counter. The cover is blue and white, and it's every bit as thick as the first book.

A year ago, if someone told me I'd be excited to be holding a book in my hands, I'd have laughed in their face.

It's taking everything I have to keep from reading it right here on the spot.

I dig my student ID out of my wallet so he can scan it.

"So when you're done," Mr. London says, his tone implying we're best pals, "you need to come talk to me. I just finished the sequel, and I have a theory about the cook."

I have a theory about the cook, too, from the first book, but I still can't tell whether he's patronizing me. I don't know why he's talking to me at all. The words burn on my tongue.

As always, I stand silent too long. He scans my card, then scans the book, and then he hands it to me.

What's sad is that I *want* to talk to him about the book. But with Mr. London, I feel like anything I say should be preceded by some kind of apology on behalf of my family. And I don't know how to do that.

Ever the coward since eight months ago, I shove the book in my backpack and walk out.

It's pouring rain outside, so the cafeteria is packed. I hate when this happens. At least I have a new book. I find my usual table and sit at the end. It's empty for now, because I pack a lunch and most people buy, but it won't be for long.

Sure enough, after a minute, a shadow falls across my book, and the table creaks and shifts as someone sits down. I keep my eyes on the page.

A snack bag crackles open. A familiar voice says, "You really like reading, huh?"

Owen Goettler. He's eating a bag of potato chips. An orange sits next to it.

"Yeah," I say.

"What's that one about?"

I turn the book around. "I'm literally on the first page."

"Oh." He says nothing to that. He eats his chips methodically. One at a time. With a noticeable break between each.

Some underclassmen come and sit at the other end of the table. They're carrying on about something hilarious that happened in health class, and I lock my eyes on my book to keep from giving a heavy sigh.

After a moment, I consider that Owen is still silently sitting across from me with his sad little bag of chips and his orange.

He must see my eyes on his food, because he says, "So, my plan was to get all the snacks in one day, and then have a side dish for my cheese sandwich."

"Good plan."

"Yeah, well, the lady guarding the lunch line disagrees. She said I should have been more judicious with my money."

He says this without emotion, like he's discussing the weather, but it lights a fire of anger inside me. It's not like the lunch lady personally buys the bread and the cheese.

I tear a strip off my lunch bag, and like yesterday, I slide it across the table with half my sandwich.

"Thanks," he says equably.

Then he reaches across the table and pours half his chips onto the remainder of my bag.

I hesitate.

"It's okay," he says. "I can share."

Not really true, and I'm literally the last person he should be giving anything to, even a handful of potato chips. But I don't want to shove them back at him. "Thanks."

He jerks his head toward the freshmen at the end of the table and leans in. "Are they seriously laughing about some kid losing his boxers?"

"I've been trying to ignore them."

"Oh right. Because you're reading."

I don't know if that's a dismissal or what, but he's not looking at me anymore.

"Right." I look back at my book. Pick up the remaining half of my sandwich.

Across from me, Owen keeps eating like it's a surgical procedure.

I read. He sits in silence. At first, my eyes keep skipping around the page because I sense him watching me, but when he says nothing, I relax and lose myself in Serra with Laia and Elias.

I'm turning page six when he says, "Wait, I wasn't done with that page."

I freeze and look up at him. "Are you reading this upside down?"

"Well, it was that or listen to their plot to superglue some guy's locker shut." He nods at the book. "It's not like you're making conversation."

I can't figure this kid out at *all*. "Do you *want* me to make conversation?"

He shrugs. "Whatever."

It's possible he's completely screwing with me, so I look back at the page.

Which I can't turn until I know he's done.

I sigh heavily.

"Okay," he says after a moment. "Go."

With dramatic flair, I flip the page. We read for a few minutes. The chapter ends.

Without preamble, Owen says, "So, your friend Connor is kind of a prick, huh?"

He's not my friend anymore, but I say, "I think he's moved past 'kind of.'"

That makes him smile. "We might be the only two people who think so." His eyes flick past me, across the cafeteria, where dozens of kids crowd around two tables by the wall. Connor is there, standing beneath a large, hand-painted banner that proclaims Athletic Department Bake Sale. A cookie for a dollar. A cupcake for two. He's taking cash by the fistful from kids looking for a sugar rush.

I know from experience that he's flirting with every girl who approaches. Half of them will make a donation for the chance to talk to him.

What a rip-off. Especially since it's for the athletic department, which is the best-funded division in school. When the marching band has a bake sale, their cookies are a quarter. Even then, they can barely get anyone to buy anything.

The real irony here is that Connor is manning the table. His dad once wrote a letter to the school board to say that kids who couldn't afford to buy lunch should have to work with the janitor to earn it. He told my dad about it. *Teach them a little work ethic*, he said.

Owen sets down his sandwich, then picks up another chip and eats it.

I wonder what it's like to watch other kids hand over disposable cash when you're condemned to eat cheese sandwiches every day.

And then the lunch lady judges you for trying to make the most of the money you get.

Suddenly I want to give him the rest of my food.

"You look like someone kicked your dog," Owen says.

I have to clear my throat. "I don't have a dog."

My eyes drift across the cafeteria again. I remember those bake sales. I bet they'll pull in over a thousand dollars by the end of the day. Especially if they set up again after dismissal.

And for what? New jerseys? A few new lacrosse sticks?

"You going to turn the page again or what?"

Owen's voice pulls me back.

"Sorry." I turn the page automatically, though I haven't read the one before it. "What are you doing here, Owen?"

"I'm eating lunch." His voice lowers and turns serious, an obvious mockery of my own. "What are you doing here, Rob?"

I don't try to hide the tension in my voice. "Why are you eating with *me*?"

"Because your mom makes a mean roast beef sandwich."

"I made this."

"Fine. Because *you* make a mean—"

My voice lowers further. "Don't mess with me."

Any mockery disappears from his face, and he almost draws back. For one split second, I remember what it was like to be the kind of kid someone like Owen wouldn't dare speak to. Even the underclassmen at the end of our table pick up on my tension.

"I'm not messing with you," he says earnestly.

"I'm not going to be some secret path to popularity and hot girls," I say tightly. "No one talks to me anymore."

"Okay, for the record, I don't need a path to girls."

Oh.

Owen puts another chip in his mouth. "I wouldn't mind a secret path to Zach Poco, though. Any chance he's speaking to you?"

Zach Poco plays right wing for the varsity soccer team. His parents own several strip malls in the county, and they're close with Connor's parents. I don't know Zach well, but even if he'd talk to me, I know for a fact he's not gay. "No."

Owen shrugs. "Long shot."

"The longest." I pick up a chip.

"What about you?" he says.

"What about me?"

He rolls his eyes as if I'm being dense. "Do you need a path to Zach Poco?"

"Oh. No."

"Oh, right. You used to date that girl with the purple streaks in her hair. Karly or Kaylie or something?"

Callie, but I'm not going to correct him. She wanted us to have a Serious Relationship. You could hear the capital letters every time she brought it up. Between sports and school and interning for my father, I didn't have time to be serious. Or any desire, if we're getting down to details.

Then my life fell apart and took *serious* to a whole new level.

I haven't talked to Callie since it happened. When Connor didn't return my texts, I didn't reach out to anyone else.

None of them reached out to me.

I don't want to think about the past. "Are you some kind of stalker, Owen?"

"My best friend graduated last year. I have a lot of time to watch people."

I guess that's true.

Owen's eyes glance up, over my head. "Prick alert. Twelve o'clock."

"What?" I say, just before a hand smacks me on the back of the head.

I whirl. Connor walks right past me. "Heads up, Lachlan." Then he cracks up.

I watch his departing back. It's not that he hit me very hard or that I can't take it.

Like everything else, it's a pointed reminder of our dead friendship. Something he would have done in the locker room, if we were joking around. Words once said without any vitriol.

Heads up, Lachlan.

I'm striding away from the bench before I realize I'm moving. Walk right up behind him.

I smack him on the back of his head so hard that he stumbles and drops what he was carrying: the cash box from the bake sale.

It bursts open on impact. Coins tinkle all over the laminate floor. Cash flutters out and away from the box. Money goes *everywhere*.

Connor finds his balance and turns. His eyes could generate laser beams. He looks truly furious. "You *asshole*."

For some reason, his ready anger lessens mine. "Takes one to know one."

"Rob Lachlan!" Mr. Kipple, the vice principal, is storming across the cafeteria. "I saw that. You'll clean up this mess, right now."

"You sure you want him to do that?" Connor snaps.

Now I want to hit him again—but I don't want to get suspended. I don't have much pride left, but I don't want to be labeled a troublemaker. Mom has enough to deal with.

I drop to a knee and start scooping the cash into a pile.

Connor stands over me, holding out the cash box, waiting for me to fill it.

Hell, no.

Luckily, Mr. Kipple has reached us, and he says, "You too, Connor. You're not completely innocent here."

He gets down on one knee beside me. He's muttering under his breath the whole time. I'm sure he thinks I can hear him, that his words are having some huge impact on me, but my heartbeat is a roar in my ears, and there's too much gossip going on around us.

I shove a stack of cash into the box, then reach for a couple of errant twenties. They curl in my palm as I grab some loose quarters, too.

"I'm going to count all of this," Connor says. "Don't get any ideas."

My teeth clench so hard I can feel it in my neck. Mr. Kipple is standing over us, and Connor was loud enough that he has to have heard him.

He says nothing. Not the ally I thought he might be a moment ago.

I think of Owen being denied a cheese sandwich. Everything is so messed up.

I put my hand over the cash box and let go of the quarters.

The two twenty-dollar bills stay in my palm.

Sweat collects under my collar as I curl my fingers tighter and reach for more change. I'm waiting for one of them to call me out, to snap that they saw me hang on to the cash, but neither says anything. I chance a glance up, and Connor is picking up pennies. Mr. Kipple isn't even looking at us. Something across the cafeteria seems to have caught his attention.

Someone had to see.

No one says anything. We've lost the attention of the students nearby. Watching people clean up grows old pretty quick.

Connor slams the cash box closed. He makes no eye contact.

Then he straightens and turns away, leaving me standing there with the money wrapped up in my suddenly sweaty hand.

I stole forty bucks.

This isn't the same as the other day. This isn't money he refused to take.

I *stole* this.

I return to the table and drop onto the bench across from Owen. The underclassmen are gone. I thought he'd have been watching the clean-up effort, but Owen's taken over reading the book.

No one saw. I still can't quite believe it.

Owen's eyes glance up. "Like those kids need the school to buy them gear."

"Seriously," I say. It makes me wince inside, because I was once one of those kids, and while it doesn't feel right to align myself with Owen, it doesn't feel wrong, either.

He's peeled his orange and divided all the pieces, and he's eating them as methodically as everything else.

The cash is searing hot against my palm.

I slide my hand under the cover of the book and let go of the money. My heart is pounding like I'm being recorded and the cops are going to spring a trap any second.

Owen frowns. "Dude. You look like you're going into shock."

I flick my eyes at the book. "Make sure your lunch choices are more judicious this time."

He hesitates, then slides his hand beneath the cover, then slides it back out. He peeks under his palm like he's caught a bug.

He goes still. His eyes meet mine.

This is a *moment*. I can feel it. He can rat me out. He can shove it back. He can storm away from the table.

He can take the money and be complicit in what I just did.

I have no idea what I expect. Time stretches into infinity as I wait for Owen Goettler to determine my fate.

His fingers close around the cash. He slides it into his pocket.

Then he shoves the book back across the table to me. "Catch up on the last three pages. It's getting really good."

CHAPTER FOURTEEN

Maegan

When I get home, Samantha is tossing balls at the rebounder again. I haven't seen her since she stormed away from the table last night, and I wonder what kind of mood she'll be in.

Mom and Dad aren't home yet, though, so if I'm going to talk to her, now would be my best chance.

I pour chocolate milk into a cup and carry it out to her. My feet sweep through dead leaves as I walk. The air is heavy and cold, a bite with a taste of smoke from a neighbor's fireplace.

"I don't really want to talk right now," she says tightly, without turning. The ball slings against the rebounder with a hard snap.

I hesitate. "Okay. I brought you chocolate milk, though."

She catches her latest throw, then turns. "Oh. Sorry. I thought you were Mom."

"Nope."

She takes the cup from me and drinks half of it in one swallow. "Thanks."

"You're welcome."

She looks down at the cup and swirls it in her hand for a minute. "Thanks for last night, too. I really appreciate it."

"Last night?"

"You didn't tell them." Her eyes lift to find mine. "About David."

No one is home, but I keep my voice quiet anyway. "No." I pause. "It's not my secret to tell."

She twirls the lacrosse stick in her hand, then chucks the ball across the yard. "If you're going to get on my case about it, you can go hang out with Mom."

"I'm not getting on your case." I pause. "I'm trying to be your sister. I'm trying to be supportive."

She catches the ball as it sails back to her. She looks like she wants to make a crack about my sister comment—but then she must see my face.

She kicks at the leaves underfoot. "You want to be supportive? Want to run some drills?"

I snort. "Yeah, okay, so you can bean me in the head? I can't play with you." Samantha left me in her dust *years* ago.

Her face falls a little, but then she shrugs. "No, I know. I mean, I could go easy."

That's like asking a blizzard to stick to flurries. "Yeah, sure."

But then I think of someone who probably wouldn't mind running a few drills—and probably isn't doing anything more interesting than watching paint dry.

"Wait," I say to Samantha. "I have an idea."

Rob arrives faster than I expect. I'm surprised to learn he has his own car. It's a sleek black Jeep Cherokee. Not exactly top of the line, but when I get up from the porch steps to walk over to greet him, I can see the pristine interior, all tan leather and a sweet sound system.

I can't help staring.

He can't help noticing.

His expression was easy when he got out of the car, but now his eyes are guarded, his shoulders tense. He hasn't closed the door yet, like he might need to make a quick getaway. He speaks quickly. "It was my dad's car first, and he bought it before . . . *before*, so they couldn't seize it—"

"You don't owe me an explanation." I have to shake myself. "It's fine. I shouldn't have been staring."

"Everyone stares." He hesitates. "It's eight years old and it's got over a hundred thousand miles on it, so we can't sell it for a whole lot. And Mom says it's better to stick with a car that we know runs well than to give it up for something—"

"Really," I say. "You don't have to explain."

He shuts up.

This feels like the moment I showed up at Wegmans and found him without any books. I'm always a little guarded, but Rob seems permanently set at DEFCON 1.

Samantha appears at my side and bumps me with her shoulder. She's got her lacrosse stick in hand, and she's tossing the ball in the air, twirling the stick, and catching it.

"You bring your stuff?" she says. No *thanks for coming* or *hi, I'm Samantha*. When there's a lacrosse ball involved, she's all business.

Rob doesn't seem to mind. "Yeah." He slams the door and opens the tailgate. He's brought two sticks and a pile of pads and a helmet. All of it is dirty and grass stained.

She's not wearing anything more protective than a sweatshirt, so he slides a stick free. "I'm out of practice," he says. "It's been a while."

Samantha backs up, swings her stick wide, and flings the ball at him.

His stick was hanging by his side, but he's fast, and he whirls to snatch the ball out of the air.

He snaps it right back to her.

She catches it and grins. It's the first real smile I've seen on her face since she got home from school. "You'll do," she says. "Get the rest of your stuff on. I'll go get my goggles. Megs, come help me out."

I absolutely hate when she calls me Megs and she knows it. "Why can't you get them yours—"

She seizes my arm and drags me toward the porch. Once we're inside, her voice drops to a hushed whisper. "Maegan. You said you were texting your calculus partner. I thought you were dragging some math geek over here. Rob Lachlan is *hot*. Are you dating him?"

I snort. The idea of Rob having even a fleeting romantic interest in me is laughable. "No. And he *is* my calculus partner."

"Does he have a girlfriend?"

"Don't you have enough boy problems?"

"Not for me, you idiot. Come here. Put on some lip gloss."

"Aren't you supposed to be getting your goggles?"

"Like that'll take more than two seconds. Come here. Let me do your eyes."

I smack her hand away. "You don't think that will look a little suspicious? If I show up outside with full makeup on?"

"I'll be subtle."

"Sam—"

"Maegan." Her eyes are fierce—and also a little hurt. "Let me be *your* sister for five minutes, okay?"

That shocks me into compliance. For months, I've felt like she was pushing me away. Has she felt the same?

While I'm turning this thought over in my head, she's stroking eyeliner and shadow onto my lids, then flicking at my lashes with mascara.

Guilt has been pricking at me since she thanked me for keeping her secret from Mom and Dad, and I can't be silent in the face of all this sisterly love. "Sam, I need to tell you something."

"Are you carrying *his* baby?"

"No, seriously."

She unscrews the cap of a tube of lip gloss. "What's up?"

"Rob knows. About you."

Her hand goes still.

"I didn't mean to tell him," I rush on. "I was upset after dinner last night, and he made a guess, and I think he was joking, but it was right on the mark, and—"

"I don't care." She brushes gloss across my lips.

"You don't?"

"No. Mom and Dad are the ones who don't want the truth to get out. But I'm not a nun. I know what I did. I'm not going to dance around in a maternity shirt yet, but I'm not upset." She hesitates. "I'm actually a little jealous that you have someone to talk to. I can't tell anyone from school because I don't want them to yank the scholarship until I know what I'm doing."

"Rob's not—we're not friends. I don't really *talk* to him."

"Yeah, well, you need to change that. Look. Subtle."

I turn and look at myself in the mirror.

"This looks so obvious." I don't wear much makeup to school, and now my eyes are dark-lined and my lips are glossy. "He's going to wonder what's taking so long."

"Trust me. He won't. Shake out your hair."

"Sam . . ." But then I see her look and sigh. "Fine." I shake out my hair.

She goes to get her goggles.

While she's doing that, I put my hair back in a loose ponytail and head downstairs. I mean, honestly.

Rob is out back tossing the ball against the rebounder. Black pads broaden his shoulders and cling to his rib cage, but his helmet is in the leaves beside a tree. Like Samantha, every toss and catch looks effortless; the only indicator of speed is the flip of his stick and the indentation of the elastic.

Okay, fine. He's attractive.

"You put your hair back up!" Samantha says.

"Yeah. Well. You can't have everything."

"Fine, then. Have it your way." She yanks out her pony tie and flings it on the table, shaking out her blond waves as she pushes past me to slide the door open.

I stare after her, gape-mouthed, then get myself together to follow. I'm scowling and I'm not even sure why. I just spent five minutes telling her I'm not interested. And I'm not.

I mean, not really.

Okay, maybe *a little*.

Samantha is skipping across the yard, her hair shining gold in the fading sunlight. Her goggles, striped with pink and blue, hang from one hand.

Rob turns when he hears her rustling through the leaves. "Why do I need pads? Girls don't get physical—"

Samantha slams into him with her shoulder.

He grunts and falls back a step. "Okay, fair enough."

Ugh. I'm going to have to go back into the house.

What is *wrong* with me?

But then Samantha turns. "Hey, Megs? I forgot to put my ponytail tie back in. Loan me yours?"

Oh, she is something else. If I don't give her mine, I'll look like a weirdo.

I mean, more of a weirdo than I look right now, standing on the porch, staring at them.

I carefully unwind the elastic and shake out my hair, then walk it over to her. My cheeks feel warm, and I can't look at Rob. I'm super conscious of the eye makeup suddenly. "Here you go."

She winds her hair up, and I watch, because otherwise I'm going to be looking at Rob, and he's clearly looking at me.

I don't understand how this got all awkward.

Because of my sister. That's how. I wasn't even thinking of him that way, and then she had to go into makeover mode.

Then he says, "I know some great drills, but we need three people." All casual directness. "Do you play at all?"

Oh. He was looking at me because he had a lacrosse question.

"No—I mean—not really." I stumble all over my words like I'm falling down the stairs again. "Not enough to play with the two of you."

"Okay." He shrugs and turns back to Samantha. "What did you have in mind?"

Then they're lost to the game and talks of drills and ground balls and defense. They run the length of the yard, throwing the ball back and forth to each other from all angles. I've seen Samantha play a billion times, so today my eyes are locked on Rob. I can see why he and Connor would have been thinking about scholarships: he's as athletic as my sister, and the ball whips back and forth from his stick like he's got it on a string.

Then they start a new drill where they're running parallel, then one of them chucks the ball way out into the grass, and they race to see who can get it off the ground first.

Samantha is more aggressive at first, shoving Rob out of the way, and I can tell he's trying to go easy.

"Are you sure you should be doing that?" I yell to her.

She ignores me and puts her shoulder down and gets him right in the gut.

He yields and lets her scoop the ball off the ground, but he's smiling, spinning the stick in his hands. He got rid of his sweatshirt twenty minutes ago, leaving his arms bare. My eyes are transfixed by the way his biceps move.

He's breathing hard, but he says, "I feel like I'm at a disadvantage here."

"Why?" says Samantha. She's breathing equally hard, blinking sweat out of her eyes. She doesn't smile. "Because of the baby? I'm not a china doll. Play for real or get the hell out of here."

My sister, the master of tact.

Rob loses his smile. "Fine."

"Fine." She twists her stick, then tosses the ball far ahead. They sprint for it.

He's faster, but not by much. This time, when Samantha tries to shove him away, he ducks inside her movement, his stick flying out to capture the ball. She tries to jab him in the side, but he twists and shoulders her away.

She refuses to yield. Their legs tangle. They go down.

Oh, crap. I'm on my feet.

The porch door behind me slides open. My father's voice booms across the yard, some mixture of worry and anger. "Samantha! Are you okay?"

Then he's rushing past me, still in uniform.

Double crap. I go after him.

By the time he gets to them, Rob is pulling Samantha to her feet.

They're both red-faced and breathing hard, but she's smiling. "That was awesome."

Rob's eyes are wide and concerned. "Are you all right?" he's asking her. "I didn't— I didn't mean to—"

"You're damn right you didn't mean to," my father says. "What do you think you're doing here?"

Rob falls back a step, but he doesn't flinch from my father's eyes. "Maegan invited me."

Uh-oh. Dad turns his eyes to me. "Are you crazy."

So rhetorical there's not even a question mark. I babble anyway. "Samantha was bored. She wanted to play. Rob is my math partner—"

"Enough." He turns to Rob. "Do you know what you're doing? You could really hurt someone."

"It was an accident," Rob says. "We got carried away." Then he tacks on, "Sir."

"Well, it's not going to happen again." He glares at Samantha, who hasn't said a word. Her breathing has returned to normal. Any joy has died from her eyes, leaving nothing but righteous anger.

"What on earth are you *thinking*?" my father demands.

"I was thinking I wanted to play a game," she snaps. She shoves her lacrosse stick into Dad's chest, and he catches it automatically. "No one got hurt. Not even the 'little problem.'"

He looks like he wants to break the stick in half. His jaw is clenched. "Come inside. We're going to talk about this." He looks at Rob. "And *you* are going home."

Rob takes a step back. He nods quickly. "Yes, sir."

"No." Samantha loops an arm through Rob's and holds him there. "He's Maegan's friend. And we're going to dinner."

Rob takes a breath. He looks to me as if for help. "I, uh . . ."

My father ignores him. "You are doing no such thing. You are coming into this house, and you are going to—"

"No!" cries Samantha. "I'm eighteen years old, and I'm going to get something to eat. I didn't do anything wrong. I was playing a *stupid game*. You're not telling me what to do, Mom isn't telling me what to do, and this dumb baby isn't telling me what to do." Her voice cracks, and she starts crying. "Okay, Daddy?" Her breath is hitching. "It was a stupid game. And now I'm going to go get some stupid dinner."

Dad takes a long breath and runs a hand back through his hair. "Samantha—"

"Come on," she says to me. "I need to get out of here." Then she turns and starts dragging Rob toward the driveway.

I follow, though I'm not sure if I'm doing the right thing. My father's anger hangs in the air and seems to follow me all the way to the car.

Rob doesn't bother to strip the pads, he just tosses his helmet into the back seat. I move to let Samantha ride shotgun, but she finally lets go of Rob's arm and shoves me at the passenger door.

Once we're all inside, I realize my father is still in the middle of the backyard, glaring at the car.

"Are you sure about this?" Rob says under his breath.

"Yes," Samantha says fiercely. "I can't go back there *now*."

"Okay." He starts the engine. Pulls out of the driveway. Pushes sweat-spiked hair out of his eyes.

We drive in complete silence for a minute.

Then Samantha bursts out laughing. "*Sir.* Oh my god, that was too much. You're no dummy, Rob."

He shrugs and glances at her in the rearview mirror, then over at me. "Well. You know." He smiles, and butterflies go wild in my abdomen. "He did have a gun."

CHAPTER FIFTEEN

Rob

I should be thinking about how good it felt to run with a stick in my hands again. Or maybe about how shitty it felt to have a cop in my face. Or the fact that I could have really hurt Maegan's sister—though Samantha could legitimately kick my ass. On the field or off.

Honestly, I should be paying more attention to the fact that Maegan looks really pretty with her hair loose.

Instead, I'm thinking about the fact that her father was the first man I saw after finding *my* father, and seeing him tonight brought everything back in a flash of gore-soaked memory. They teased me for calling him *sir*, but it wasn't respect. It was me trapped in a memory, when my eyes didn't want to see and my shocked brain ran on autopilot.

I'm also thinking about the fact that I've got three dollars in my pocket, and according to this stupid menu, a soda is a dollar ninety-nine.

These thoughts tangle together and go nowhere good. Some days I truly hate my father.

I wish I'd split that forty bucks with Owen.

As soon as I have the thought, guilt washes over me. The money we once had was *stolen*. It's not like Dad gambled it away or lost it in the stock market. I've taken enough, and I don't need to buy dinner at a rinky-dink Mexican restaurant on someone else's dime. Mom will have something on the table in an hour. A soda is fine. Hell, water is fine.

I shouldn't regret giving Owen all of it.

If I regret anything at all, it should be the stealing.

But I don't.

The lunch lady said I should have been more judicious with my money.

I'm still angry about that. If some kid with money came through the line and bought six orders of french fries, would she make a dig? Of course not.

But then again, some kid with money wouldn't have been eating free cheese sandwiches all year. I still can't decide if that matters. That's not Owen's fault. It's not like he picked his mom.

Then again, it's not like I picked my dad.

I wonder if my father made justifications like this.

"Are you okay?" Maegan says.

I run a hand through my hair, ruffling the sweat out of it. "Yeah, no. I'm fine." I set the menu aside and take a sip of my water. At least that's free.

She doesn't stop studying me. "So, was that a yes or a no?"

Her sister can pummel me on the field, but Maegan is the one who can pin me down with words. She's quieter, but that just means she spends more time thinking. I dodge her gaze. "I'm all right."

"Dad's buying dinner," Samantha announces. "He gave me his credit card yesterday to fill the car up with gas, so now it's on him."

"You don't have to do that." I can't take money from a cop. Especially a cop who was kind to me once.

"Oh, we're doing it," Samantha says. "I'm sick of being cooped up in the house with them. And I owe you for coming over to play. I've been dying just tossing a ball at the bounce-back."

"Anytime," I say. "I know the feeling."

"Tomorrow?"

Maegan nearly chokes on her water. I can't tell if that's a good thing or a bad thing. I can't tell if I *want* it to be a good thing or a bad thing. I've completely forgotten how to be around girls. There's no challenge when most of them are throwing themselves at you. It's a little different when none of them will give you the time of day.

My thoughts are all over the place. Maybe I'm misreading simple courtesy for flirting. Like when she sat in the back of class, under the pretense of being *fair*.

Or maybe not.

Samantha is still waiting for an answer. As usual, I've been sitting here twisting my thoughts into knots for too long.

"I can't ditch my mom every night," I say. "Friday?"

"Deal."

"As long as your dad isn't going to be waiting on the porch with a shotgun."

"I'll check his schedule first," says Maegan.

That's reassuring.

A waiter comes to the table. He's around our age, but I don't know him. He looks like he'd hang with the hipster crowd, with wild orange hair and thick-rimmed glasses. His name tag reads *Craig*.

"Hi, again," he says, his eyes locked on Samantha. His voice is almost breathy.

Wow. I may have forgotten how to act around girls, but I can at least keep from slobbering. This guy isn't even subtle.

I mean, I get it, but Maegan's sister is a little too intense for me. She's definitely too intense for him.

Especially since she blinks at him. "Again?"

Maegan smacks her on the shoulder. "Hi, Craig."

"Oh. Right." Samantha folds her menu closed. "We want the guacamole. And the taco platter. And the flauta platter. And the fajitas. And the—"

"Are we expecting a crowd?" Maegan says.

"I'm hungry." Samantha looks at me. "What do you want?"

Now that we're talking about food, I'm starving. It's like the mention of guacamole turned on the food receptors in my brain. "I'm fine. Nothing. I'll eat with my mom."

Samantha looks at Craig. "Two taco platters." Then she turns to Maegan. "What do you want?"

"I'm pretty sure there will be enough to share."

Craig makes a note on his pad and rushes off. But not before offering a quick smile for Samantha.

"He is so obsessed with you," Maegan says under her breath to her sister.

"Oh my god. He is not."

"He is," I offer.

Both their eyes shift to me, and I almost blush. I'm still getting used to having company around me. "I'm surprised he didn't 'accidentally' fall into your lap."

Samantha's eyes light up, but only for a moment. Then her face falls. "Too complicated. I still don't know what to do about David."

I hesitate. "The father?"

"Yeah." She rubs her hands over her face. "I keep wanting to call him, but he's blocked me. Megs says I can use her phone, but . . . What do you think?"

For a minute, I don't realize she's asking my advice. "What do *I* think?"

Her hands slide down her face. "Yeah. You're a guy. If you got a girl pregnant, then blocked her calls, and then she called you from another phone, what would you do? Is he going to hang up on me?"

"That's one hell of a hypothetical."

Her eyes don't leave mine. "So?"

"If I got a girl pregnant, I wouldn't block her calls."

Her eyes look wounded. "You're not helping."

"It's her professor," Maegan says softly. "And he's married."

Ever since I found my father in the den, it takes a lot to shock me. This is doing it. I have no idea what expression is on my face right now, but it must not be good.

Samantha slaps her hand on the table. "You said he *knew*!"

"He knew about the baby. I didn't give him the whole sordid story."

I clear my throat and straighten. "You should call."

Samantha snaps her head around. Her eyes are hopeful, like this is what she wanted me to say. "Really?"

"Yeah. It's his kid, right? And he's not some college freshman. He can man up and take a phone call."

Jesus. I sound like my father. The thought makes me scowl.

Samantha doesn't notice. "Okay. Okay." Her breathing accelerates. "Megs. Give me your phone."

Maegan slides out her cell phone. "You're going to do it right here? Right now?"

"I have to or I'm going to chicken out." She starts to dial. "I'll go outside. Come get me when the guacamole gets here."

"You want me to interrupt your call with David for *food*?"

"Shut up. It's ringing." She walks away from the table.

Leaving me and Maegan alone.

I have to clear my throat. I pull apart my straw wrapper just for something to do with my hands. "So. Her married professor, huh?"

"Yeah." She hesitates, and her voice is very soft. "My parents don't know *that* part."

I consider the way her father was angry about the fact that we were playing lacrosse. This would probably be a whole new level. "I'm guessing this David won't be able to 'sir' his way out of that."

"No."

"Is the guy, like, sixty? Because *professor* is making me think of someone with a white beard smoking a pipe while climbing on top of your sister."

Maegan chokes on her soda, then laughs. She's so serious all the time that it feels like a reward to make her laugh. I have to smile in return.

I completely forgot what this felt like, to sit in a restaurant and laugh.

The thought is sobering. God, I'm such a loser.

"No," she says, still smiling. "But he's in his late twenties. My parents will flip."

"What's your sister going to do?"

"I don't know. I don't think she knows. And it's making the house really uncomfortable." She hesitates. "No one wants to live through the abortion debate at the dinner table. That's why this is our second time here this week."

Wow. She's considering ending it, and this douchebag won't even take her calls. Wouldn't he want to know? I think I would.

Maegan grimaces. "I'm sorry. I'm sure this is the last thing you want to think about. I didn't mean for her to force you into coming to dinner with us."

"You didn't force me." I shrug and use my straw to poke at the bottom of my water glass. "And it's nice to fixate on something other than whether my father needs a diaper change."

She goes still. Her face pales a shade.

Now it's my turn to grimace. "Sorry. Overshare."

"Do you have to . . . do that?"

I meant it as an offhand comment, but I wish I hadn't said anything. I shift in the chair and keep my eyes on my glass. I don't talk about this with anyone. Ever. "We have a nurse who comes during the day. But at night I have to help my mom."

There is absolute silence for a moment. The restaurant isn't crowded, but our table seems shrouded in quiet regret. If we were in the grass and Samantha slammed into me right now, I'd shatter into a million pieces.

Then Maegan places her fingers over mine. "Rob. I'm so sorry."

My throat tightens. It's too much, after the memories her father dragged up. I take a breath and shrug. "It's fine. It's life. You know."

"I know."

But she doesn't let go of my hand. It's the first time in months someone other than my mother has voluntarily touched me. Her fingers are a warm weight over my own.

I forgot what this felt like. My breathing goes shallow. I don't deserve this, but I can't bear to pull away.

"Hey, you guys!" a girl says brightly.

I snatch my hand away. Sniff back tears I didn't realize sat so close. Slam the vault on all that emotion.

A girl and a guy approach the table. I don't know them, but I've seen them around school. I think the girl's name is Rachel. She's tall, almost as tall as I am, with spiral curls. The guy is even bigger, all muscles and gut, wearing a plaid fleece and jeans. I think he plays football, but I could be wrong. His expression is unreadable.

Not that I'm trying too hard to read him. My brain is spinning, still trapped in the moment two minutes ago, when Maegan's hand fell over mine.

"Hey," says Maegan. She sounds thrown, which is one hundred percent better than how I feel. "What are you guys doing here?"

"I've been craving tacos, so I begged Drew to take me out." Rachel drops into the chair Samantha left, leaving the guy to sit down beside me.

"Why don't you join us," I say dryly. I mean it to be light, but I sound like a prick.

Drew pulls his chair closer to the table and says, "We will. Thanks."

Okay, good. He sounds like a prick, too. At least I'm on a level playing field.

A familiar tension settles over the table—or at least a tension familiar to *me*. It's the same tension that rides along for every classroom interaction, every discussion with someone who might have known my father.

Maegan must pick up on it, because she leans in and haltingly says, "Um. Rob, this is my best friend, Rachel. And her boyfriend. Drew."

"Hey," I say. I can do this. I can be normal.

Encouraged by that, Maegan says, "Drew and Rachel, this is—"

Drew flips open a menu. "We know who he is."

Of course they do.

I would give anything for my mother to call me with an emergency right now. The house burning down. My father speaking in tongues. The FBI on the front porch again. Anything.

My phone sits silently in my pocket. Traitor.

Rachel leans in to Maegan. She speaks softly but doesn't do the greatest job. "Are you guys on a date? How could you not tell me?"

"It's not a date," Maegan says quickly.

Drew looks at me. "Charity?"

Rachel pokes him, chastising him under her breath, but his gaze doesn't leave mine.

I'm pretty sure my eyes are sending a clear message right back.

Maegan is scrambling. "No, Samantha wanted to run lacrosse drills, so I invited Rob over—"

"Your sister hasn't gone back to school yet?" says Rachel. "Is she still sick?"

Maegan's mouth is working but no sound is coming out. I've never met someone so bad at keeping secrets. She's going to spill the beans *again*, and I'm guessing these people would be more of a gossip mill than I am.

"She said it's the first day she woke up without a fever," I offer. "I figure I can't catch strep from a lacrosse ball."

"And it's not like you've got any friends left anyway, right?" says Drew.

"Hey," says Maegan. "Stop it."

A year ago, I could have played this off as a sports rivalry—the lacrosse team and the football team always have a little less-than-friendly antagonism going on. But now there's too much history on my side, and it's impossible to ignore. I don't know if Drew has a specific beef with me—I don't keep track of *every* lawsuit pending against my family—but I torture myself enough. I don't need this douchebag to help out.

I ball up my napkin and toss it on the table. "You think you can get a ride home from your friends?" I say to Maegan.

"I . . ." She glances uncertainly at Drew, who's studying the menu extra hard, then at Rachel, who looks uncomfortable but obviously won't speak out against her man. Maegan's gaze returns to me. "Rob, wait, please—"

"Text me next time you want to work on the project."

She says something in response, but I can't hear her over the blood rushing in my ears. I knew this was a bad idea. I don't know how I let it all go so far.

Cold air punches me in the face when I storm out of the restaurant. My eyes burn from the wind, and I bury my hands in the pockets of my sweatshirt. It's dark enough that no one will see me.

Until I get to my Jeep and discover Samantha sitting on the back bumper.

She's sobbing into her hands.

Shit.

I should get Maegan. I can't even text her, since Samantha has her phone.

The last place I want to go is back into that restaurant.

I'm such a jerk that I'm standing here thinking about my discomfort when Maegan's pregnant sister is sitting alone in a cold parking lot, crying on the back of my car.

That spurs me into motion. I stride across the gravel and stop in front of her. "I'm guessing it didn't go well."

She swipes at her eyes and looks up at me. "His wife answered."

Whoa. All the breath leaves my lungs in a cloud of steam.

I turn and drop onto the bumper beside her. I barely know this girl, but at least I'm not the only one with problems.

It's such a selfish thought that I want to kick myself.

She brushes more tears off her cheeks. "I'm so stupid."

"You're not stupid."

"You just met me. Trust me. I can be pretty stupid." She swipes the last of the tears on her cheeks and points at her abdomen. "Case in point."

"You didn't put it there yourself." I sit back against the tailgate. "What happened with the wife?"

She looks over at me. Her eyes are still watery. "Do you really care?"

I'm kind of morbidly curious. "I'm listening."

"So at first, I asked to talk to David. I almost couldn't talk, so I sounded like a total mess. It was so quiet, for like the *longest* time. I pulled the phone away from my face because I actually thought she hung up. But then she demanded to know who I am, and I—I lost it. I started crying. And then—*and then*—she said, 'Oh great. Another one.' And hung up. Can you believe that? *Another one.*" She starts crying again, sobbing openly. "This stupid baby keeps making me cry. I hate crying."

"You're really good at it."

She laughs through her tears, then looks up at me, her lashes shining. "Did you come out here to check on me?"

I wish I could claim compassion. I look away. "No. I came out here to leave."

"Why?"

"Some of Maegan's friends showed up. They don't like me much." I kick at the gravel of the parking lot.

"Is it Rachel and Drew? What's their problem? They're usually pretty nice."

"I've only known them for thirty seconds, but *nice* isn't the word I'd use."

The front door of the restaurant bursts open, and Maegan comes out, huddled in her jacket. She spots us across the parking lot, and her steps slow for a moment.

"You're still here," she says to me. But then she must notice her sister's tear-streaked face and rushes on with, "Sam! Are you okay?"

"I'm better. Rob made me laugh."

I'm not even trying to be funny. I push off the bumper and straighten. "I'll let you guys go eat."

"Wait." Maegan puts a hand on my sleeve. Her eyes shine in the darkness, and our breath forms a cloud between us. "Drew was being a jerk. I'm sorry. I shouldn't have let him say that stuff."

"It's not a big deal."

"There are like four hundred tacos. Will you come back?"

I glance at the door to the restaurant.

Drew's voice is like an ice pick in my brain. *Charity?*

I can't. I shouldn't have done this at all. I don't belong here.

I shake my head. "I need to go. I don't like leaving my mom alone."

Maegan's expression evens out. I'm sure she's thinking of what I said about my dad. I'm sure she's considering what her friends said right to my face.

I don't know where I stand with her. I don't know why it matters, but it suddenly does. Too much. I let myself want something for five minutes, and now it's like losing everything all over again.

"My life is a mess," I say to her. "Let's keep it to calculus, okay?"

She blinks. Her eyes are still shining. But then she takes a step back. "Okay. Whatever you want."

Then she and her sister move out of the way, and I lock myself into the Jeep, leaving them standing there in the cold.

CHAPTER SIXTEEN

Maegan

Last night with my parents was a nightmare. But this dinner with my friends and sister is coming close.

Especially since Samantha isn't pulling any punches with Drew.

"What's wrong?" she says when we all sit back down. "Another guy at the table made you feel inadequate?"

He snorts and picks up a taco. "If you're talking about Rob Lachlan, the last thing he makes me feel is inadequate."

Rachel's eyes are on me. "Two days ago, you were pissed that he was your partner, and now you're eating dinner together?"

"I invited him to dinner," Samantha says. "Not Maegan."

"Trust me," Drew says to my sister. "You can do better."

"Funny," says Samantha. "I said the same thing to Rachel."

"Sam!" I snap.

But Drew laughs. "It's fine. I can take it. I don't have to walk away from the table."

That's definitely a dig at Rob. I want to defend him—but I'm not sure how. "Why do you have such a problem with him?"

"Why do *you* feel so sorry for him? His dad stole millions of dollars, and the kid still lives in a mansion." Drew snorts. "If *my* dad stole something, I guarantee you no one would be all like, 'Poor little Drew.' They'd be waiting for me to show up at the gas station in a ski mask."

That shuts me up. I'm not sure what to say.

Drew grabs another taco. "See? You know I'm right. *You* cheated on the SAT and you didn't even get suspended. You get to take it again! No questions asked! You think that would've happened to a black kid? Hell, my freshman year, some other kid lost his wallet in gym class, and they searched my locker first."

I swallow.

"She didn't get suspended because it was a first offense," says Samantha.

"And she's a straight-A student," says Rachel. "She made a mistake."

I fix my eyes on my plate. I do not like the turn of this conversation.

Especially because I know Drew's right.

"A mistake." Drew wipes at his mouth with a napkin. "That's my point. You guys get to *make* mistakes. Rob Lachlan looks guilty as hell all the time. There's no way he didn't know what his dad was doing, but he's walking around without an ankle bracelet." He snorts. "Poor Rob. Give me a break."

There are so many things I want to say.

He didn't do anything wrong.

He's lonely.

He's sad.

He's living with the mindless body of his father.

But none of that means that Rob is innocent. He can be sad *and* guilty. I don't know anything about investing, or what an internship—if that's what it was—would entail. If Rob was working for his dad, would he have known? How could he not?

With the whole school against him, it's hard to stand up for him. He barely stands up for himself. Drew was right: Rob *did* walk away from the table. Is that a sign of weakness or guilt? Or is that a boy so beaten down that he can't take any more?

Drew's words weigh all these thoughts down with another: Am I only giving Rob the benefit of the doubt because of the color of his skin?

"He can't help that he's a white kid," Samantha says. She's spooned a massive pile of guacamole onto her plate, and she's now dipping her taco into it.

"No one says he has to *help* it," says Drew. "I'm just saying being white cut him some slack. A lot of slack."

This all feels so complicated suddenly. Drew's not wrong. Consequences seem to fall all over the map. Look at Samantha. Look at Rob.

Look at me.

I love Rachel and I like Drew, but I don't want to be at this dinner table.

My phone is sitting by my hand. I want to text Rob to see if he's okay.

Rachel is watching me. "You like him," she says quietly.

"What?" I snap my head up. "No. I don't."

"You're not saying anything."

I'm irritated. "I just said something."

"You're turning red." I expect her tone to be teasing, but it's not. She doesn't like the idea. We've never really talked about Rob Lachlan, but I consider how she didn't say anything when Drew was being so mean.

"You're pretty red," agrees my sister. She loads another taco with guacamole. I wonder what that's going to look like when it comes up later.

Drew laughs. "Your dad would lock you up if you tried to date Rob Lachlan."

"No, he wouldn't," I snap. "And I don't want to date him. He's my math partner. He ran some drills with Samantha since she was home. The end."

My voice is too loud, too tense. Silence falls over the whole table. Rachel and Drew exchange a look.

Forget this. I stand up. "I'm going to call Mom to come get me."

"Maybe you could call Rob," says Drew. Then he cracks up. "Maybe you two would make the perfect couple."

Now *that* is a dig at me. I storm away from the table.

The fact that I was considering texting Rob doesn't make me feel any better.

The air bites into my skin when I step out of the restaurant. Maybe Rob does deserve to be the senior class social pariah. He wasn't exactly friendly and all-welcoming when he was popular. I can't reconcile dude-bro jock Rob Lachlan with the boy who looked ready to cry in the middle of Taco Taco.

The door to the restaurant bursts open, and feet crunch across the gravel. I expect Rachel to be coming after me, especially when an arm falls across my shoulders, but it's Samantha.

"Are you okay?" she says.

"It's a weird night."

"He was being kind of mean," she says.

"No. He's right." I pause. "Maybe I am giving Rob a free pass. Maybe he did help to rip off the whole town."

Samantha falls quiet for a minute. "Do you really believe that?"

"I don't know what to believe."

"I remember when Dad came home that night. When Rob's dad tried to kill himself. He was really upset."

I nod. I remember that, too. We walk in silence for a few minutes.

"Everyone at school hates him," I finally say. "Everyone thinks he had to be in on it."

"People love finding the weak link that makes them feel superior. I see it in lacrosse all the time. Girl can't keep up? Cut her down even more. If someone else is weak, it means you've got the advantage."

Her voice is sad. We should be calling Mom, but we keep going, turning out of the parking lot to walk along the road.

"Do you think that would happen to you?" I say.

"Of course." She kicks at road grit. "Hasn't it happened to you?"

I frown. It's the first time she's asked me about cheating. Honestly, I wasn't even sure she was aware of how things have changed for me. "Yeah." I pause. "I didn't think you'd noticed."

"Of course I noticed." She hesitates, then blows out a long stream of steam into the air. "Megs—"

"I don't want to talk about it."

As soon as I say the words, I realize I'm lying. I actually want her to push.

She doesn't. The silence swells between us. I need to break it.

"Do you want to end your pregnancy?" I ask her.

"*I* don't want to talk about *that*." She keeps her arm around me, and we keep walking. "You do like Rob, don't you?"

"He's . . . interesting." I look over at her shadowed profile. "Do you think there's a chance he really didn't know what his dad was doing?"

"Do you know everything *our* dad is doing?"

"No, but that's a little different. Dad's a cop. I'm not doing ride-alongs every night."

"Yeah, well, even if you were, do you think Dad would involve you in something illegal?"

"I doubt it . . . but Dad wouldn't do that. He's too honest. We can't compare him to some guy who stole millions of dollars."

"He was still a dad."

The thought is jarring. It rattles me along with Rob's comment about having to change his father's diapers. I can't even imagine. I don't *want* to imagine.

"This is so complicated," I say.

"Trust me." Samantha pats her still-flat stomach. "I know all about complicated."

We call Mom from the little strip mall down the street, but she doesn't come to get us.

Dad does. In his police cruiser.

I get in dutifully, but Samantha walks up to the driver's side window and knocks until he rolls it down.

She leans on the window ledge. "I called Mom."

"Your mother's in her pajamas." His voice is much harder with Samantha than it ever is with me. Especially now. "You got me."

"I'm not getting in here if you're going to give me a hard time about playing lacrosse."

He sighs. "The last thing I'm worried about is you playing lacrosse."

"Are you worried BECAUSE I'M PREGNANT?" She all but yells this, and an elderly couple leaving the dry cleaners next door glances over curiously. Nothing like a teen girl screaming at a police officer to generate a few stares.

"Get. In. The. Car." My father's voice could cut glass.

"Not until you promise you aren't going to interrogate me."

"I'm about to *arrest* you. Get in."

"YOU'RE GOING TO ARREST A PREGNANT TEENAGER?"

My father gets out of the car with such speed that Samantha actually blanches and falls back a few steps. His voice is lethally quiet. "You will get in this car or I will drive to that school and question every boy I see until I find the one who did this to you."

"Oh yeah?" Samantha snaps. "Go ahead and try."

"Watch me."

"Can I get out first?" I call.

It breaks the tension. My father sighs. Raises his hands. "Fine, Samantha. You win. You want your mother? Fine. I'll tell her to get dressed and come get you." He pulls a cell phone out of his pocket.

I expect that to spur Samantha into motion, that she'd climb into the car. She doesn't. She stands there with her arms folded while he calls. Listens as he explains the situation.

Poor Mom.

He only speaks for a few moments—"Yeah, she's refusing to leave with me. I'm not having a video of me shoving my daughter into a police car showing up on YouTube"—then presses the button to end the call.

He flings the phone into his cup holder and rolls up the window between him and Samantha.

I expected her to get in the front—big sister privilege, as she used to call it—so I'm in the back seat, like a prisoner. He's not on duty, so the radio is turned down, but he always has it on. Codes come across the wire about problems all over the county.

When he closed the window, I expected him to shift into gear, but he doesn't move. We sit in the quiet warmth, listening to a report about an alarm going off at a convenience store in Linthicum.

We sit here long enough that I wonder if I should have gotten out to stand with my sister. Solidarity or something. But I can't open the door from inside, and she's still beside the car, arms folded across her chest. Breath streams out of her mouth in a long cloud.

I want to ask if I can get out and give her my coat, but I don't want Dad to yell at me. He can see how cold she is.

"Are we waiting for Mom?" I say softly.

"Of course." His voice is gruff. "I'm not leaving your sister in the middle of a parking lot."

It'll take Mom at least ten minutes to get here. And that's if she were dressed and ready when he called.

I sit back against the seat and sigh.

"What are you doing with that boy?" he asks me.

Uh-oh. "Can I get out and stand with Samantha?"

"Maegan."

"I told you. He's my math partner. Sam was saying she wanted to run some drills, and he plays lacrosse, so—"

"Last night, you needed to borrow the car to go to Walgreens. You were meeting with Rob Lachlan?"

"Yes." I pause. "Is that a problem?"

He's quiet. Thinking.

"It's not like he's some violent criminal," I say. "We have to calculate dropping a ball from different heights. He's perfectly polite."

"I'm not worried about him being polite."

"Then what are you worried about?" After Drew's attitude, this is almost too much. My voice finds an edge. "Do you think he's guilty, too?"

"I don't know. That wasn't my investigation." His voice softens. Mom and Samantha have always been close, but Dad's always been gentler with me than my sister. "I do know that boy's had a rough time of it, and it's not getting any easier anytime soon." He turns in his seat to look at me through the gridded mesh. "I know you had a rough time of it last year, too, and you need to get yourself back on the straight and narrow."

"So you think I should cut him off like everyone else?"

"I think desperate people do desperate things." He shrugs a little. "You know what his father did. Growing up with that as a role model . . . you don't know what that can do to someone, sweetheart."

I don't know if my dad's talking about the millions of stolen dollars or the attempted suicide or both—and I'm not sure if it matters. I swallow. "Okay, Daddy."

"Do your project. Be kind to him like you always are. But don't invite him to the house anymore. Okay?"

"Okay." My voice is soft. "You think . . . you think he'd do something wrong?"

"I don't want to think so, but he's lost everything. So has his mother. From what I understand, they're hanging on by a thread."

Rob flinched over a ninety-nine-cent cup of coffee at Wegmans. Tonight, he studied the menu at Taco Taco and then declined dinner, choosing to sip from a glass of water. "I know. I know they are."

Headlights flash across the storefronts, then Mom pulls her minivan into the space on the other side of where Samantha is still standing.

Dad unlocks his door. "When you've lost everything," he says, "sometimes you don't see anything wrong with taking a little back."

CHAPTER SEVENTEEN

Rob

Mom is making a chicken Caesar salad. Great.

There's nothing wrong with chicken Caesar salad, but it's kind of depressing when your stomach thought it was getting tacos and guacamole.

She always cheats and adds bacon, though, which makes it better, and dumps on a ton of generic parmesan cheese. I remember when she'd grate her own, but I know better than to mention that. She's got some kind of R&B music playing in the kitchen, and she's singing along while she assembles the food. I want to tell her she's too old for this kind of music, but it's rare for the house to feel anything but tense and solemn, so I'm not going to rock the boat.

Dad's in the family room, his wheelchair pointed at a rerun of *The Daily Show*. I don't pay much attention to politics, but I do know he hated political comedy. I wonder if Mom stuck him in front of it on purpose or if the show changed over while she was cooking.

I don't change the channel.

When I make my way into the kitchen, she's dancing around, slicing the chicken in rhythm.

"You're in a good mood," I say.

"Robby!" She sets the knife to the side, then dances over to me to kiss me on the cheek. "I thought you'd be later. I was going to wrap your salad up."

"Nope. I'm here." She dances her way back to the cutting board.

Then I notice the glass of red wine on the counter. The half-empty bottle behind it.

Wow.

I don't care if she drinks—hell, I'm surprised she's not lit every night. I have half a mind to ask if I can join her. But there hasn't been a drop of alcohol in this house since Dad pulled the trigger. I don't know if it's a money thing or if she's worried about what people would think—or some combination of the two—but she's always been pretty conservative.

"Stop at the liquor store?" I say.

"A client gave my boss a bottle, and he gave it to *me*." She's a little too emphatic on each word, and she goes back to singing along with the music.

I could go the rest of my life without hearing my mother sing about licking someone's skin.

I clear my throat. "You want me to slice that chicken?"

"Nope, I've got it."

I watch her anyway, worried she's going to take off a finger.

Then she says, "How's Connor doing?"

Just when I thought my night couldn't get any more irritating. "Why the hell would I know how Connor is doing?"

She glances at me over her shoulder while the knife flies through the food. It takes everything I have to keep from snatching it away from her. "You said you were going to run some drills with a friend. I assumed you were meeting up with Connor."

"No, Mom, no." I grit my teeth. "I know you're hammered right now, but maybe tomorrow you'll remember that Connor's dad is the one who—"

"Whoa." She turns and points the knife at me. Not in a threatening way. More to make a point. "First of all, I'm not even a *little* hammered. Second—"

I snort. "Yeah, okay."

"*Second*, what Connor's dad did and what *your* dad did shouldn't have any bearing on your friendship. You boys were thick as thieves."

"Nice phrasing, Mom."

She winces, then picks up her glass to take a sip. "When it was all going to hell, I'd hoped you'd be able to lean on him."

A pause, and her voice softens. "We were all so close, Rob. You know that. It was hard for Bill to blow the whistle—but I don't blame him. I can't blame him. What Dad was doing was wrong. Marjorie even came to sit with me the day after the FBI showed up." Mom's expression turns solemn. "Did you know that? It took a lot for her to do that. It meant a lot that she didn't treat me like—"

"I don't want to talk about this." Connor and I were best friends because our fathers were best friends. I've often thought about what I would have done if our situations were reversed: if Bill Tunstall was the one who'd been stealing, and Connor was the shamed son.

I consider the way Connor rags on me at school. The way he smacked my head and stood over me, waiting for me to clean up the spilled money. His smug superiority.

I would like to think I'd never act that way. But I consider how I used to look at kids like Owen Goettler and I realize I'd probably be exactly the same.

This thought gives me no comfort whatsoever. It makes me glad I told Maegan to keep our relationship to schoolwork. I don't deserve her friendship. I don't deserve kindness. Not from anyone.

But her fingers were so warm on mine. The air so quiet between us. The beginning of trust.

Then her friends showed up.

We know who he is.

My father used to say, "I don't carry a grudge, but I have a functioning memory."

He was talking about people who screwed him over in business, but that expression always stuck with me. I won't let bitterness over Drew's comment stew in my gut—but I'm not going to forget it, either.

"Do you want to talk about when you're going to go see a counselor?" Mom says.

I freeze. No. I want to talk about that even less. I almost fell apart when I made an offhand comment to Maegan about Dad's care. I can't sit in a room with a stranger for an hour. I can't do it.

"Because I made you an appointment," she continues. "A girl at work says her pastor works with a lot of troubled youth in the community. It's not religious, just someone—"

"I already made an appointment," I say quickly.

The words fall out of my mouth automatically.

I expect her to call me on the lie immediately, but maybe the wine is working in my favor. Or worse, maybe I've never given her a reason to think I'd be dishonest. Her face brightens. "You did? Where?"

"The school psychologist." Another lie. But I can fix it. Tomorrow. I can make an appointment.

I think. I think we have one. I'm sure we have something.

In the back of my head, my conscience is at work with a pickax. Did my father lie so easily? Did my mother believe him so easily?

"Really?" she asks.

I nod. "Yeah."

For some stupid reason, I'm thinking of Maegan at the restaurant, how she nearly spilled all her sister's secrets right out on the table. She's honest. She's good.

I'm standing here lying to my drunk mother about something completely inconsequential.

I should take it all back. Promise to see this pastor and not mention it again.

But I've buried myself in the lie. She's already enveloping me in a hug.

"You're such a good boy, Rob. I don't know what I'd do without you."

"Well." I clear my throat. "I made a promise. I kept it."

I'm a horrible son.

Tonight, my father's eyes seem to follow me. It's in my imagination, I'm sure, but I feel like he knows I lied. He's judging me.

I want to get up and turn his chair around.

No, on second thought, I don't. I want him to sit there.

I want him to watch what he's created.

The next morning, I need to hit the library again. I couldn't sleep after everything that happened, so I sat up in bed and read that whole book. I didn't drift off until after four in the morning, so it was a real treat when the alarm blared at six.

My phone sat beside me when I was reading, and I kept hoping Maegan would text me, but of course she didn't. We're doing a math project together—and I specifically told her to keep it to that. Her closest friends believe I helped my father embezzle seven million dollars. No big deal.

Lack of sleep is doing nothing for my mental state.

"Mr. Lachlan! Back again so soon!" Mr. London's false cheer is like a dart gun. Every word pierces. *Pew. Pew. Pew.* "What did you think?"

Today, I have no tolerance for this. "You don't have to do that," I growl. "I know you hate me. Just own it, okay?"

He snaps back. Any happiness falls off his face. Now he looks like I've shot *him*.

I wish I could say I felt vindicated, but I don't. I feel like a jerk.

A girl's voice speaks from around the corner. "I need to find a physical source for this sociology project. Come on, Con-con."

Con-con. It's Lexi Miter. Connor's girlfriend. I used to mock him for that nickname. I have no idea how he's tolerated it for so long. Honestly, I have no idea how he's tolerated *her* for so long.

Lexi is the kind of girl who thinks everything is funny—even things that really *aren't*. If I had money to gamble, I'd bet she made a joke about the way I found my father. She has a credit card that her parents pay without question. Someone online got ahold of her number once and racked up $3,000 in charges from Amazon. Her parents paid it all and didn't realize for six months the charges were fraudulent.

At that point, the credit card company wouldn't reverse the charges. They said it was the Miters' responsibility to review statements in a timely manner.

I only know all this because Lexi thought it was *hilarious.* "Who has time to read a bunch of stupid statements? I've got a *life.*"

Three thousand dollars. Hilarious.

The worst part is that at the time, I remember thinking my dad would chew the credit card company a new one for refusing to reverse the charges. I wasn't thinking about how Lexi had been careless. Or that her parents were.

A few days after that all happened, Lexi texted her credit card number to our inner circle. She said, "If my parents don't care, you all should be able to reap the benefits."

I still have it saved somewhere. I remember being tempted but never used it.

It felt too much like stealing.

The irony.

"I need to ask Mr. London where they keep the older

periodicals," Lexi is saying, and her voice gives me a little jolt. In a second, they'll be in view.

I remember again the expression on Connor's face when he stood over me, the open cash box in his hand. I'm torn between ducking behind the counter and balling up a fist to clock him upside the head.

I must look like it, too, because Mr. London steps back and raises the counter. "Want to hide in my office?"

I suck in a breath, startled. I've basically just told Mr. London to go to hell. The last thing I deserve is compassion.

But then Connor says, "Whatever, Lex. But hurry. I want to get a bagel."

I slip through the opening and into Mr. London's darkened office.

My breathing is too quick, loud in the space around me.

After lying to my mother and stealing from the fund-raiser, it shouldn't feel so humiliating to add *hiding* to the list, but it does. I listen as Lexi asks for directions, and Mr. London offers to show her whatever she needs.

Then I'm alone, standing here in the quiet dimness.

His office is tiny, with no windows, but it's homey. His desk takes up most of the space, and one of the school's ancient computers occupies almost half of that. Books and slips of paper are stacked everywhere, but there are three chairs: one for him, and two for whomever else.

Dozens of photographs are tacked to the wall. My eyes flinch from the ones of him and his husband—the husband my father ripped off. I swallow, and it hurts. I need to get out of here.

Mr. London appears in the doorway. "They're gone."

"Thanks." I can't quite meet his eyes. "I didn't touch anything." My ready anger from a minute ago feels foolish, but I can't quite work out how to apologize.

He leans against the doorjamb. "I wouldn't have told you to wait in here if I was worried about you touching anything."

Suddenly, I feel trapped. Confronted. My skin is all prickly. I wish he'd get out of the doorway. My breathing quickens again, and I rub a hand over the back of my neck. I still haven't been able to meet his eyes. My fingers tighten on the strap of my backpack.

"Hey," he says, and his voice is low. "Sit down a minute."

"I need to go to class."

"I can write you a pass."

I shift my feet. "It's okay. You don't have to."

"Rob . . . what you said—"

"I didn't know, okay?" My chest is so tight that the words fall out of my mouth like they're trying to escape. "Everyone thinks I knew, that I was helping him. But I didn't know. I didn't help. I wouldn't . . . I wasn't . . ."

I choke to a stop. I have to swallow this emotion before it pours down my face. I'm nearly shaking from the effort.

I hate my father so much.

Mr. London hasn't moved. "Rob. Sit. Take a load off."

His voice is no-nonsense, and maybe I needed someone to tell me what to do, because I drop into a chair and dump my back-pack on the ground beside me. I press the heels of my hands into my eyes. I'm distantly aware of Mr. London sitting in his desk chair, when it gives a squeak of protest.

Then the room falls into silence, only broken a moment later when the first bell rings. After a minute, I lower my hands. I keep my eyes on the edge of his desk. "Sorry. I didn't mean to lose it."

He's still quiet, and the chair squeaks again as he shifts his weight.

He's quiet so long that my emotion dries up and my breathing steadies.

I finally look up. He's studying me, his expression inscrutable.

"What?" I say.

"I don't hate you, Rob." He pauses. "I won't lie—it was . . . hard at first." Another pause. "Especially when you kept coming into the library." He grimaces. "I thought . . . I thought maybe you were taunting me."

I frown. That never occurred to me. A new kind of shame sets up shop in my stomach. I shake my head quickly. "I didn't. I wouldn't. I—"

"No, I know that now. At first I didn't think you were really reading the books. I thought you were coming in every other day to screw with me." He catches himself and half smiles. "To *mess* with me. But then you checked out the Harry Potter books in order, and then the Winner's Curse series, and then all the Throne of Glass books, and I realized you were actually reading them. I mean, if you were trying to get to me, you'd grab any book off the shelf and check it out. You wouldn't spend fifteen minutes reading book jackets." He hesitates. "You would have given up when you didn't get a reaction from me."

I consider how brightly he asks about every book I return. "So, you've been screwing with *me*. Got it." I grab the strap of my backpack.

"At first, yes. But not now. I can't read everything. And I really am curious to hear what you think."

I hesitate. I'm not sure what that means.

"I didn't realize you were hurting," he says.

"I'm not." But I am, and we both know it. I almost sobbed all over his desk.

A part of me wishes he would press the point, but he doesn't. It's probably inappropriate for me to want anything from him. I should be holding a tissue box while *he* cries.

"Did you finish *Torch Against the Night*?" he asks.

"Yes," I say. "But I can't return it yet. Owen Goettler wants to read it."

His eyebrows go up. "You're friends?"

"I have no idea."

That makes him smile, but his eyes are a little sad. "You don't have to dash in and out of here, okay?"

"Okay."

"Really."

"I know." But I don't. In a way, his honesty has put me on edge. A little.

He hesitates. "You want to bolt now, don't you?"

"Yeah."

"Okay." He pulls a pad of late slips out of a drawer. He signs his name.

I take it and go.

CHAPTER EIGHTEEN

Maegan

My father's warnings are still rolling around in my head on Thursday morning. I keep up my end of the bargain and take a seat in the back of Mrs. Quick's class, waiting for Rob. I'm still not sure whether to apologize—because I want to—or keep it to math, because that's what he wants. I keep hoping I'll see him and my path forward will be clear.

But then the bell rings and he doesn't show up. Mrs. Quick calls the class to order. I'm sitting in the back by myself.

Great.

I'm still on pins and needles. There's a text on my phone from Rachel last night, asking me why I'm so upset. She points out that I was the one upset about him being my partner.

I don't know how to respond to that.

So I haven't.

I've left the text go unanswered so long that it's going to be awkward when I see her at lunch. The thought makes my stomach roll.

Maybe I should forget the last few days. We were assigned

to do a calculus project together. It's not like Rob asked me out or we've been flirting over coffee. It's math. And he's not even here.

I hope he's okay.

The thought comes unbidden, wrapped up in imaginary scenarios of his father having some kind of emergency—medical or otherwise.

The worst part of me wonders if he's cutting class. He said he has an A in calculus, but it's not like he whipped out his transcript to prove it. Maybe he knows how to lie so thoroughly that I'd believe anything he said. Dad's words about Rob's losing everything weigh heavily on my mind.

That boy's had a rough time of it.

I chew at my lip. I can't decide whether to feel sorry for Rob or to steel my emotions against him or to be wary of him.

I wonder if people feel this way about me, too.

Then he appears in the doorway. He looks tired and drawn. He raps on the door frame, and when Mrs. Quick pauses to look at him, he holds out a pink slip of paper. A late pass.

She nods and resumes her lecture.

He makes his way down the row of desks and drops into the chair beside me.

He says nothing.

I say nothing.

Now it's awkward.

I pull a slip of loose-leaf out of my binder and write a quick note to him.

Are you okay?

When I slide it on top of his notebook, he stares at the words for the longest time.

I wish I could crawl inside his head and figure him out.

He gives me a brief nod, folds the note in half, and tucks it into his backpack.

And then, for the rest of the period, he keeps his eyes focused forward and never once turns to look at me.

By lunchtime, I feel as though a line has been drawn in the sand. Well, on the tile floor. I carry my tray away from the cashier and spot Rachel and Drew at our regular table over to the right—and Rob sitting with Owen Goettler way at the back to the left.

That seems like an odd combination. For an instant, I hesitate and consider heading left. I don't like how things ended last night, and I don't like how tense he was in calculus.

When I swing my eyes back around to the right, Rachel is looking at me.

Her expression says she's already followed the line of my gaze. She knows exactly what I was considering.

If I sit with Rachel and Drew, it feels like I'm taking a stand against Rob. It shouldn't, but it does.

But if I go sit with him, it feels like I'm taking a stand against my friends. I don't like the way that feels, either. Drew was kind of a jerk to Rob last night, but his points were valid.

Finally, I take my tray and head to a table to sit by myself. I point myself in a direction so I'm not looking at Rob *or* Rachel.

Then I pull out my phone to scroll mindlessly.

The whole time I'm sitting here, I expect Rachel to come over. To ask what's wrong. To put her arm around my shoulder and ask if we're okay after last night.

Maybe she's waiting on me, and I went and sat all the way over here.

Does she owe me an apology? Do I owe her one?

Does Drew owe Rob one? I think he does—regardless of everything he said after Rob left.

No one texts me.

No one apologizes.

I pick up my fork and start eating.

CHAPTER NINETEEN

Rob

Maegan isn't eating with her friends. She's at a table by herself.

I, however, am not.

"Why do you keep looking at that girl who cheated on the SAT?" says Owen.

"I'm not." I keep thinking about what she said when we were at Wegmans, how her dad expects a lot from her. I never felt unfairly pressured by my father, but I know Connor did. I put my eyes back on my food.

"Did you know that when they caught her cheating, they had to scrap the scores of everyone in the room?"

I did hear that. "I don't care."

"They couldn't prove whose tests had been compromised, so—"

"Leave it, okay?"

"Okay." He pulls a bag of chips out of his backpack and tugs it open.

I frown, realizing he doesn't have a tray of food in front of him. "Wait. Why didn't you buy a lunch?"

"I feel like we've been over this."

"But . . ." I hesitate. "Did you give that cash to your mom?"

"No." He pops a chip into his mouth. "I didn't realize there was a mandate attached to it."

I flush. "There wasn't. I just . . . sorry. Forget it. Do what you want with it."

Irritation pricks at me, though. My neck is on the line for that money—not his.

I can't shake this feeling, though. I'm eating my sandwich, with an orange and a bag of cheese curls waiting, while he's picking at a bag of chips like they're being rationed.

"It's really bothering you, isn't it?" says Owen.

"No."

"Liar."

I set down my sandwich. "Look, what do you want from me?"

"I want you to admit that you want to know what I did with the money so you can judge me for it."

"Fine."

"You admit it?"

"Yes." I do not like this feeling at all. I shove the sandwich into my mouth and take a bite so I don't have to say anything else.

He shrugs. "Okay. I gave it to Sharona Fains. She sits next to me in history."

I rack my brain but can't come up with any idea of who this girl is—or why he'd give her money. I wait for more of an explanation, but he just keeps eating his chips.

"Why?" I finally say.

He shrugs. "She was crying to a friend that she *needed forty dollars*, and I happened to have forty dollars, so I gave it to her."

"She didn't ask you where you got it?"

"I'm a poor kid. She probably assumed I stole it."

I stare at him. He puts another chip in his mouth.

I sigh, then rip my paper bag in two, then give him half the sandwich.

"Thanks. What is this, egg salad? Do you live in a nursing home?"

"Shut up. Why did she need the money?"

"I have no idea. But she was crying, so it seemed important."

I'm trying to picture this interaction and coming up with nothing. "But now you don't have money to buy lunch."

"And how is that different from any other day?"

I open my mouth. Close it. I have no idea what to say. My brain is spinning with thoughts of Lexi Miter and her credit card number—offered to kids who really didn't need it. Or the lunch lady who wouldn't let Owen get a cheese sandwich because she disagreed with how he spent the first money I gave him.

"I have never before witnessed an existential crisis," says Owen. "I feel like I should take your picture right now."

"Would you shut up?"

"Look." Owen puts down the sandwich and sucks mayonnaise off his thumb. "The first day, when you gave me the money. You said you felt bad, right?"

"Yes."

"Before your life blew up, did you know who I was?"

I did, though only in a passing way. Some of the girls from our group used to call him "Cheese Sammich," but never to his face. I heard a guy once mutter that he was sick of Owen holding up the cafeteria line. None of these memories are ones I want invading my brain. "A little. I guess."

"I'm guessing you occasionally had ten bucks in your wallet, then, huh?"

Yeah. I did. I don't know what to say.

I wish I were still staring at Maegan across the cafeteria. I cut a glance her way. She's still alone, eating by herself at a table near the far wall.

I wonder what happened with her friends. I'm the cause of it, I'm sure. Did they cut her out? Or did she cut herself away from them? Owen's words aren't sitting well with me. I knew what Maegan did, of course, but I've never considered how that would affect her social standing, just like my father's actions affected mine. If I moved across the cafeteria to go sit with her, would that make things better or worse?

"You going to answer me or what?" says Owen.

I shift my eyes back to him. "Yeah. I occasionally had ten bucks in my wallet." I pause, and an edge enters my voice against my will. "Do you want an apology?"

"Nope." His eyes flick up and past me. "Prick alert. Twelve o'clock."

I'm quicker on the uptake today, and I swivel my head around to see Connor striding toward us. I expect him to smack me on the back of the head or something equally moronic, but instead, he's glaring at Owen. "What did you just say?"

Owen snaps his eyes back to his sandwich and doesn't say anything.

Connor moves closer. He's never been a bully, but he has a

pretty short fuse for people jerking him around. It's because he can't do anything about how often his father does it.

He's all but looming over Owen. "I asked you a question. What did you just say?"

"Leave him alone," I say.

Connor ignores me. "Did you call me a prick?"

Owen's gone still, the sandwich suspended between the table and his mouth. His eyes seem fixed on the bread, the yellow-and-white line of egg salad. It reminds me of the way bunnies go still when they sense a predator. Like a complete lack of motion will render him invisible.

"Leave him alone, Connor."

"New boyfriend, Lachlan?"

"Why? Jealous?"

That gets his attention. He swings his head around in my direction. "Are you trying to start something?"

"You're the one who came over here."

He puts his hands on the table and leans down. I'm sure he expects me to back off and wither like Owen is doing, but something has changed since Mr. London's office this morning. Maybe it's knowing I have nothing more to lose. Maybe it's realizing I'm not the only one with problems. I have no idea.

I do know I'm sick of hiding from Connor and his friends, like I did something wrong.

I hold his eyes. Keep my voice even. "How's your dad?"

He jerks back. It sounds like an innocuous question, but it's a low blow, because I know more about Connor's relationship with his father than anyone else, including Lexi Miter.

Emotion flickers in Connor's eyes, some combination of rage and regret. "Go to hell, Rob."

"Tell him I said hi."

Connor draws himself up. For an instant, I think he's going to shove me off the bench and slam me into the ground.

Mr. Kipple must notice us, because his voice calls out from forty feet away. "Mr. Tunstall. Mr. Lachlan. Is there a problem?"

Connor's hands are curled into fists at his sides. If we were in a cartoon, steam would be coming out of his ears. "No problem," he calls back tightly. He looks back at me. "Tell him yourself."

"Is that an invitation?"

He gives me a cynical look and takes a step back. "Yeah, sure. Come on over. Big party Saturday night." Then he snaps his fingers. "Oh wait. You can't. Don't you have to chew your dad's food or wipe his ass or—"

"Stop. Rob. Stop." Owen's voice, a low rush across the table. He's grabbed hold of my forearm.

I'm halfway out of my seat, and I didn't even realize it. My jaw is clenched so hard it hurts. All I see is red.

Connor laughs and walks away.

"Sit," says Owen. His eyes are as big as saucers. "Kipple is still looking over here."

I ease back onto the bench of the cafeteria table. I know better than to provoke Connor. I might know how to push his buttons, but he knows all of mine, too.

I pick up my sandwich. "Sorry." My voice sounds like I've been eating gravel. "Thanks."

"Don't mention it."

We eat in silence for a while.

Eventually, Owen lets out a nervous laugh. "I thought he was going to break my jaw for calling him a prick."

"Nah, Connor's usually all talk." It's so weird to discuss my former best friend like this. Like he's a specimen I once studied, not a guy I grew up with like a brother. "It would take more than that."

"Why did he get mad when you brought up his dad?"

I hesitate.

Owen picks up on it. "You don't have to tell me."

"No, it's—it's fine." I don't owe Connor anything. In fact, a dark, angry part of me wants to spill all his secrets on the floor of this cafeteria so our classmates can see who they're idolizing. "He and his dad don't get along. He used to try to pit us against each other. 'Why can't you be more like Rob?' That kind of thing. It used to make Connor nuts."

"Oh."

I can tell from his voice that it doesn't sound like enough. I hesitate again. "It's not just that. Connor's dad is . . . hard on him."

"What, like he knocks him around?"

"No, it's not like that. He . . ." I rack my brain, trying to think of a suitable example. "Last year, Connor got a C on a midterm and his dad locked him out of the house all night."

"Oh."

"In January. In the freezing rain." He made him go to school the next day, too. Connor texted me and asked me to drive him to school, and I remember thinking it was weird because he had his own car. He climbed in the passenger seat and shivered the whole way to school, then came down with the flu the next day.

His dad made him take Motrin and go to school anyway. Made him play lacrosse, too. The coach benched him when Connor puked in the middle of the field.

Owen picks up a chip. "I'm having a hard time drumming up sympathy."

"Maybe because he wasn't crying over forty dollars."

Owen doesn't take the bait. "You going to go to his party?"

"What? No."

"Don't you miss your friends?"

"What, are we six? No. It's fine." But I'm lying. I don't miss all of them, but I do miss some of them. I miss the camaraderie.

It feels like a weakness to admit that. I give him a look. "Why? Want to go?"

"No offense, but you're not my type."

Wait. "I'm not—"

He gives me a look right back. "I know. I'm kidding."

I can't tell if we're fighting or bickering or messing with each other. Owen is the last kid I thought I'd ever share lunch with, but I suddenly can't stand the thought of losing . . .

Losing what? A friend?

I reach out and steal one of Owen's chips. "Don't worry. I know you're holding out for Zach Poco."

He looks startled, then smiles. "Seriously, there's no contest." He hesitates. "What do you do after school?"

I look back at my food, but my appetite dries up in a heartbeat. "Didn't you hear Connor?"

Owen freezes. "Oh." Another hesitation, heavier this time. I wonder what he's thinking. At the same time, I avoid his eyes because I don't want to know.

I breathe. Swirl the water in my bottle. Listen as the weight of the silence around me settles in.

Then Owen says, "Do you have to do that every day?"

I shrug. My brain supplies the repetitive image of me going through the front door of the house. Being greeted by the sound of soap operas, which the nurse watches with my dad in the afternoons. If he's aware of what he's watching, I guarantee he hates it.

"My mom works late on Thursdays," Owen says. His voice falters. "If you want to come over and play Xbox or something. Or not. If you're busy. Don't worry. Forget it."

"Did you just invite me and uninvite me in the same sentence?"

He looks abashed. "Maybe."

"I don't have to be home until five, really." That's when the nurse leaves, and we know from experience that they'll leave at five on the nose, regardless of whether anyone has come home. Once Mom asked me to stop at the store and I didn't make it back until ten after. I walked into a pitch-dark house, my father sitting in the middle of the living room, alone. It should have been sad, but it was actually creepy as hell.

I hate when these memories invade my thoughts. "Well. If it was a real invitation . . ." Now I sound as faltering as he did. I tell myself to knock it off. "I could play some Xbox."

Owen lives in a two-story duplex south of the school. He says he usually walks, but it's windy and freezing and I don't want to leave my car, so I drive us over there. If he's surprised about the car, he doesn't say anything. I'm surprised that someone who can't buy lunch has an Xbox, but I can return the courtesy, so I keep my mouth shut.

His fridge is mostly empty, but a whole shelf is bowing from the weight of three cases of generic diet soda. He offers me one, and I take it. "My mom loves them," he says. "Her weakness. Come on, we can crash on the sofa."

His living room is small, with older furniture, but it's tidy. Owen fires up the television and suddenly we're killing Nazis in *Call of Duty*. I've never been huge into gaming—lacrosse and school took up too much time. But I can hold my own.

Or, I thought I could. Owen is kicking my ass.

"I can run the tutorial for you if you want," he says.

"Shut up."

I want to ask if *he* has any friends. The invitation to come over here took me by surprise every bit as much as the invitation to come play lacrosse with Maegan's sister.

"Can I ask you something?" I say.

He swerves with the controller like an opponent on screen is actually attacking him. "Sure."

I stop pressing buttons and study him. "Why did you invite me over here?"

"What, did you think my mom was going to be waiting in the kitchen with a revolver?"

"Um. No. Not until you said that."

He taps a button and the screen goes still, then he looks at me. "The same reason you gave me the ten bucks on Monday."

Because I felt bad. That's what I said when he asked me.

My cheeks feel warm. I stare back at the controller in my hands.

"And you seem like an all-right guy," Owen says. He's unpaused the game, and his arms swerve again. "Honestly I always kind of thought you were the asshole and Connor was the nice one."

"Wow, Owen, don't hold back."

He grins. "I guess you can be wrong about people."

"I guess you can."

"I used to hang out with Javon Marshal. Do you know him?"

I search my memory banks and come up with nothing. My expression must give it away, because Owen says, "He graduated last year, so he kind of left me on my own. He lived down the street."

"Did he go away to college?"

Owen hesitates. "No. He enlisted. Army. His mom says he might not be able to come home for Thanksgiving, but maybe Christmas."

I can't read anything in his voice. I wonder if Owen plans to enlist after he graduates.

I wonder what *I'm* going to do after I graduate. I remember being hopeful about lacrosse scholarships, because I definitely have the grades to back it up. I could possibly look at academic scholarships, but I'm not sure if I could leave Mom. Besides, even if I could get a scholarship, there are other expenses to consider. Housing. Food.

"Are you going to join the Army?" I ask.

Owen hesitates, then shrugs. "I don't know. It's a guaranteed job and free tuition, so . . ."

A key rattles in the lock of the front door, and Owen swings his head around. "Crap. She's home early."

I draw back, startled by his sudden change. "Are you not allowed to have people over?"

"No, it's fine. Just . . ." He winces. "Don't tell her who you are. Okay?"

"Oh. Sure."

The lock finally gives, and Owen's mom bursts through, bringing a gust of cold air with her. She looks to be in her forties, with tired eyes and streaks of gray threading her dark hair. It's pulled back into a tight ponytail. She's wearing nursing scrubs with lollipops all over them, the kind you'd wear if you worked in a pediatrician's office. She's fighting to get her key back out of the lock.

"Hi, Mom," Owen calls. "Why are you home early?"

"Oh, it's so *stupid*. The whole bottom of my shoe came off. It's a safety hazard, so—" She stops short when she sees me. "Oh. Hello. I didn't know you had a friend over."

Her voice puts the tiniest bit of weight on the word *friend*. I stand. I almost hold out a hand to shake hers. Old habits die hard. "Hi." I hesitate. "I'm Rob."

She smiles. Her eyes flick to Owen and back to me. "Rob. Hello."

Ms. Goettler is completely getting the wrong idea here.

And what am I supposed to say? *Oh, yeah, no, I'm Rob Lachlan. My dad stole your money. I'm not macking on your son. Thanks for the soda.*

Owen saves me. "He's just a friend, Ma. Don't start printing wedding invitations."

I cough. "I should probably go."

"You're welcome to stay for dinner," she says.

"No, I promised my mom I'd be home by five."

"Ah, so you're a good son." She comes over to the couch and ruffles Owen's hair. "Maybe you could give Owen some lessons."

You're a good son. I almost flinch.

He shoves her hand away, then rolls his eyes good-naturedly. "I'm home by five, too. Come on, Rob. I'll walk you out."

"Take my shoes by the door and toss them in the dumpster," she calls after us. "I can't believe I'm going to have to find a hundred dollars to replace those—"

The door swings closed, cutting her off, leaving us with cold silence between us.

"You didn't have to walk me out," I say to Owen.

"Nah, it's fine. I like to keep her guessing."

"Hilarious."

We stop by my Jeep. Owen's got her shoes in his hand. They're white clogs. Some kind of nursing shoes, I guess. They look like they've been beat to hell, and one is completely falling apart.

"Are those really going to cost her a hundred bucks to replace?"

"Probably. They're special shoes. She works in the hospital. They're really strict."

I think about the forty dollars he gave away. I wonder if he's thinking about the same thing.

I remember when a hundred dollars was a drop in the bucket. I had lacrosse cleats that cost twice that much, and my mother never batted an eye.

I know what a hundred dollars would mean to my mother right this moment. Hell, what it would mean to *me*.

I think about Lexi Miter's credit card, the number sitting unused but still saved in my phone.

I swallow.

"What's wrong?" says Owen. "You look like someone kicked your dog again."

I take a breath. This is more than forty dollars from a cash box. Stealing from the athletic department's fund-raiser isn't different from stealing from another student, but it feels different just the same.

Somehow, I can't stop myself. "I want to help your mom."

"Yeah? You've got a hundred bucks?"

"No." I hesitate. "But I know where I can get it."

CHAPTER TWENTY

Maegan

Friday afternoon, five o'clock. Normally, I'd be hanging out with Rachel and Drew, making plans for the weekend.

Today, I'm hiding in my bedroom with a book. My social life took a bullet last spring, but apparently I took it from gasping on the floor to DOA.

An insistent knock raps at my door. Samantha pokes her head in without waiting for an answer. "What time is Rob getting here? Is that what you're wearing?"

"What are you talking about?"

"He said he could come run drills on Friday, right?"

"Don't you remember Dad chasing him out of here? Or maybe the way Drew treated him? Or—"

"It's not a date. It's lacrosse. Text him."

I haven't spoken to Rob since Thursday morning, when he barely nodded at my note in class. "No way. Dad's downstairs. He'd lose his mind."

"Then we'll go to Quiet Waters. *Please*?"

I sigh. "He's not really talking to me since Drew ran him out of Taco Taco."

"I thought you were doing a math project together."

"Sam, he probably wants to be left alone."

Her face falls. "No, Megs. He doesn't." She pauses. "He doesn't want to be humiliated, but he doesn't want to be left alone."

Now *my* face falls. She's right.

A note in her voice tells me she's not just talking about Rob, either.

It's cold and near dark by the time we get to Quiet Waters, one of the largest parks in the county. It's usually closed at night, but they offer ice skating in the winter, so we park by the rink, which sits at the edge of the open fields.

The lot is crowded since it's Friday night, but Rob is already there, sitting on the tailgate of his Jeep. His lacrosse stick spins between his hands, jumping from palm to palm. Despite all the motion, his expression is closed down, like when he was waiting for me in the Wegmans parking lot. I was surprised that he still wanted to meet up, but Samantha was right. He *is* lonely. I know he is.

When we get out of the car, a cold breeze eats through my jacket, and I shiver. "Thanks for coming out."

He shrugs and looks across the parking lot at the shadowed field. "I didn't think about how dark it would be. We'll have a hell of a time seeing the ball."

"Let's try anyway," calls Samantha. She's already pulling on her goggles.

Rob shifts off the tailgate and grabs his helmet. "Your sister doesn't mess around," he says to me under his breath.

The low voice is encouraging. Maybe we're okay.

I open my mouth to whisper back, but he turns away to jog after Sam.

Well, then.

He was right. They can't see the ball. They both keep missing, then running after it, breath clouding in the air as they sprint across the darkened field.

Their joy from the other night is missing. Samantha is no closer to making any kind of decision about the baby. She hasn't mentioned David or school or what she's going to do. Each day that passes seems to be a ticking time bomb for her—or maybe it's a ticking bomb for our whole family.

As for Rob . . . I don't know what's up with him. This can't *all* be about Rachel and Drew—at least, I don't think so.

But no one is happy. No one is settled. No one can focus.

He doesn't want to be humiliated.

Samantha's words are nudging me with guilt. I wish I'd spoken up in his defense earlier. I just didn't know how, or if I was even doing the right thing.

Samantha and Rob have broken apart, and they're walking the field, looking for the ball. I uncurl from the bench where I've been frozen into a statue, then stride out across the darkened grass to help.

"I've got another one," Rob says as I approach. "I can get it."

"No," says Samantha. She's breathless, and I'm worried she's been pushing it too much. "It's too dark."

"Sorry." He makes a face. "I should have figured."

Samantha swallows. She suddenly looks a little green. "That might have been too much running. Or not enough dinner. Or too much—" She breaks off and takes a long breath through her nose. "I will not throw up. I *will not* throw up."

"Samantha." I put out a hand. "Here, give me the stick."

She all but slams it into my chest. "Go over there so I don't do this in front of you."

Rob frowns. "Do you need something—"

"Go." Samantha punches him in the shoulder.

I grab his arm and drag him away. "Come on."

Almost immediately, my sister throws up in the grass behind us.

Rob winces, then says, "Are you sure we should leave her?"

"I tried to hold her hair back yesterday, and she asked me if I have a puking fetish. I promise she wants to be left alone." I pause and glance up at him. The helmet leaves most of his face cloaked in darkness, the face guard painting shadow lines across his mouth.

I have no idea why I'm staring at his mouth.

A blush crawls up my neck, and I jerk my eyes forward. "There are benches by the ice rink. We can sit there."

The benches are large rectangular planters that overflow with flowers during the summer. Now, they're swarming with people lacing skates or drinking hot chocolate, but we're able to carve out a corner for ourselves. Speakers stationed around the rink blast pop music.

Rob pulls off his helmet, then roughs up his sweat-dampened hair. I expect him to say something, to make some kind of conversation, but he doesn't.

As I consider every word Drew said at Taco Taco, I wonder if Rob thinks I feel exactly the same as they do.

I sit there waiting for words to magically form in my mouth. They don't.

Rob stares out at the ice rink and eventually says, "Should we check on your sister?"

I pull out my phone and text her.

MAEGAN: You OK?

Her response comes almost immediately.

SAM: Made it to the restroom
I'll be here for a few minutes

MAEGAN: Do you want me to come there?
SAM: NO

"She's fine," I say.

"Fine?" he echoes.

"Well, she's in the bathroom. She doesn't want me to go there. So."

"So."

That's all he says. He's bouncing his stick against the slate walkway along the benches. A mother walks past us with a toddler in tow, and the little boy in a puffy snowsuit stares at us while gumming a cookie.

I take a breath. "Rob?"

His eyes don't leave the stick. "Yeah."

"I don't . . ." I hesitate. "I'm really sorry about my friends."

He glances over. "I'm used to it."

That hurts more than it should. "I know . . . and I'm sorry."

"You don't have to apologize." He's quiet for a minute. "Is that why you've been eating lunch by yourself?"

"Yeah." I blush. "You noticed?"

"I'm not exactly sitting at a crowded lunch table myself." He pauses, his expression bemused. "Though somehow I've become friends with Owen Goettler."

"I saw that," I say without thinking.

"Did you?"

Somehow his voice has grown a little . . . deeper, maybe. Softer, but more intense. Or maybe it's the cold and the dark and the uncertainty between us.

"Yeah," I say, my voice barely more than a whisper. "I did."

He studies me for the longest moment, then turns back to stare out at the night. "You could have joined us. You don't have to eat by yourself."

"I thought . . ." I swallow.

He looks back at me. "What did you think?"

"I thought maybe you were mad about what happened with Drew and Rachel."

"Oh. No. I mean, not at you." He takes a breath. "I thought maybe you were mad because I messed up your friendship."

The music from the skating rink is so loud and raucous, but we've found this little cocoon of honesty, and I lean closer to him, not wanting to break it. "Is that why you aren't talking to me?"

His eyes widen, but then he shakes his head and stares at the ground. "My whole life is complicated. I didn't mean for that to rub off on you." He inhales like he's going to say more . . . but then he doesn't.

I watch the stick spin between his hands, and for the first time I notice the tension in his forearms, the way his knee is bouncing.

I reach out and grasp the stick above his hand, gently forcing it still. "You can talk to me, Rob."

He takes a long breath and lets it out, then turns his head to meet my gaze dead on. "Do you think I knew, Maegan?" His eyes narrow slightly. "Do you think I knew what my father was doing?"

I don't know. That's what I want to say. But that's not an answer. I don't know what exists between us, but I do know Rob isn't a boy who entertains many gray areas in his life.

He's not really asking about his father at all, I realize.

What he's asking is, *Do you trust me?*

As soon as I figure that out, the answer is obvious. It's been obvious since the day I realized he was waiting for me in the Wegmans parking lot instead of letting me walk in alone.

"I don't think you knew." As I say the words, I realize they're true. All week, it hasn't been my gut telling me to be wary of Rob Lachlan. It was everyone else's gossip.

I slide my hand down half an inch until my fingers brush his. "I don't think you helped him." I pause. "I think you're kind. And honest. And thoughtful."

His dark eyes hold mine, and I wish I had a map of the emotion I see there.

Boots stop with a slide of grit on the walkway in front of us, and a girl's soft voice says, "Rob?"

We both turn and look up at the same time. Callie Rococo is looking down at us. I don't know Callie well, but we've had a few classes over the years. She's on the varsity dance team, with the body to match. She's what Samantha always calls "basic": clear skin, bright blue eyes, impeccable makeup, completely forgettable face. Right now she's wearing tight jeans tucked into Uggs, her blond hair spilling over the neck of a North Face down vest. A pair of ice skates hangs over her shoulder—definitely not rentals.

"Callie," says Rob. He sounds thrown. "I . . . hey."

"Hey," she says softly. "I was skating with my sisters on the other side." She gestures vaguely at the other side of the rink. "I thought that was you."

After a beat, Rob stands. Damn his chivalry. "Yeah, it's me."

Her eyes flick to the lacrosse stick, and a tiny frown line appears between her brows. "You still play?"

"A little."

Callie moves closer by a fraction. She touches his arm. "I've been thinking about you. How've you been?"

"I'm good." If he's surprised at the question, I can't tell. His voice is even and gives nothing away. A shadow of the old Rob Lachlan sneaks into his voice. "I was running drills, but it got dark."

Then Rob turns to look down at me, and he holds out a hand as if to pull me to my feet. "Maegan, do you know Callie?"

No boy has ever offered a hand to me, so it takes me a moment to get it together to take his, even though I can stand from a bench on my own. "Yeah, we've had a few classes together over the years."

"Sure," she says. "Hey." I brace myself for some kind of nasty comment about cheating or screwing over my classmates, but her expression isn't dismissive. Maybe my edges are too raw from everyone else, and now I'm the one who looks unkind.

I offer a small smile. "Hey."

Her eyes flick back to Rob. "I've been wanting to call you, but I wasn't sure . . . ah . . ."

"I'm around," he says.

I'm around. What does that mean?

Her eyebrows go up. "Oh! Well, great. Are you . . ." She hesitates. "Connor's having a party tomorrow night. I was going to check it out. Any chance you might want to . . ." Her voice trails off, and I can tell she's waiting for him to fill the silence.

He doesn't.

But he waits for her to finish.

"Well," Callie says, her voice faltering. Her eyes flick to me and back to him. "Maybe I'll see you guys there?"

It takes a moment for her words to register. I'm so used to people giving me a wide berth that it's a shock to be treated like I'm part of a couple.

"I don't think I'm invited," Rob says.

Samantha appears beside us. She smells like she's chewed an entire package of spearmint gum. "Invited where?"

Callie glances at Samantha, then back at Rob, and her cheeks turn pink. "Sorry—I didn't mean to get in the middle of a . . . of a . . ." Those words trail off, too. She shifts her feet. "It's been a rough few months. I just—I think a lot of people miss you being around. You should come."

"I don't think so," he says.

"Are you talking about a party?" says Samantha. Despite the fact that she spent the last twenty minutes puking, she sounds interested. "Tonight?"

"Ah . . . tomorrow," says Callie. "At Connor Tunstall's." That little frown line appears on her forehead. "Aren't you Samantha Day? I thought you went away to school."

Samantha wraps an arm around my neck. "I did. God, I need to get out. Can we come, too?"

I glance at Rob. Samantha has no idea about the dynamics here, but I would bet money that Rob would rather rip his fingernails out with pliers than go to a party at Connor's house.

I clear my throat. "Sam, you're in college." *And pregnant*, I think. "We don't have to go."

"No, it's okay," says Callie. "There are some other college kids coming, too. You know Connor has connections."

"I remember," says Rob. I can't read *anything* from his voice.

"It's fine," says Callie. "Connor won't care."

"Pretty sure he'll care." For the first time, a dark note creeps into Rob's tone.

"Well, he won't be the only one there. Come if you want, stay home if you want. No pressure." She glances across the rink. "I need to get back to my sisters." She turns and strides away.

Samantha hooks an arm around Rob's neck, too, and pulls him into our bizarre hug, like we've been hanging out together all our lives, and not just for the last few days. "Rob, my friend, you have to take us to that party."

"No way." The hard-edged confidence is gone from his voice. He sounds as off-balance as I feel.

"Who was that girl?" says Samantha. She still hasn't let go of his neck—or mine. "Do you know her?"

"Ah . . . my ex-girlfriend."

My face warms again. I didn't know that. Not that I ever kept track of that crowd, but still. It explains the tension. Worse, I can see them together. Preppy girl, preppy guy. Dancer plus athlete. They'd go to college, get degrees, then buy a six-bedroom mansion and have generically beautiful children.

Then he adds, "I haven't talked to her in months. Not since before . . . *before*."

I frown. "She broke up with you because of your dad?"

"No. She broke up with me because I was more into lacrosse than into her."

I duck out of my sister's hold. My face is still warm from all these realizations. I shouldn't even care. Rob has never done so much as flirt with me. "We can't go to a party."

"We can." Samantha gives Rob a shake. "You *have* to take us."

"You are soundly out of your mind."

"Please?" She presses her forehead against his face and mockingly pouts. I wish I had a shred of her confidence. "Please, Rob?"

He glances at me like she's not attached to his neck. "Is something on me? I feel like there's something on me."

Now I'm blushing for an entirely new reason. I don't know why she's being like this. If she wants to go so badly, she could go by herself. No one is going to throw Samantha out of a party.

Samantha stage whispers at him. "If you don't take us, I'll tell everyone this is your baby."

He bursts out laughing. "Let me warn my mom first."

"Please," she says more seriously. "Don't you have any idea what it's like to be cooped up in your room with no one to talk to?"

That hits its target. He sobers immediately, then sighs.

"Please?" Samantha whispers.

Rob looks at me. My sister is literally hanging off him, but his gaze finds mine and holds me there. "Do you want to go?"

I wish I could read his mind. I wish I knew the right answer.

Samantha lets go of his neck and attaches herself to mine. "Please?" she says. "Please, Megs."

Please, Megs. I stare back at Rob. "Okay."

Samantha squeals.

Rob sighs, then runs a hand through his hair. His expression is dark and inscrutable. I expect him to refuse again.

Instead, he says, "I'll pick you up at nine."

CHAPTER TWENTY-ONE

Rob

Mom raps on my door frame when I'm buttoning my shirt. Her eyes widen when she sees me, and she smiles. "You look nice."

"Thanks." I feel like a poser. I'm wearing a forest green button-down and jeans that I got for Christmas last year. Everything brand name, everything from a different life.

I've spent most of the day thinking of ways to use Lexi's credit card number to buy things for other people who need them. I feel like I should grab a ball cap and a hooded sweatshirt from my closet.

"You're going out?"

I try to ignore the interest in her voice. "Yeah." I hesitate. I had a lot of freedom before, and it never occurred to me to ask permission before going anywhere. I never got in trouble, so I had a long leash. "Is that okay?"

"Of course." A pause. "I'm just surprised."

Me too. But I don't say that.

I told Owen that Connor isn't the type to get physical, but I feel like he'd make an exception in my case.

Mom is still hovering in the doorway. "You look upset."

I glance at her. "I'm okay."

"You haven't mentioned how your meeting with the school psychologist went."

I turn away—but that leaves me looking back at myself in the mirror. That's almost worse. My eyes are full of self-censure. "It was fine."

"I really appreciate you doing this, Rob. I know it will be difficult at first, but I think talking—"

"Mom."

She raises her hands. "Sorry, sorry. But I do appreciate you keeping your word. You've been running every morning, you made an appointment—"

"Mom." I grab my keys and wallet from the top of my dresser before I can watch myself flinch. "I really need to go."

She doesn't move from the doorway, though, so I need to stop in front of her.

"You haven't gone out on a Saturday since it happened," she says. She straightens the collar of my shirt. "I don't want to jinx it, but . . . I'm glad you're getting back to your old self."

Since it happened. I hate how we always talk around everything. As if my father isn't lying in bed in the room next door, staring at a darkened ceiling.

As if going to a party means everything is back to the way it was.

As if I'll ever be my old self again.

Do I even want to be?

"We'll get through this," she says softly.

Maybe we're both deluded. I do know I can't douse her hope

any more effectively than I can my own, no matter how unrealistic it is.

"I know," I say more gently. "I really do need to go. I'm picking some people up."

"People?" Her eyebrows go up.

Great. Now she sounds even more excited. "Just some friends from school. I won't be too late."

"Am I a bad mother if I tell you to be as late as you want?"

My steps almost falter. "You're not a bad mother," I call back. *I'm a bad son.*

I can't remember the last time I picked up girls for a party, but I'm having the most bizarre sense of déjà vu.

Maegan told me to park on the street and text her when I got to her house. She and her sister must have been waiting by the door, because they come out immediately. It's pitch-dark outside, but they're both in skintight jeans and tops that catch a little sparkle from the distant streetlight. Samantha is practically skipping across the lawn in the heeled boots she's wearing, while Maegan follows more sedately, her arms wrapped around her midsection.

When they climb into the Jeep, cold air swirls in with them, carrying girlish scents of vanilla and oranges. I could close my eyes and imagine it's a year ago. Connor in the back seat with Lexi, Callie up front with me. Connor would be half-lit already, because he really did have connections, while I usually stayed straight sober because I never wanted to disappoint my father.

Samantha claps me on the shoulder from the back seat, and

my brain returns to the present day. "Thanks for going," she says, leaning forward to all but whisper it in my ear. Her blond hair is a cascade of curls falling over one shoulder, and dark red lipstick makes her look five years older than she is. Her eyes are dark-lined and heavy-lidded. Athlete Samantha is gone, leaving Bombshell Samantha in her place.

Maegan climbs into the front seat beside me, her eyes trained on the windshield, a soft blush on her cheeks, though I can't tell if that's makeup or reserve. Her brown hair is curled as well, her eyes lined with green and gold. I don't know her well enough to know if she goes out like this usually, or if Samantha got to her, but she never looks like this at school. A lace maroon top clings to her curves, with a silver necklace dropping a green pendant right at the start of her cleavage.

Her hands rest on her thighs, picking at a flaw in the denim. She's nervous.

I think of the way she brushed her fingers over mine and want to do the same thing.

"Hey," she says shyly. Her eyes shift my way. "Thanks for driving." A pause. "You could have backed out."

You're kind. And honest. And thoughtful. She's all those things. Not me.

"He's not backing out," says Samantha. I cast my eyes at the rearview mirror. She's applying lip gloss, using a little hand-held mirror.

"You can," Maegan says, a little more firmly. "If you want." She hesitates, and her voice softens. "You don't have to put yourself through hell because Sam wants to get out of the house."

My eyes flick down her form again, and the part of my brain

that is very much not a gentleman wishes we were going some-where more private—and leaving her sister here on the lawn.

"Don't let her fool you," says Samantha. "*She's* trying to back out."

That snaps my eyes back to Maegan's face. "You don't want to go?"

"No one wants me there," she says. Her cheeks redden, and she looks away from me. "I know a lot of people think I'm some kind of rebel, but I'm not—I'm not a party person."

"We don't have to go. No one wants me there, either."

"If we keep sitting here, Mom is going to get suspicious," says Samantha.

I put the car into gear and roll away from the curb. I was jit-tery before, but now that's doubled.

"It's a party," says Samantha. "Not a funeral. Listen to some music, drink some beer—I guarantee that after an hour no one will even care who you are."

"More like thirty minutes," I say under my breath.

"Really?" Maegan murmurs at my side.

I shrug and hit the turn signal as we roll to a stop at the end of her street. "Yeah." The first hour, I'll need to lay low if I don't want to be fair game for Connor and the rest of his crowd. There's no Mr. Kipple around to keep everyone in line at the Tunstall house. But after that first hour, everyone will be too drunk to care who shows up.

"So let's go," says Samantha.

I wait for Maegan to say a word of protest. I haven't pulled away from the stop sign yet.

I hold her eyes. She holds mine.

She doesn't say a word.

I sigh. Off we go.

Connor lives in a McMansion on the other side of Highland, a huge brick-front colonial with white pillars supporting the front roof. His yard is four acres of meticulous landscaping, complete with a long driveway, a four-car garage, and a swimming pool. Spotlights line the front of the house, tastefully aimed up at the brick, creating cones of light and darkness. Cars already line his driveway, but the last thing I want is to get trapped here, so we park on the road to walk up.

Everyone at this party probably has Lexi's credit card number.

I doubt anyone needs it.

The instant I have the thought, I regret it. When Owen gave Sharona Fains the forty dollars, I judged him for not knowing why she needed it, and here I'm doing the same thing, just in reverse.

Samantha glances over her shoulder, because Maegan and I are ambling along like we're heading to our execution. "Come on, guys. It's freezing."

"Go ahead," Maegan calls. "We're coming."

Samantha turns and jogs across the lawn.

"I don't know why she wanted to come so badly," Maegan says. "She's been throwing up all day."

"I thought about doing the same thing."

Maegan catches my hand and draws me to a stop. "Should we wait for her in the car?"

The words aren't meant to be suggestive, but my brain hears it that way anyway. I have to force my gaze to stay north of her neck. "We can," I say. "If you want."

"What do *you* want?" she says, then bites a shiver through her teeth.

"I want to burn this house down." I wish I had a coat to offer her.

She looks startled. "Do you really?"

"Why? Want to help?"

"Sure. Maybe I could one-up my reputation from cheating to arson."

Her voice is self-deprecating, and I frown. "Can I ask you something?"

Her eyes meet mine. "Of course."

"Why did you do it at all?"

Her eyes flare wide. "What are you talking about?"

"You're in a bunch of AP classes. You were shocked when I suggested splitting up the homework the other day. It's not like you *needed* to cheat on the SATs. I mean . . . I don't get it."

She swallows and looks away. "That's the problem. I don't know if *I* even get it."

"Someone said they had to scrap the scores of everyone in the room."

When she looks back at me, stars glitter in her eyes, and I realize it's because tears sit there, waiting. "I know. They all had to take it again. I have to take it again. I just—Samantha had just gotten her big scholarship. Everyone was celebrating. There was . . . there was so much pressure. For once, I wanted to be the one who succeeded. I wanted to be the one who came home with a big success that my parents were celebrating. When I think back on that day, it feels like a dream. I'd been up all night studying, and then they put me next to Randall Briggs. He already had a flipping fifteen hundred! I was so tired, and I needed a good score. I didn't mean to screw it up for everyone else. I didn't."

"Oh, Maegan." I don't even know how to finish that.

"Please don't. Please don't pity me. I don't deserve it. I know what I did was wrong."

I stare down at her and let out a breath. "I think you should stop punishing yourself."

"*You* should stop punishing yourself," she says. "You're the one who didn't do anything wrong. These were your friends. Your father—what you went through . . ." She takes a breath. "They shouldn't have turned their backs on you."

Maegan wouldn't have turned her back on me. I'm sure of it. "They all think I'm a criminal."

"Well, they all think I'm a cheater."

"You're not a cheater."

"Yeah, Rob. I was. Once."

"One mistake doesn't define you."

She sniffs and carefully swipes at her eyes. "You're going to wreck all of Sam's handiwork."

That makes me smile. I want to touch her so badly that my hand aches, but I still can't tell if she feels the same way or if she's saying these things out of kindness.

"You look very pretty," I say instead.

That blush blooms on her cheeks again. "Thanks. You look . . ." Her blush deepens. "Never mind."

"Oh, now you need to tell me."

She sobers. "I almost said you look like the old Rob Lachlan." That makes me wonder what the new Rob Lachlan looks like. "I wish I felt like him."

Feet swish through the grass nearby, undercutting a low murmur of conversation. A guy and a girl stride across the yard behind Maegan. The guy is carrying two six-packs of something in a red carton. He glances at us dismissively—just another couple having a discussion or an argument or whatever—but does a double take when his eyes land on my face.

"Rob. Wow." It's Zach Poco. I should have brought Owen.

My defenses snap into place like a brick wall assembling in a cartoon. I can almost hear the stones clinking together. "Hey," I say.

I barely recognize the girl he's with, but her eyes widen, then go from me to Maegan and back.

For a breath of time, I wonder if Zach is going to cop an attitude like Connor.

But then he shifts a six-pack under the opposite arm and extends a hand. "Hey, man. Haven't seen you in a while."

We literally go to the same school and cross paths at least once a day, but okay. I can play this game because it's preferable to the alternative. I grasp his hand and do the awkward pull that's not really a handshake and not really a hug.

"You know Lily?" he says, nodding to the girl with him.

"No. Hi," I say. "This is Maegan."

"Hey," says Zach. "You guys going in?"

I look at Maegan. "You ready?"

Her eyes say she's ready to bolt. But there must be some of her sister in her, because instead of dragging me to the car, she straightens and says, "Sure. Let's go."

CHAPTER TWENTY-TWO

Maegan

Rob leads me through the front door into a wall of darkness and sound and writhing bodies. The smell of beer hangs in the air, thick and almost sickly sweet. None of the house lights are on in the main foyer or the large room beyond, but light shines from a side hallway, offering enough illumination so we don't run into anyone. The music is all-encompassing, bass pulsing the floor. The house is massive, but I can't get a handle on the layout in the dark. People are *everywhere*, but I barely recognize half of them. Shadow cloaks every face, and I'm pretty sure we've already lost the couple Rob knew from the front lawn.

A few people glance our way as we move through the foyer, but no one stops us, and no one says anything. Eyes flick over my face and either lose interest or skip down my body.

I draw closer to Rob, tense. I'm not sure what I expect to happen. Armed guards with barely restrained Dobermans? No one is paying any attention to us.

We make it to the edge of the large room at the back. The family room? Living room? I can't tell, and in a house this big, it might be called something pretentious, like a great room. Windows take up most of the back wall, beyond which I can see a sprawling patio and a covered pool, all lined with flaming tiki torches. A few classmates are braving the cold to chat on the patio, but in here, everyone is dancing.

Then I spot Samantha, in the center of the crowd, because *of course*. She's dancing with two boys, all but pressed between them. Her eyes are closed, and she's lost to the beat and the movement. I want to roll my eyes, but at the same time, I'm glad we came. Maybe she really did need this.

Rob leans down close to speak over the music. He's never been this close to me before, and he smells like spices and warmth and every dirty thought I've ever had.

Then I realize he's asked, "Do you want anything?" and he's waiting for an answer.

I want you to keep breathing against my neck like that.

"No," I say quickly. "I'm fine."

"You sure?" His hand finds my waist, and I'm sure it's to keep me from moving away, but my world narrows down to the feeling of his palm against the half inch of skin between my shirt and jeans. "I never drink," he says. "So you can. If you want. I'll be okay to drive later."

I never drink either, but I'm so keyed up about his hand and his breath and the heady scent of his neck that I'm nodding without thinking about it.

"Okay," he says. "I'll be right back." He vanishes, leaving me there against the wall, bodies shifting all around me.

I'm about ready to melt into the floor. This is ridiculous.

Samantha appears in front of me. There's a red cup in her

hand. "Where did Rob go?" She sounds both curious and demanding.

"To get me something to drink." I home in on the plastic cup she's holding, and realize her breath is too sweet. "You're *drinking*?"

"Oh stop. It's Coke. I need something to keep me from puking."

A boy shifts through the crowd to stop beside us. He's tall with light hair and he's vaguely familiar, but I can't place him. "Hey, Samantha," he calls over the music. "I didn't expect to see you here."

She blinks at him. "Um. Hi."

"Craig." He hesitates, and any confidence slides out of his expression. "Ah . . . from Taco Taco."

"Hi, Craig," I say.

He gives me a kind smile. "Hi." He looks back at my sister and runs a hand through his hair. "Do you . . . ah, would you like to dance?"

"Maybe a little later?" Sam hooks her arm through mine. "I was going to dance with my sister."

She hauls me into the throng of dancing people.

I'm not a great dancer, but I can hold my own. "You're kind of rude to him," I say to her.

"He's too nice, Megs."

"Sure, that's what you've got too many of." I roll my eyes. "Nice boys."

"What?" she calls over the music.

"Never mind." We move to the beat, and it starts to pull some of the tension out of my body. No one knows me here. No one cares who I am.

They know who Rob is, though.

The instant I have the thought, the worry comes roaring back. He went alone to get me a drink. I shouldn't have let him go by himself.

But then Samantha smiles and takes me by the shoulders and turns me around. Rob is pushing through the dancers, and I all but end up walking straight into him. I have to put a hand on his chest to steady myself.

Hi, Rob.

I haven't had a sip, but I feel like I'm already drunk.

He presses a closed can of ice-cold beer into my free hand. He leans down to talk. "Is this okay?"

"Yeah. Of course." I don't really want it, but I also don't want to reject it after he went to get it for me.

"I was going to open it for you, but I know girls are sometimes particular about that."

He smells so good that I can barely register what he's saying. "Oh. Yeah. Thanks." I quickly snap the top and take a deep swallow. I'm already warm from dancing, and the beer goes down easily. Too easily.

Rob's eyebrows go up.

Samantha whoops from behind me, but then reaches out to take it from me. "You need to be hot and dancing," she calls, then starts dancing away, taking the beer with her. "Not unconscious on the floor."

Now I'm blushing. I hope he can't tell.

Rob moves closer. We're kind of moving to the music, but not dancing. Not touching. He leans in. "It's nice that Sam looks out for you."

"She has her moments." I don't know how fast half a can of beer can hit you, but my brain feels like it's tripping over itself. "Thanks for the drink. I was worried about you."

He's closer suddenly. Still not touching, but I can feel his warmth. "Worried?"

"I know you're anxious about being here."

He makes a face. "I ducked in, grabbed a beer, and walked out. It was okay." Half a shrug. "And now we're in the dark and dancing. It makes for a good cover."

Does that mean I make for a good cover? I'm so off-balance. I still have no idea where I stand with Rob.

I have plenty of ideas where he stands with me. A lot of them involve taking his shirt off. Some of them involve him taking off mine.

Okay, I'm definitely feeling the beer.

The music changes, shifting into something pulsing and sensual, with a beat I can feel all the way through my body. Rob doesn't ask me to dance; he takes my hand and spins me into the music. The bodies around us become a blur. I can't seem to focus on anything but his eyes, dark and shadowed and fixed on mine. His hands brush my waist, my hips, my shoulders, but never more. Just enough to drive me crazy.

The music shifts into a new song, but Rob shows no intention of wanting to stop. His hand brushes the line of my jaw. My shoulder. Falls on my waist. Stays there.

Another song. More people. Closer. The living room is a pulsing wave of bodies. The beat controls my heart. His body brushes mine as we move.

Then he's against me. His hand brushes my hair back, and

his lips drift along my neck. A gasp escapes my throat. I might catch on fire right here.

"Hey," he says, his voice low and just for me. "Can we get off the dance floor?"

I nod, unable to speak. He tows me through the people, toward a darkened hallway. Suddenly, we're away from the press of people, and the music softens. My heart rockets along in my chest, and my whole body feels like a live wire. I don't know where he's taking me, and right now, I don't care.

Every door along this corridor is closed, leaving us in near pitch-darkness. Rob stops at the end, in front of a set of double doors.

He runs a hand through his hair and takes a deep breath. "Sorry," he says. "Connor showed up, and I didn't . . . I didn't want something to happen."

My brain needs a few moments to process those words. They don't compute.

That was all a diversion? My breath comes quick and panicked, and I force myself to calm down. I feel so foolish. I was letting myself get carried away for no reason. Rob's not interested in me. He's trying to stay hidden until we can get out of here.

I wish I had the second half of my beer. I feel about ready to cry.

"Hey," says Rob. He moves closer. It's darker in the hallway than it was in the living room, so it's easy to dodge his eyes. "Are you okay?"

"Yeah. Just—" I have to sniff. *Damn it.* "Just out of breath."

He's even closer somehow. "What's wrong?"

"Nothing. Nothing's wrong."

"Maegan." He breathes my name like a promise.

I can't say anything. I want to be bold and brassy and confident like Samantha, but I'm not. I'm honest and open and I wear my heart on my sleeve. So I fix my eyes on the collar of his shirt and feel my cheeks burn as I say, "I'm an idiot. I got—I got carried away."

He's quiet for a moment. "I don't understand."

I lift my eyes to meet his. "I forgot you were using me as a cloak so no one saw you."

"Is that what you think?"

"You said you needed to get away from Connor."

"I *wanted* to get away from Connor." His hand lands on my waist, warm and sure. The other finds my face, and his thumb strokes across my cheekbone. "Because I didn't want to be interrupted."

Oh.

And before I can fully process that, his hand slides into my hair and he presses his lips to mine.

Rob kisses like everything else he does: slow and deliberate and full of confidence. No fumbling, just the warm addictive pull of his mouth. When his tongue brushes mine, there's an unspoken question, and I answer by fisting a hand in his shirt and pulling him against me. A low sound escapes his throat, and my back finds the wall. I can't stop touching him. My fingers trace the line of his jaw, the slope of his neck, the smooth skin of his collarbone before it disappears under his shirt.

His hands are equally invested in me, a strong weight at my waist, sliding under the edge of my shirt. The feel of his palms against the bare skin of my lower back pulls a gasp from my lips, and Rob draws back half an inch.

"Good?" he whispers.

I draw a shaking breath. "Very good. Don't stop." But I grab the collar of his shirt and say the words so fast they all run together. *Verygooddontstop.*

Rob smiles and obliges.

My shirt slides higher as he gets more daring, his thumb skirting across my abdomen to light me with warmth while making me shiver. He's kissing my neck now, whispering my name in a way I'll be replaying over and over again later. One hand shifts lower, tracing the edge of the skin beneath the waistband of my jeans. I'm all but panting against the wall, and I'm glad it's here to hold me up. I'm a little dizzy and a little dissociated, like I've stepped outside this moment and I can't believe it's happening. Then his fingers find the back strap of my bra and stroke beneath.

"Rob," I whisper. "Rob."

His hand slides free. His eyes are dark and heavy and fixed on mine. "Too much?"

Not enough. The music from the party seems louder suddenly, and I'm very aware someone could walk down this way any time. "No, just . . . we're in a hallway."

He smiles, his eyes questioning. "Do you want to not be in a hallway?"

I nod rapidly, and his smile turns into a wolfish grin. He takes my hand and turns for the double doors. A pin-code type lock mechanism sits over the doorknob. I expect him to turn for one of the other doors, but Rob starts punching numbers, and the lock gives immediately.

I hesitate. "Do you know where you're going?"

"I pretty much grew up here. Come on."

I expected a bedroom, possibly a master suite, but the doors lead to a dim hallway beyond, lined with floor-to-ceiling windows. Another set of double doors are at the other end. I can see out to the side of the yard on one side, and the torch-lit pool to the other. The door swings closed behind us, and the lock clicks into place. The sounds of the party are gone, and we're trapped in a silent fishbowl of windows.

"This is an addition to the main building," Rob says. "It leads to the pool house." This time when he tugs on my hand, I follow. The second set of doors doesn't have a lock on it, and we slide through quickly, into a huge room with a cathedral ceiling crossed by wooden beams. The floor is all gray ceramic tile, the walls lined with stone, but my eyes are drawn to the massive hot tub throwing off steam in the center of the room. The jets are running, creating a rushing white noise that echoes off the walls. The only light in the room comes from the lights in the center of the hot tub, throwing blue-and-white aquatic patterns across the stones.

"Holy crap," I whisper. We're not poor, but I don't know one single friend who has something like *this* attached to their house. My eyes flick to Rob's. "Is your house like this?"

"I don't have a pool," he says. But that's *all* he says, which leads me to think that his house isn't much less extravagant.

A big-screen TV is attached to the wall on the other side of the room, above what looks like a wet bar, complete with a full-size refrigerator, two rows of liquor bottles, and two dozen wineglasses hanging upside down from a rack. A door to the right of the bar is closed and dark.

"Connor won't let people back here during the party," he says. The rushing water softens every word. He nods at the closed door. "His dad would lose his shit if anyone got into his office. But his close friends will come back here once everyone starts to leave."

I step away from him and trail my fingers in the water of the hot tub. This whole room is like a secret paradise.

My hand stops at the corner. Diamond earrings are sitting in a little divot in the plastic. I touch them with a finger. "Someone will be missing those."

"Connor's mom is kind of careless."

"With *diamonds?*" But then my eyes glance around the room again and realize that Connor's mom probably *can* be careless with diamonds.

"With everything." Rob speaks from right behind me. His hands close on my waist, and he leans down to kiss my neck. In half a second, I'm flushed and wild with attraction, and I've completely forgotten what we were talking about.

"Is this okay?" he whispers, his lips a soft brush against my skin. His hand is flat against the front of my abdomen, his body a warm weight behind me.

"Yes," I say. "Yes."

But then my brain clicks into place and I turn in his arms. "Wait. What am I saying yes to?"

His eyes widen in surprise, but then he laughs, a little. "You're a cop's daughter, that's for sure." He brushes a stray hair out of my eyes, his fingers lingering as they stroke along the curve of my ear. "Whatever you want," he says. Then he makes a sheepish face.

"Well. Not *whatever* you want, because I didn't come prepared for all that, and the tile floor is *cold*, not to mention *hard*—"

I giggle breathlessly and put a hand over his mouth. I'm blushing fiercely. "I don't think I'm ready for all that."

He nods behind my hand, his eyes serious. Then he takes my wrist and kisses my fingers gently. "We can go back to the party if you want."

"I want to stay here. Just . . ." I'm blushing again. "Slow." I blush harder. "Slowish."

"I can do slowish."

Oh, yes he can.

He's more sure now, if that's possible, his hands stroking the length of my back under my shirt. Every time his mouth falls on mine, I feel ravenous. I could spend the rest of my life like this, kissing Rob Lachlan in the dark, with the sound of rushing water behind us.

When he breaks free again to kiss his way down my neck and across the bare line of my shoulder, I whisper, "Did you bring Callie here, too?"

"Callie who?"

God, I could fall in love with him. I fist both hands in his shirt and pull it free from his jeans, and then my hands are on the curved muscled slope of his back.

I'm rewarded with a gasp. "Jesus, Maegan." His chest is against mine. I can feel his breath. His heart, tripping along as quickly as my own.

Without a thought, I jerk my shirt over my head and move to fling it away from me.

Rob snatches it out of the air before it can go flying. "Maybe don't throw that into the hot tub."

I burst out laughing. I'm suddenly self-conscious and giddy. I close my arms together over my chest, then press my hands to my mouth. "Sorry. I'm the one who said slowish."

He doesn't bother unbuttoning his shirt, he simply pulls it over his head. "Don't worry. I can catch up."

Then he pulls me against him, and this time, his mouth is *everywhere*. I've gone this far with a boy before, but never like this. Never with this electricity in the air, this heady rush of adrenaline and attraction that has me wanting to take the rest of my clothes off. My hands stroke across his shoulders, the corded muscles of his arms.

His hands close on my waist, and before I'm ready for it, he's lifting me to sit on the edge of the hot tub. I squeal with laughter, but he holds me still, then kisses fire across my stomach.

I'm so drunk on him that I don't notice the click of a door—or maybe there is no sound. I hear a footstep, and then a man's voice.

"Well now. Is that Rob Lachlan?"

CHAPTER TWENTY-THREE

Rob

Well, damn.

Before everything happened with my father, I never had a bad relationship with Connor's dad. I could fill a diary with the stories Connor has told me about him, but the guy has never been anything but polite to me. Sometimes I'd complain to Dad about him, especially after the sleeping-outside-in-freezing-rain incident, and Dad would sigh and say, "Bill's a good man, Rob. I didn't always see eye to eye with your grandfather, but now I can respect the choices he had to make. Connor might be upset, but a man's relationship with his son can get very complicated."

No kidding.

I have no idea where Bill came from, but he's by the wet bar, looking like the perfect corporate dad in khakis and a polo shirt, dark-framed glasses perched on his nose. For a brain-splitting moment, I wonder if he's been there all along and I somehow missed him. I'm still standing beside the hot tub, but Maegan has slid off the ledge. Now she's clinging to my back, hiding behind me.

Her breath is a hot rush against my shoulder. "Oh my god, do you know that guy?"

"Yes." I have to clear my throat. My body was not prepared for the abrupt 180 of emotion. I'm flushed and hard and angry and humiliated. Maegan's breasts pressing into my back are not helping. Then again, neither is the knowing look on Bill's face.

I can't read his expression, but there's no disguising what was going on here. Maybe he'll call the cops and sell out a second member of the Lachlan family.

I have to clear my throat again. "This is Connor's dad."

The man looks over his glasses at us. "It's been a while, Rob. Shall I give you and your . . . *friend* . . . a moment to arrange yourselves?"

He doesn't wait for an answer, just turns and walks through the door to his dimly lit office.

Was he in there all this time?

His voice floats out to us. "Come in and talk to me for a minute when you're done, Rob."

That doesn't sound promising.

Maegan is scrambling to grab her shirt off the floor. "Is this going to be okay?" she whispers quickly. "Are we going to be in trouble?"

"Taking your shirt off isn't a crime." My voice is edged, but none of my anger is at her, so I run a finger along her jaw to soften the words. "It's okay. It'll be okay."

I have no idea whether that's true.

She pulls her shirt over her head in a rush. "Why does he want to talk to us?"

"Not us. Me." I'm fumbling to get the buttons undone on my

shirt; they don't go back on anywhere near as easily as they come off. "You don't have to go in there."

"But he said—"

"I don't care what he said. I'm not dragging you into this."

"Are you still getting dressed?" Bill calls.

I pull my shirt on, then give Maegan a quick kiss on the cheek. "Find Samantha. Just wait for me in the living room."

My shirt is only half-buttoned when I get to the doorway of Bill's office. The room is shadowed and dim, thanks to a tiny desk lamp sitting by his computer. The furniture in here is all rich red leather and sleek polished wood. Diplomas and awards hang framed on the wall behind him, along with a painting of a moon-lit harbor that's a real Chagall.

I never gave these things much thought a year ago. Now, they're hard to reconcile when I think about Owen asking if I ever had a ten-dollar bill in my pocket when I saw him with a cheese sandwich. Connor's mom can be careless with a pair of expensive earrings, while Owen's mom was stressed about walking through a hundred-dollar pair of work shoes.

I have to shake these thoughts free.

Despite prompting me twice to come talk to him, Bill doesn't look up when I stop in the doorway. A few documents sit on the desk in a near-perfect line across the blotter. A pencil is in his hand, and he's looking at one of the documents. It's a passive-aggressive move. *You're not important until I decide you are.*

I have zero tolerance for this bullshit. I rap my knuckles on the door frame. "You wanted to see me?"

"Rob! Come in. It's been ages." He shuffles the papers together into a pile and turns them facedown. When he looks up at me, he removes his glasses, and his eyes are troubled. "I've been worried about you. We haven't seen you around, and I know things have been difficult."

Things.

I don't move from the doorway. "Mom and I are doing all right."

"Marjorie called her the other day. She said your mom's been encouraging you to get some help."

I bristle. I don't like the thought of Mom talking about me with anyone in this family. I know my father is responsible for what he did, but Bill Tunstall is the one who brought it crashing down. Maybe Mom can separate that in her head, but I sure can't.

"I should go check on Maegan," I say.

"I didn't mean to interrupt your little . . . ah, *rendezvous*, but I'm glad you're here." He rocks back in his chair. "Connor said you've been avoiding him. It's good to see you boys are spending some time together again."

"I wouldn't say that." I hesitate. "Have you been back here this whole time?"

"I'm always here when Connor has friends over. Too much liability otherwise."

I shuffle my feet, then tell myself to knock it off. Being here, standing in front of Bill, is reminding me of my father in ways I don't appreciate. I can almost feel him clapping me on the shoulder, saying, "Stand tall, Rob. Be a man."

I feel like I'm the one who drank half the can of beer instead of Maegan.

Bill nods at the chairs by his desk. "Sit down. I've been wanting to talk to you."

I want to bolt, but in a different way from how I wanted to run from Mr. London's office. Bill Tunstall represents everything we once had. If he could have warned my father—if he could have warned *us*—if he could have helped turn it around . . .

These thoughts are choking me. My hands are tight. I take a step back. "I really don't want to leave Maegan alone too long."

He doesn't move from his chair. "Rob. Please. You were like a son to me."

The words hit me like a bullet, lodging in my chest with a lump of pain that's difficult to breathe through. "No," I say, and it's tough to speak through it. "I wasn't."

"Yes." His expression doesn't change. "I kept you out of it."

"Yeah." My voice breaks, and I have to breathe to cover it up. "Sure, you did. I really feel like I was kept out of it."

"I did." He pauses, then removes his glasses and folds them on the desk. "You worked for your father. You're a smart kid, Rob."

It takes me a moment to work out what he's saying, and when I do, it's like taking a second bullet to the chest. "I didn't know what he was doing. I didn't."

Bill raises his hands. "Like I said. I kept you out of it. It was the least I could do for you and your mother."

My hands have curled into fists. "Don't act like you did us a favor."

"This wasn't an easy situation for any of us, son."

"Don't call me that." My voice has grown heated. I'm never one to rage out, but right now I prefer anger to crying. "You have no idea."

He's quiet for a moment, but his expression shifts into one of pity. "I can see I've upset you. I'm sorry. I want you to know that

I'm here if you need anything. What your father was doing—that was wrong, Rob. Whatever he had you doing—"

"I wasn't doing anything!"

He continues as if I didn't interrupt, his tone quiet and even. "—you're better than that, Rob. I know what was going on. But you're better than that. Okay?"

I'm glaring at him, my breathing so quick and my pulse pounding so hard that I feel like I'm going to hyperventilate. Or maybe turn into the Incredible Hulk.

He thinks I'm a thief. He thinks I was helping my father. He really *does* think he somehow protected me from the investigation.

"I didn't know," I say, my voice dark.

"Okay, Rob. If you say so."

I turn away from him, somehow managing to walk without breaking ceramic tiles in my rage.

"Prove me wrong," he calls from behind his desk. "I'm just looking out for you."

"I don't need to prove you wrong," I yell. "My father was the thief. Not me."

I storm toward the hot tub.

And then, as I round the corner where Maegan and I were making out, I prove myself wrong. I slide my fingers along the edge of the hot tub, scoop up those forgotten diamond earrings, and shove them in my pocket.

Then I slam through the double doors and leave Bill Tunstall behind.

♥

In my fury, I nearly miss that Maegan is waiting for me in the glass-walled hallway connecting the pool house to the main home. It's probably a miracle I didn't hit her with the door. She has to grab my arm to stop me, to get my attention.

"Hey," she says. "Stop. Are you okay?"

I'm a ticking bomb with seconds left until detonation. I picked up those earrings. I *stole* those earrings. They're all but weightless, but my pocket feels like it's filled with lead. We need to get out of here. "Yes. No. Where's your sister?"

"I don't know. I was worried about you—"

"I'm fine." I take her hand and lead her forward.

She follows, almost stumbling to keep up with me. "Rob—you're not—your shirt isn't—"

"It's fine." I shove through the second set of doors, and music slams me in the face. It's louder than it was before—or my nerves are more on edge. The lights flickering from the living room have already given me a headache.

Maegan squeezes my hand. "What did he do to you?"

"Nothing." I finally stop spinning and look down at her. "Do you think you can convince your sister to leave now?"

I must look like a wreck, because Maegan nods quickly. "Let's find her and get out of here."

Dancing people pack the living room from wall to wall. Earlier I found it intoxicating: the music, the clinging darkness, the feel of Maegan's body brushing mine. Now it's dizzying, the music too loud, the room too hot. The scents of beer and liquor and smoke thread through the room, battering my senses. I can't make out anyone's face. I hope Maegan is looking for Samantha, because I can barely think straight.

I'm just looking out for you.

Sure, Bill. Thanks a lot.

At the same time, these thoughts fill me with guilt. My father wasn't a good man. He hurt a lot of people. I have to look them in the eye every day. I should be *glad* at what Bill did.

I'm not. I have to live with the fallout. I'm not glad about any of it.

"There," says Maegan, and this time she tows *me* forward, into the crowd. I'm jostled by the dancers, but I cling tightly to her fingers, and she propels me right to the middle of the dancing.

Samantha's eyes are closed, that red plastic cup hanging precariously from her fingers, and she's dancing with her back against some guy I've never seen before. He's grinding against her, a hand splayed across the front of her abdomen.

Maegan lets go of me to step up to her sister. "Sam. Hey! Sam!"

Her sister's eyes open lazily, but she doesn't stop dancing. "Hey, Megs."

"We need to go."

"No way. I'm having a good time." Her eyes fall closed again.

"Sam. Seriously." Maegan is yelling over the music. "We need to go."

The guy dancing with Samantha opens eyes that light with irritation. His voice is a low rumble that carries over the music. "She said we're having a good time. Okay?"

"Maegan. It's fine." I don't want to get into it with a stranger. I don't want anything drawing attention to us. My nerves are so shot that I want to say I'll go wait in the car. These earrings feel like little balls of fire in my pocket.

Maegan jerks her head toward me. "He's our ride, and we need to go. Come on, Sam."

Samantha pulls away from tall-dark-and-surly and gives Maegan a light shove at her shoulders. "Don't you know I'm sick of people telling me what to do?" She takes a drink from her cup, then gives me the same light shove, speaking right into my face. "Leave if you wanna leave. I'll get a ride." Then she turns back to her new friend.

It takes me half a second to realize she's drunk.

It takes me a full second to realize the implications of that. Once again, I'm so tangled up in my own problems that I forget it's not all sunshine and roses for everyone else.

Maegan's just as quick on the uptake. Her eyes are wide. "Oh my *god*. Sam. Are you out of your *mind*?"

"Would you just go?" Samantha snaps.

Maegan steps forward and grabs her arm. "I can't leave you here like this. I can't believe you're drunk."

"Hey," says the guy. He pulls Samantha behind him. "She said she doesn't want to leave with you."

"She's my sister," Maegan snaps. "And she's hammered."

"Easy," I say, putting a hand on her arm. Maegan has a fire inside her that rivals Samantha's when she chooses to set it free, but the last thing we need is a fight in the middle of Connor's living room.

"Everyone is drunk," says the guy. "She doesn't want to go with you."

Maegan pulls free of my hand. "Yeah, well, she's *pregnant*."

The guy jerks back. His eyes go from Samantha's face to her belly and back. "You're what?"

"Forget it!" says Samantha. "Just forget it."

She moves to push past her sister, but Maegan grabs her arm. "Please, Sam. Come on. Let's go—"

Samantha whirls and slaps her square across the face.

She stumbles into it, so it's not a hard slap, but Maegan cries out and falls back. Her hand flies to her cheek.

"Whoa." I step in front of her, blocking Samantha before she can wind up for another hit.

"Get out of my way, Rob," she says.

"You need to calm down." We've started to draw the attention of everyone around us. There's not much dancing going on. There's a lot of staring.

Samantha shoves me in the chest. She's strong, but she really is drunk, so she doesn't rock me back.

I catch her wrists. "Stop. We're leaving."

"Go to hell."

I want to get out of here so badly that I consider physically dragging her out the front door. "Fine. Stay here. I'm taking Maegan home."

"No," Maegan cries behind me. "We can't leave her here like this."

"I'm not a baby!" Samantha yells. "I'm eighteen years old, and you're not my mother."

"Lucky you," Maegan says. "Mom will *kill* you."

Samantha jerks her hands free. "Good. I guess that'll solve a lot of problems, then, won't it?"

I've run out of tolerance for this—but I also don't want to leave Maegan's drunk sister stranded. "Please," I say to Samantha, and

I can hear the urgency in my own voice. "Please, can we get out of here?"

She takes a breath. Her eyes are a little unfocused.

And then, because life likes to kick me even when I'm down, Connor shoves his way through the crowd. His eyes lock on me, and he pushes around Samantha to get in my face. "Should have known it was you causing a problem, Lachlan."

"Give it a rest, Connor. I'm trying to leave."

"Yeah? Doesn't look like you're trying too hard. Looks like you're hassling this girl." When *he* shoves me, he definitely has the strength to knock me back a step. I have to grit my teeth to keep from retaliating.

"What the hell are you doing here?" he demands.

"Ask your mom," I snap. Then I turn, catch Maegan's hand, and start plowing through the crowd.

I should know better. Connor never backs down, especially when he's got a few beers in his system. He grabs my shirt by the shoulder and spins me around. His mouth is open, his eyes are dark with fury, and he's about to unleash some comment that will make me want to wither into the carpeting.

I don't give him a chance. I draw back and hit him right in the face.

Maegan gives a little yip of surprise behind me. Connor goes down. Blood, almost black in the shadows, glistens on his mouth.

He's trying to get back to his feet. Most of the crowd has sucked back. Nothing draws an audience like a fight. But Connor has friends here—and I don't.

"We need to go." My voice is almost breathless.

"Okay," says Maegan. "Okay. But Sam . . ."

Her voice trails off. Sam is gone.

"Go," says Maegan. "Go."

She doesn't need to tell me twice.

CHAPTER TWENTY-FOUR

Maegan

We've been driving for a while, and the car is heavy with warm, silent darkness. My head is spinning with so many things that I don't realize Rob isn't heading toward my neighborhood until he hits the turn signal and I see the sign for the interstate.

"Where are we going?"

Rob takes a shaky breath. "I don't know. Sorry. I was just driving." He glances over at me, oncoming headlights flickering across his features. "I can take you home."

"No!" I swallow. "I can't go home without Samantha."

"Tell me what you want to do," Rob says.

"I don't know." My voice is barely a whisper.

He keeps driving aimlessly. Now I get it.

I want to pull my phone out of my bag, but I'm terrified of what I'll find. Would Samantha have gone home? I can't imagine her going home drunk—but I also couldn't have imagined her drinking while pregnant, so my imagination isn't worth a whole hell of a lot. Could my parents be looking for me? Dad told me to stay away from Rob Lachlan, and now we're rocketing down the highway at seventy miles an hour.

"Slow down," I say. "Please. The last thing I need is for us to be pulled over."

He eases off the accelerator. "Sorry."

"No. It's—it's fine." I rub my hands across my face. My cheek still stings from where Samantha hit me. I can't believe she did that. "Maybe we shouldn't have left Sam there."

"Text her."

"I don't want to look at my phone."

He's quiet for a moment. "You think she might have told your parents?"

"It would serve me right."

"No." For the first time since getting in the car, his voice is sure and steady. "Why? Your pregnant sister was drunk at a party, and you tried to get her out of there. She had no right to hit you." He grimaces, and his hands flex on the steering wheel. "I shouldn't have hit Connor, either."

I can't figure out all the dark notes in his voice, and I wonder what happened with Connor's father, before everything went to hell in the living room. "Does your hand hurt?"

"I'll be all right."

I've spent enough time around police officers to know that's guy code for "It hurts, but I'm not going to admit it." I reach out and take his hand off the steering wheel, laying it across my palm, then stroke my fingers across his knuckles. It's too dark to see anything, but they feel swollen.

His hand closes around mine, and he laces our fingers

together, then brings my hand to his mouth to brush a kiss across my knuckles. Goose bumps spring up all the way down my forearm.

"Does your face hurt?" he says.

"No," I say, and I mean it. "She didn't hit me hard." I swallow. "I was more shocked than anything."

"Good." He kisses my hand again.

I'm glad his eyes are staying on the road, because I'm melting in the passenger seat.

Then he very deliberately puts my hand on my knee and lets go. "Would you mind checking your phone? Your dad is a cop. Everyone already thinks I conspired with my father to steal millions of dollars. I'd rather not add kidnapping to the list."

There's no amusement in his voice, so I know this must be weighing on him. It's so strange to sit here judging my own choices, while he's sitting beside me worried about how other people are going to judge his.

I tap the button to unlock my phone. "No messages."

He sighs, but he doesn't sound relieved.

I slide my fingers across the screen, typing out a quick message to my sister.

MAEGAN: Please tell me you're OK.

Nothing. I type another.

MAEGAN: Sam. Please. I'm worried about you.

Nothing.

MAEGAN: If you don't tell me you're OK, I'm calling
Mom.

For a moment, nothing happens, and I'm worried I'm going to have to make good on that threat. But then the little dots appear to let me know she's typing.

SAMANTHA: I'm surprised you haven't called Mom
already.

The words hit me harder than her slap did. I hadn't considered Samantha doing the same thing, hiding out because she's afraid to go home. I slide my fingers across the screen quickly.

MAEGAN: I'm not trying to hurt you. I'm trying to be
your sister.
SAMANTHA: I'm fine. Craig is taking me to Taco
Taco so I can sober up before he takes me home.

Craig. My eyebrows go way up. I read that out to Rob.
"Huh," is all he offers.
"Do you think she'll be okay?"
"He seemed like an all-right guy." He pauses, then looks over again. "Your sister is pretty good at getting people to do what she wants, huh?"
I snort. "That's a nice way of putting it."
We fall into silence again, but now that I know Mom and Dad don't have the Maryland State Troopers out looking for us, we relax into the white noise of the highway. My hand still tingles

from where he kissed it. Every time my brain replays the feeling of his hands and mouth on my body, my cheeks warm and I have to look out the window. I'm glad it's dark and he can't tell.

I want to know how long he plans to drive around, but I'm worried he'll think I'm ready to go home. I'm not. Not by a long shot.

Eventually, I glance over. "What did Connor's dad want to talk to you about?"

"He wanted to make sure I'm staying on the straight and narrow." His hands flex on the steering wheel again. "Said he was trying to look out for me. Yeah, sure."

I know what Mr. Lachlan did, of course, but I don't know enough about the details between the Lachlans and the Tunstalls to figure out the dynamics of what that means. "You don't like him?"

Rob glances over in surprise. "Bill Tunstall is the one who blew the whistle. He figured out what Dad was doing."

Wow. "I didn't know that." I pause. "Is that why you hate Connor so much?"

"Yes." He flinches. "No. It's complicated."

He says nothing more, so I say, "It's just you and me in the car."

He's quiet for a while, the car eating up the miles. His silence is weighted this time, though, so I wait.

Finally, he speaks. "I don't hate Connor." Rob pauses and runs a hand through his hair. "Sometimes I do. I don't know. He was my best friend." He laughs without much humor. "That sounds so stupid. Like we're in third grade, right?"

I think of Rachel, who hasn't spoken to me since the night it all fell apart at Taco Taco. "It's not stupid."

"Dad and Bill were always close. I wasn't kidding when I said I practically grew up in that house. We were always over there—or they were at our house. Dinner parties, cookouts, you name it. We used to have a vacation home right on Bethany Beach, and we'd spend half the summer there."

I don't ask him what happened to the beach house. Dad once said that anything Mr. Lachlan had bought with stolen funds would be seized by the FBI.

"I don't know how Bill figured it out. They were both financial planners, but they weren't partners or anything. They didn't even work for the same firm." Rob rubs a hand across the back of his neck. "I used to intern for my dad, so everyone always thinks I knew what was going on, but I didn't. I didn't realize until tonight that even Bill thought I knew." He glances over. "I'm not really even answering your question."

"It's okay. Just talk."

"Mom thinks Dad confessed to Bill. She didn't know anything either, but she says the guilt had to be tearing him up. She thinks they were probably shooting the shit over a few drinks, and Dad probably gave it up." He hesitates. "Bill called the authorities the next day. I didn't even know what was happening. The FBI dragged me out of school. I remember thinking—"

His voice breaks. He stops talking. I don't even think he's breathing.

Eventually, he clears his throat, but his voice is still rough. "I remember that the week before, there was this story in the news about a guy who walked into his broker's office and shot up the place. Mom and Dad talked about it at dinner. She said something about how people lose their minds when it comes to money. When they called me to the principal's office and there were all these FBI agents there, I thought—I thought that's what had happened. But it wasn't. I mean . . . obviously."

"Yeah," I whisper.

"They arrested him. They froze everything. Mom had a trust fund from her parents, so they couldn't touch that, but that was complicated. It took a week for Mom to be able to bail Dad out of jail. Even when he got home, we had no access to anything. Everything of value in the house had been taken. Computers, jewelry, you name it. But that's not the worst." Rob's voice hitches, but he gets it together. "People started showing up at the house." He glances over. "People who lost their money to him. They would bang on the door at all hours of the night. Once, they broke in and came after Mom—it was awful. She had to call nine-one-one, and one of the cops made a dig about how she shouldn't be too surprised that people wanted their things back. Like *she* was the one who stole everything. Once he was out of jail, Mom stood by him in public, but inside the house, she was always screaming at him. On the last night, she was raging out so hard that I couldn't even understand what she was saying. He was crying. I could hear him through the wall. I'd never heard my father cry before. I put a pillow over my head."

He stops there. His voice doesn't break or anything, he just stops. Any emotion has vanished.

That doesn't feel like a good sign.

"What happened?" I say softly.

"She stormed out. I heard the door slam. Then the garage door cranking up, and then back down. Then silence. And then a gunshot."

His voice is so quiet and level and even, but the air in the car is dense with dread. We're flying down the highway, but I feel like we're heading for a brick wall. I want to brace my feet on the floorboards and stop whatever is coming.

But of course it already came. His father pulled the trigger last February.

I want Rob to stop. I don't want to hear this. Not in this cool, dispassionate voice. I want my own pillow to pull over my head.

But then he says, "You know the rest."

No. I don't. I really don't. But I feel like he's given me a pass. Or maybe he doesn't want to relive it, either.

He shakes his head. "And I still haven't said anything about Connor." Rob takes a breath. "I couldn't reach Mom that night. After Dad—after." He swallows. "I couldn't reach her. I was—I was all by myself. The house was full of cops and paramedics and the blood was . . . well. You can imagine. I didn't know what to do. So I called Connor. I hadn't been allowed to talk to him since everything happened, but I had no one else to call. So I called him."

"What did he say?"

"Nothing." Rob glances over. "He didn't answer. I left some pathetic rambling voice mail, begging him to call me back."

"And he didn't." Not even a question. I already know the answer.

Rob sniffs and looks out at the darkness. "No. He didn't."

I don't know what to offer, what kind of platitudes would

make this better. There aren't any. I can't fix Rob's father. I can't fix his friendship with Connor—if there's anything worth fixing. I can't imagine getting a call from a friend needing help and not responding. I can't even imagine it about my worst enemy.

I frown. "Why?"

My question seems to surprise him. Rob looks away from the road briefly. "What?"

"Why didn't he call you?"

His hands tighten on the steering wheel, and he looks back at the road. He must punch the accelerator because the car picks up speed. "Because he's an asshole."

"No, but—" I bite my lip. I don't want to make him angry. "He was your best friend, right?"

"Yeah."

I think of Rachel. "Like—a *real* friend, though, right? The cry-on-your-shoulder kind?"

Rob's eyes flick my way. He looks like he wants to deny it, but he also said Connor was the first friend he called after finding his father lying in a pool of blood. "Yes," he says evenly, dragging the word into three syllables.

"And he ditched you because of what your father did?"

"He ditched me because he thought I was part of it. Just like everyone else." Rob glances my way. "You realize you're, like, the only person who's speaking to me at school?" He rolls his eyes. "You and Owen Goettler."

"Maybe Connor was never really your friend at all." Because I still can't figure out how a close friend could turn his back on someone so absolutely.

Rob flexes his hand. "I don't think we're on our way to making up anytime soon."

We fall into silence again.

"What do you want me to do?" he asks eventually. "Do you want me to take you home?"

I blush again, and I'm glad he can't see it. "Is it wrong if I say no?"

"Is it wrong if I tell you my mom said to stay out as late as I want?"

Okay, *now* I'm blushing. "No. But I think my mom would have a problem with that." I pause. "Want to get coffee?"

He picks up my hand and kisses my knuckles again. I wonder if it'll ever feel normal.

"Wegmans?" he says. "They're open until midnight."

"Yes," I agree, relaxing down into the seat. "Wegmans."

CHAPTER TWENTY-FIVE

Rob

Somehow, I forget about the earrings. I forget that I'm a thief.

Then I get home after midnight and shove ice-cold hands into my pockets for the walk to my front door. I feel the square edges against my fingertips.

Fear and guilt plummet through my body, like a rock dropping into my gut.

This is bigger than a few twenties from the cash box. This is bigger than a pair of shoes.

My breathing is tight and shallow, and I'm frozen in the space between my car and the front door.

I want to undo it. I can't undo it.

Another thought strikes me: I wonder if my father had a moment like this. I wonder if he ever had these identical thoughts.

The realization is enough to make me move. I climb back into the car, open the glove box, and shove the earrings deep inside. Then I lock the glove box, lock the Jeep, and head for the front door.

It's fine. It's fine. They won't even notice. I *know* they won't notice.

These thoughts do nothing to loosen the pit of guilt that's formed in my abdomen. It refuses to dislodge.

What did Bill say? *I did my best to keep you out of it.*

Anger swirls around the guilt and swallows it up. I put my key in the lock.

After the noise of the party and the close warmth of sharing space with Maegan, my house feels like a crypt. Mom kept her word and didn't wait up. The only light on in the main level is the tiny light over the stove. I grab a bottle of Coke out of the refrigerator and press the pedal on the recycling bin to raise the lid.

There's an empty bottle of wine sitting on top. It's different from the one Mom was drinking the other day.

Huh.

I turn for the stairs in the dark. I kind of want a shower, but I want sleep more. It's been a long night. The best thing about sleep is that I don't need to think about anything.

My father's bedroom door is open, his feeding pump making a low rhythmic clicking every few seconds. I don't look in on him. Sometimes he's just staring at the ceiling, and it freaks me out.

Mom's door is closed.

Something must have happened tonight. While I was gone. Either a mess or an inexplicable panic attack or something she wouldn't have wanted to deal with on her own. A new stab of guilt catches me under the ribs.

Not like I can do anything about it now. I walk past their

bedrooms and into the darkness of my own, tilting the bottle of Coke back to take a sip.

Something solid slams into my midsection, hard. I choke on soda and cough. Another hit, and I double over. The bottle goes flying.

Then a fist cracks into my face. I go down. I've barely registered the impact of the floor—polished hardwood, thanks, Mom—before a booted foot kicks me right in the abdomen.

All the breath has left my body. My nose is burning from choked soda. Nothing hurts yet, but I feel the promise of pain. Any second now. It'll come back with the oxygen. I remember from taking hits in lacrosse.

A hand grabs my collar and slams me into the floor again. I need to shout for my mother. She has to get out of the house. She has to call nine-one-one.

I can't make a sound. I still can't breathe.

Then a husky male voice speaks right into my face. "How's it feel, Lachlan?"

Connor. It shouldn't be a surprise, but it is.

Oxygen finally fights its way into my lungs, and every organ in my abdomen feels like it's been rearranged. I want to curl in on myself, but he's still got a fist gripping my collar. Painful little gasps are escaping my throat.

This is retaliation. He must know what I stole. I'm trying to get my brain to fire the right neurons so I can either punch him back or yell for help. His next hit could put me out.

But he doesn't hit me again. He lets go and straightens, leaving me lying there on the floor.

"What were you doing at my house?" he demands.

"You—you invited me." I make it to my knees, but the pain in my stomach keeps my forehead pressed to the floor. "How did you get in here?"

"I still have a key, you asshole." He shifts his weight, and the sound makes me flinch. I'm ready for another kick.

It doesn't come.

He's not demanding his mother's earrings. He's not accusing me of theft.

"What were you doing there?" he says again. His voice is lower. Threatening.

"I ran into Callie. She mentioned it. Asked me to go." I break off to wheeze. Connor waits, like some kind of hit man in a movie. "Samantha Day wanted to go, and she convinced me and Maegan to go with her."

That must not be what he's expecting—or maybe it's too boring or too honest. He doesn't hit me. He doesn't say anything.

I can hear him breathing. Thinking.

Judging.

Oxygen has cleared my brain. I realize I've been drooling on the floor. Nice. I put a hand against the hardwood and push myself upright. The entire side of my face aches, and I touch a hand gingerly to my lip. Maybe I've been *bleeding* on the floor.

"Is this all you wanted?" I say. "To hit me back?"

"What's the real reason you were there?"

"I just told you."

"Yeah, well, I don't trust you." He's got me there. In the dark, his mismatched eyes are shadowed and glaring. "You're lucky I didn't kill you."

I glare back at him. "You would've been doing me a favor."

Those words hit him hard. I'm not sure how I can tell, but they do. He says nothing.

An intermittent beeping comes from the hallway. *Be-beep. Be-beep. Be-beep.*

Connor drops back a step. "What's that?"

I should scare the shit out of him and tell him it's an alarm system. "Dad's feeding tube."

He takes another step back. He's not glaring now.

The beeping only means there's a kink in the line, and it's not like Dad will starve to death if I don't go fix it. Depending on the night, I usually wait to see if Mom will get up and take care of it. But her door is closed, and that empty bottle of wine is probably guaranteeing she's not waking up anytime soon.

I turn away from Connor and head into the hallway. I have no idea if he's going to wait or follow me or leave altogether, and I really don't care. I step into Dad's room and click on the little nightlight beside his bed.

He's awake and staring at the ceiling. His breathing is a little quick. I wonder if the beeping woke him up, or if it was the scuffle with Connor. Either way, his breathing has an anxious quality to it.

I might resent my father, but I don't like it when he's afraid. "You're all right," I say gently. "I'll fix it."

A tap on the screen of the feeding machine silences the alarm. I pull the tubing free, work out the kink, and refeed it through. After a moment, the rhythmic clicks begin again. His breathing steadies.

"See?" I say, even though he gives me absolutely no acknowledgment. "All better."

I wait for a moment, as if *this* will be the time that he blinks and turns to me and says, "Thanks, Rob."

But of course he doesn't. He never will.

I click off the light and turn for the doorway.

Connor is standing there.

I'm glad the light is off. This is more humiliating than when he stood over me in the cafeteria. "Don't start something here," I say to him, and I make an effort to keep my voice low. "If he gets really upset it can be challenging to calm him down."

Connor doesn't move. If I stand here, I'm going to start something myself. So I push past him and head back to my bedroom.

This time I flick the light switch. That full bottle of Coke landed on my bed and leaked all over my quilt. From the looks of it, it's soaked all the way through.

Great.

I'm so tired.

"I didn't know he was like that." Connor speaks from behind me, in the hallway.

"Yeah?" I say without looking. "What did you think he was like?"

"I don't know. I didn't—I didn't know."

"Would it have made a difference?"

"No."

At least he's honest. I sigh and start stripping my bed. Connor vanishes from the doorway.

Good. I hope he locks up.

I make a pile of bedclothes in the corner, then get a towel from my bathroom to lay over the wet spot on the mattress. Just as I'm about to go down the hallway to the linen closet, Connor reappears with folded sheets and a comforter.

This might be more shocking than the fact that he was staking out my bedroom.

"Did you lace these with anthrax?" I ask, making no effort to hide the surprise in my voice.

"Shut up." He picks up a fitted sheet and shakes it out, then moves to the top corner of my bed. "Are you just going to stand there, or are you going to get the other side?"

I want to stand here, to watch him burn off some of the guilt he's obviously feeling. I want to feel superior, just for one fraction of a second.

But I also want to go to bed. I know if I'm a dick, he won't keep making the bed. He'll walk out.

So I pick up the other corner. We make the bed.

I don't thank him. My abdomen hurts the whole time.

When we finish, we're standing on opposite sides of the bed. I finally look at him in the light. A bruise has formed along his jaw where I hit him. I probably have an identical one forming on my own face.

Maegan was right. I do have questions.

How could you ignore me when I called you?

How could you let me go through this alone?

How could you think I'm a thief?

How could you?

I don't ask any of them. It's not that I don't want answers. It's that I'm scared of what he'd say.

So we stand there staring at each other, saying nothing.

A line forms between Connor's eyebrows. He inhales.

"Go," I say, before he can speak. "I'm tired. I don't have anything to say to you."

Emotions flicker through his eyes. A quick burst of anger, then pity, then acquiescence. No remorse. No regret.

"Fine," he says. "Whatever." He turns and walks out. I wait, listening to his footsteps as he jogs down the staircase. The door opens and closes gently. His key finds the lock.

I don't get into bed until I hear a car engine fire up down the street.

Thanks to those earrings in my glove box, I don't sleep at all.

CHAPTER TWENTY-SIX

Maegan

I've been home for an hour, and Samantha isn't home yet. I texted her before I came inside, because I didn't know how she wanted to handle things with Mom.

> **MAEGAN:** What do you want me to tell Mom? I haven't gone in yet.

There was a long wait before a text came back, and I was worried she wasn't going to write back at all. The phone seemed to vibrate with tension.

> **SAMANTHA:** Tell her I ran into a friend from high school who was home for the weekend.

That was easy enough. Mom was half-asleep, watching a food documentary, and she barely mumbled "okay" when I gave her the news.

But now an hour has passed, and Samantha still hasn't shown up.

I text her again.

MAEGAN: I'm going to sleep. You OK?

SAMANTHA: As OK as I can be, considering you told the whole party I'm pregnant.

I flinch. I did do that.

MAEGAN: They were all hammered. No one will remember.

She doesn't say anything. I dash out another text.

MAEGAN: All OK with mom on this side

SAMANTHA: Good

Good. Figures.

Guilt and responsibility are wrestling in my head. I quickly do an internet search on my phone. Ten seconds later I have more information than I know what to do with, ranging from fetal alcohol syndrome to reports of how having a few drinks early in pregnancy doesn't matter at all. I don't know how much she drank, but she wasn't falling down. She was able to walk out of there with Craig.

She said she wanted to go to the party because she wanted to forget everything that's going on. Maybe I should have paid more attention. She's so confident and determined that I forget she might be hurting underneath it.

A soft tap sounds on my door, and Mom pokes her head in. "I saw your light was still on."

"I was just about to go to sleep."

"Can I come in?"

"Sure."

I scoot over in bed and sit up against the headboard so she can climb in with me. She used to do this when I was a little girl and she'd read me stories. Then, in middle school, she'd listen to all my angsty grievances about first crushes and mean girls.

Now that I'm in high school, her nighttime visits haven't been as frequent, but she has an uncanny way of knowing when I'm troubled.

She puts an arm around my shoulders, and I lean into her. I sigh, already drowsy.

Then she says, "Is Samantha talking to you, Maegan?"

I go still.

"I'm not trying to get information out of you," Mom says. "I'm so worried about her. I would feel better if I knew she was talking to you."

I swallow, unsure if even this is safe.

Mom's breath hitches. "She always used to tell me everything, but now she won't talk to me."

Mom reaches up to brush at her face, and I realize she's crying.

I draw back and stare at her. "Mom."

"Can you tell me something?" More tears fall, and her voice hitches again.

I hold my breath. Indecision is surely written all over my face.

Mom breaks down crying in earnest. Her hands are pressed to her face.

"Mom," I whisper. I touch her shoulder. "Mom. It's okay."

"Is she getting an abortion?" she asks. One hand is clutched over her abdomen, and she's almost curled over. "Is she doing it tonight? Is that where you were?"

"What? No! Mom. No." I can't take her tears. I'm crying now, just because Mom is. Does Samantha know how this is affecting our mother? She needs to. "Mom. She's not. She's at Taco Taco with a boy who graduated with her. You could drive over there right now."

"Are you sure?" She's still crying.

"I mean, pretty sure. I saw her an hour ago." I pause and wipe at my own face. I can't lie like this. Not to my mother. Not when she's sobbing in my lap. "We weren't at the movies, though. We went to a party."

"A party?" Mom almost laughs through the tears. "You were at a party?"

"Please don't be mad." I hesitate. "I would've told you, but—"

"I'm not mad." She dabs tears away from her cheeks, then pulls me into her arms. "Oh, Maegan. I'm so relieved."

She's holding me so tight. She must still be crying. Her body is still shaking.

"I wasn't worried earlier, but then you came home alone, and I started thinking." Her voice breaks. "I thought she might be in a hospital or something. My imagination got the best of me."

"No. She's still pregnant." I swallow. "If that's a relief."

That makes her give a choked laugh. "It is. I can't believe I'm saying that, but it is."

When she finally pulls back, I look into her tear-streaked face. "You really don't want her to have an abortion."

"No." Her face contorts and she looks at her hands, now wringing in her lap. "Does that make me selfish? She worked so hard for this scholarship. This will complicate her life in ways she doesn't understand yet."

"It doesn't make you selfish," I whisper.

"I wish she would tell us about this boy. We could meet with his parents. We could work something out. We could help them."

Right. This *boy*. I can't say anything.

Mom zeroes in on my face. "Wait. Who is she meeting with at Taco Taco?"

"Oh! Just a boy she went to school with."

Mom's eyebrows go up. The emotion from the imagined abortion is gone, leaving suspicion in its place. "Do you know him?"

"Mom, it's not him. Trust me. It's not him."

"Then why is Sam meeting with him?"

"Because he's a nice guy." I wish I hadn't mentioned alcohol, because I'd show her the text messages.

Mom's face falls again. "So, she's avoiding me."

I hesitate.

"Please," Mom says. "Please tell me, Maegan. Whatever it is."

My thoughts are so tangled up. Rob said he wished Connor's dad had given them a heads-up—would it be better for Mom and Dad to know what's going on, before it's too late? Or is this different?

Mom frowns. "Now you won't talk to me, either."

"Mom . . ." I take a breath. I'm not sure how to finish that statement.

"You didn't answer my question," she says. "Is Samantha talking to you, at least?"

"Yes," I breathe, hoping I'm not about to face a firing line over this.

Mom puts her hands on my face, then pulls me forward to kiss my forehead. "Okay. Then I'll let you keep her secrets. I'm glad she's talking to you."

"Why?"

"Because you're a good girl, Maegan. I know you'll help her figure out the right thing to do."

You're a good girl, Maegan. My mother hasn't said something like that to me in so long. I didn't realize how desperate I was to hear those words.

Mom leans back. Her hands are still on my face. "She doesn't have to handle this by herself, though, okay?"

"Okay."

Mom kisses me again, then moves away from my bed. She leans down to click my light off. "I'll let you get some sleep."

"Thanks, Mom. I love you."

"I love you, too."

She stops by the door, leaning in before she pulls it closed. "Maegan?"

"Yeah?"

"You don't have to handle it by yourself, either."

The words fill me with emotion. I want to tell her everything.

I have to wrap my arms around my body to keep tears from spilling out of my eyes. It takes me a breath before I can speak normally. "Okay, Mom."

She hesitates. She's going to pry, and I'm going to spill everything.

But she doesn't. She backs out of the room and closes the door.

Leaving me in the darkness.

Samantha doesn't open her bedroom door until after noon. She does it softly, almost as if she's sneaking out, and then tiptoes across to the bathroom, where she shuts the door with an equally quiet *click*. She must be hiding from Mom and Dad.

I'm in my bedroom, working on a paper for American lit, and I wait for her to come back out.

She doesn't. The shower turns on.

My phone buzzes beside my laptop.

ROB: Hey

Three letters, and my heart explodes with butterflies. I haven't heard from him since he dropped me off last night, and I've been sitting on my hands all morning to keep from writing to him first.

The insecure part of me was worried he wouldn't text me at all until we saw each other Monday morning—or worse, that he'd wake up and realize he wasn't interested at all.

But he didn't. And he didn't make me wait at *all*.

I'm so ridiculous. I'm blushing before I start writing back.

MAEGAN: Hey
ROB: How are you?

How am I? Hmm.

Still thinking about his quiet voice as he confided in me.

Still thinking about making out at Connor Tunstall's house.

Still thinking about the feel of his hands and the warm corded muscles of his arms and the way my fingers stroked up his back.

I'm blushing harder.

MAEGAN: Good. You?

I'm horrible at this. My head is full of PG-13 fantasies, while my phone is full of texts that are no more illicit than what I'd send my father.

ROB: Same. I was just thinking about you.
MAEGAN: Oh yeah? What were you thinking?
ROB: I wanted to make sure everything was OK after last night.

Oh. Well, that's less exciting than I was hoping.

MAEGAN: All good. Sam got home late.

Oh . . . Is he checking to make sure everything is okay so he's not going to get involved in some family drama?

I wish Rachel wasn't being so distant. Any other boy, and we'd be crouched over my phone together, analyzing every word.

I click over to our last messages, when she was asking me about Rob. I never replied. She never spoke to me on Friday. But I'm not going to apologize about Rob. They were mean. They should be apologizing to him.

My brain refuses to forget that I was sharing in their ire on the day I was assigned to be his partner.

I click back to Rob's texts. A new message appears.

> **ROB:** Any chance you want to meet up later to work on our project?

I bite my lip and slide my fingers over the face of the phone.

> **MAEGAN:** Just our project?
> **ROB:** Like I said last night, anything you want.

Then he adds the emoji with the sunglasses.

Here I thought I was blushing before. Another message appears.

> **ROB:** That looks worse on a screen than it did in my head. I'm not a creep, I swear.

I burst out laughing.

> **MAEGAN:** A creep would send the eggplant. What time?
> **ROB:** Owen wants to go running this afternoon. After dinner?

MAEGAN: Owen runs?

ROB: That's what he says.

MAEGAN: 7?

ROB: 7

It takes everything I have to keep from pressing the phone against my chest and spinning in the chair.

Then I hear Sam come out of the bathroom.

"Hey, Sam?" I call. "You want to come in and talk?"

Silence answers me, but she's in the hallway. I can tell.

"I don't think anyone remembers," I say. "What I said." I pause. "Or they don't care. Rachel would have heard. She would have called me."

I hold my breath as I wait for a response.

"I don't want to talk," says Sam.

Then her door slides closed, and she turns the lock.

CHAPTER TWENTY-SEVEN

Rob

I didn't drift off to sleep until six a.m., when my body gave up, I guess. So when Owen called at eight, my nerves were so jangled that I almost threw the phone through the wall.

I almost did it again when he asked if I wanted to go for a run.

The alternative was sitting in my bedroom, letting guilt jab at me from all angles, so I agreed to pick him up. We're running on the B&A Trail, a long paved path that runs from Baltimore to Annapolis. I thought maybe we'd go for half an hour or something, but we pass thirty minutes and he keeps on going. I've been keeping up with him, but secretly, I'm dying. I've been running almost every day since I made the promise to Mom, but I'm nowhere near as fit as I was when I played lacrosse.

By the time we loop around to run back, my lungs start to scream, and I have less time for brooding. My brain becomes solely focused on breathing.

Owen is barely winded. He plows on like he runs a marathon every weekend.

There's a good chance I'm going to stumble and land in a pile on the trail.

"Want to race the last mile?" he says.

"No." It takes effort to speak a syllable.

He laughs. "Come on. Loser has to do a hundred sit-ups." Without waiting for an answer, he takes off.

I sprint after him. My feet shove off the ground harder with every stride. I was fast once. I can catch him.

I'm wrong—though not by much. He beats me by a hundred meters. He stops and waits at the fence post by the parking lot, offering a slow clap.

I give him the finger.

He laughs. "Toss me your keys. I'll get the water."

I do as asked, then flop down in the grass. The ground is cold; the grass tickles my neck. Now that I've stopped running, my light sweatshirt feels like a parka. I jerk it over my head, then close my eyes and try to remember how to breathe.

A bottle of water hits me in the chest, then bounces to roll into the grass beside me. "Sit-ups, loser."

I put my hands behind my head, but as soon as I sit up, I swear. It's like Connor's boot is still lodged in my belly.

"I can't do this." I roll over and put my hands in the grass. "I'll do push-ups."

"Whatever."

I'm on twenty when Owen says, "You have a bruise on your face. Did someone hit you?"

"No."

"Walk into a door?"

"You're going to make me lose count."

"Why couldn't you do sit-ups?"

"Don't worry about it."

He reaches out and pokes me in the jaw. I see it coming and grit my teeth and ignore him, but it still hurts.

When I say nothing, he says nothing.

I keep counting in my head. The push-ups are easier than the running was, but the endorphins from exercise are quickly disappearing, being replaced by irritation. It's cold enough that we're alone out here, and late enough in the year that there are no sounds of birds or insects. The only noise is the occasional rush of a passing car.

I can't read the silence at all, but I can feel Owen thinking.

"What?" I finally say.

"What what?"

"Fine, I was in a fight. I lost. Is that what you want to know?"

"Oh. No. I was just staring at your biceps."

That makes me laugh. "Okay, I'm done." I drop onto my elbows and reach for the sweatshirt in the grass.

Owen kicks it out of reach. "You only did like fifty. Finish. Talk."

I press my hands into the grass and do as ordered, but I'm still not ready to talk about Connor—or what I did. I haven't quite unpacked it all in my head yet.

"How are you in such good shape?" I ask Owen instead.

"Running is free."

Huh. I guess that's true.

Owen draws up his legs to sit cross-legged. "I started when Javon was trying to get in shape before he left for basic training. It was something to do, so I kept it up."

"You should run cross-country." I say the words without think-ing, but then I realize Owen probably has reasons for not playing sports at school. Then again, like he said, running is free. Of all the sports, running would probably be cheapest. All you need are shoes.

Owen shrugs and says, "I didn't really start running until last year."

"Indoor hasn't started yet. You could still join."

He says nothing.

"Or track in the spring," I add.

He bites at the edge of his thumbnail.

I stop at the top of a push-up and look at him. My arms are dying now, so really it's an excuse to pause for a second. "Or not."

"Perhaps it's escaped your notice, but I'm not school sports material," he says.

"You just ran me into the ground, Owen, so I'm not sure what you're talking about."

"I don't know if I could run a race. Not with a bunch of other kids." A long, heavy pause. "I have a blind spot in my right eye." He chews at the edge of his thumbnail again and looks out at the parking lot. "I see spots in my left. I can't even get a driver's license, so . . ." His voice trails off.

I'm not sure what to say. *I'm sorry* feels weird.

"I didn't know," I say.

He shrugs. Continues to stare at the parking lot.

Then he says, "Dude, it's cold. Finish."

So I finish, and he sits there staring, and when we're done, we walk back to my car.

On Thursday night, we had a conversation about his friend

Javon going into the Army. I asked Owen if *he* was going to join the Army, and he kind of shrugged it off. I don't know anything about enlisting, but I do know you need to pass a physical. I'm pretty sure a blind spot that keeps you from driving would also keep you out of basic training.

When I fire up the engine, the space between us feels awkward. My arms are tired and my legs are tired and I just want to take a nap right here while the car warms up, but I sense that Owen is uncomfortable. I shift into drive.

"I was in an accident when I was three," he says.

I glance over at him. "I'm sorry."

"No, it's just . . . I want to explain."

"I'll shut up."

He runs his finger along the seam in the upholstery on the door. "My dad was driving, and apparently he was reaching back to touch me or hand me something or take something away from me—I don't know. I was three and I don't remember it. We can only go by witness reports. But he wasn't looking at the road and he ran a red light. It was a major intersection. We were hit from both sides. He was killed instantly. I had a skull fracture. Traumatic brain injury. I was in the hospital for months."

"Holy shit." I glance over. I think of my father and wonder if this is worse. I don't know.

"Yeah, I don't tell a lot of people. And I don't even really remember him, you know? Apparently another guy died in the accident and they sued Mom, so she lost whatever life insurance Dad had in place. And with me being in the hospital so long, insurance stopped covering it . . . you know how it goes."

Until this very minute, I had never really considered *why* Owen was poor. I just accepted that he was.

Then he glances over at me and says, "Or maybe you don't."

My throat is tight. I don't know if that's a dig or a pass or what. My father stole from Owen's mother. I knew that. It feels doubly wrong now.

I'm not even sure why. It was wrong. It's still wrong.

When we get to his house, I throw the car into park, but I don't kill the engine. Owen makes no move to get out of the car. I can't read the silence at all.

"What do you want me to say?" I finally scrape out.

"Who hit you?"

"Connor Tunstall." The words are almost pulled out of my mouth against my will. Owen just unloaded this monumental life secret and it feels awful to keep one from him.

"Why?"

"I took Maegan to a party at his house last night. He was being a dick, so I punched him." I pause. If I mention the earrings out loud, it makes the theft real. I take a breath. "Connor was waiting in my bedroom when I got home." I glance his way. "He still had a key."

Owen says nothing.

I fix my eyes on the windshield. "You want me to get out so you can take a swing, too?"

"What the hell are you talking about?"

His answer surprises me.

Even more so when he says, "You want to come in and play Xbox?"

"I thought . . . never mind. I'll come in." I turn the key and the engine dies.

He still doesn't move. "You thought what?"

"I don't know." And I don't.

He shrugs. "Then come on."

Owen's mother is drying dishes when we walk in, and she stops when she sees me.

"Rob," she says warmly. "I was hoping I'd see you again."

"Stop it," says Owen. He breaks off two bananas from a bunch on the counter and tosses one at me.

"What are you boys up to?"

I have to remind myself that she's suing my family. That my dad screwed her over. That she doesn't really know who I am, because if she did, she wouldn't be smiling at me.

I'm a thief. I'm a thief. *I'm a thief.*

I break open the banana, glad for something to do with my hands. "We went for a run."

"It's cold out for running."

"That's why we're inside to play Xbox." Owen turns away from her and heads toward the narrow staircase.

I follow him, very aware of Mrs. Goettler's eyes on me.

I'm worried she's put two and two together somehow, and she's going to start throwing knives at my back, until she says, "Leave your bedroom door open," in a knowing voice.

"He's straight, Mom," Owen calls. "Give it up."

In his room, he shuts the door.

His bedroom is tiny, with a twin bed and a narrow dresser in the corner. He's got a desk under the window, with a small television taking up half of it. His Xbox is up here today, and he switches it on, then tosses me a controller.

His door opens almost immediately. Despite the fact that I'm standing in the middle of Owen's room, my cheeks catch on fire.

I expect her to yell, but she says gently, "I said open, boys."

"Yes, ma'am," I say.

Owen rolls his eyes. She leaves.

"Your mom is really friendly," I say as he turns on the television.

"She's great usually." He slides a disk into the player. "She started crying when I brought her the shoes." We had them delivered to an anonymous Amazon locker. His eyes flick up to meet mine, and his voice drops. "I told her I had been saving up for a Christmas present."

He doesn't sound happy about that. "Do you regret doing it?"

He swallows and glances at the door. "I regret her thinking I saved it."

"Lexi won't even know the money is gone."

"I know." He gives a half-hearted laugh. "I can't imagine dropping a hundred bucks on shoes without thinking about it. Without even *noticing*."

The words stick in my brain. Mrs. Tunstall isn't even going to notice her missing earrings, and those cost a lot more than a hundred dollars.

The game loads. I press buttons on my controller to select my player, then drop beside him to sit on the edge of the bed. We play in silence for a little while.

I'm still struggling with the morality of it all. Dad stole for himself. For us, indirectly, but really, the money was for him. For his image, for his enjoyment, for whatever he wanted. I stole the money with Owen, but his mom needed the shoes. Lexi won't miss it. If I sell the earrings and use the money to help other people, Mrs. Tunstall won't miss them. Does that make a difference? That one person can afford it, but another one can't? I don't know. My father stole from people who couldn't afford it.

That is clearly wrong.

I don't know where the line is, though.

"Can I ask you a weird question?" I say finally as I'm watching his character leave mine in the dust.

"Sure."

"How do you have an Xbox?"

He presses a button and the screen goes still, and he swings his head around to look at me. His eyes are dark and angry, and I wish I could suck the question back into my mouth.

Owen sighs and turns back to the television without saying anything. He presses a button. Continues playing.

"Owen—"

"Stop." His voice is clipped. "I'm thinking."

I wait.

Eventually, he pauses the game again and gets up. He roots through his narrow closet and fishes out two game boxes. One is for a basketball video game that was hot a few years ago. The other is something I don't recognize. He slides them together in his hands and drops into his desk chair, blocking the television.

"When I was thirteen," he says, his voice low, "Mom got the Xbox off Craigslist for fifty bucks."

My throat feels tight.

"When I was fourteen," he says, "Mom had saved up some money for Christmas. Not much, but a little. The car broke down on her way home from work, though, and all that money had to fix the car. She had to max out her credit card, too." He hesitates. "It was fine. Like, I get it. I didn't believe in Santa. She's got to work if we're going to eat, right?"

My shoulders are tense. I asked for this, but I don't like what I got. At the same time, I feel like I deserve to hear this. I force myself to hold his gaze.

Owen's gaze flicks to the door, and his voice drops further. "She felt bad, though. She signed up for one of those Christmas Angel things. You know, where you list a few things you want, and some nice person buys them for you. It's all anonymous. Mom wrote two things on the list: a winter coat, and Xbox games."

My eyes go to the games in his hands. "I'm sorry. I wasn't—I didn't—"

He thrusts them at me. "Check them out. They were the hottest games that year. New games are like sixty bucks. Pretty generous, right?"

I take them from his hands, though I don't want to. "Yeah."

"Those cases were brand new when I got them. Before that, I only had two games, so I was pretty stoked."

"Sure."

"Open them up. Check out how awesome the games are."

I don't want to open them. They're empty. I can feel they're empty. I can see where this is going. "Owen—"

"Open them!"

I hold my breath and open them.

They're not empty.

No game discs. Just a note inside each.

Get a job and buy your own presents.

I'm frozen, staring at the line of neatly printed text inside each box.

"You know what kills me?" says Owen. "The boxes were brand new. Even had the tape over the edge. Whoever did that actually went to the store to buy them and took out the disks to prove a point." He snatches them out of my hand and slams them closed. "He probably had the same thought you did. 'How's this poor kid have an Xbox?'"

"No, Owen, I didn't—"

"Come on." The look he gives me could wither stronger men than me.

The problem is, he's right. I remember hearing similar comments around Dad's office when I was interning last Christmas, and the family we anonymously "adopted" asked for a Blu-ray player. *Who do these people think they are?*

"My mom works sixty hours a week," says Owen. "I can't drive, and we don't live where I can easily get a job."

My throat is so tight that it's making my chest hurt. "I don't know what to say."

He must not either, because he sits there silently.

His mom walks by the door, carrying a basket of laundry, and she must pick up on the tension, because she hesitates in the hallway. "You boys okay?"

"We're great." Owen's tone is flat and even.

All of a sudden, being here feels cruel. Like I'm taking advantage. Was I so desperate for company that I latched on to the last person in the world who should want to spend time with me? His situation was already crap, and then my father flushed it down the toilet.

This is worse than hiding in Mr. London's office.

I stand and turn for the door without looking at Owen. "I need to go home."

Mrs. Goettler stops me in the hallway, putting a hand on my arm. "What happened? Rob, are you all right?"

I can't take her kindness. Not now.

"I'm Rob Lachlan," I say. "Junior."

Her expression shifts as the impact of this sinks in. She lets go of my arm. Takes a step back.

I can't meet her eyes. "I'm sorry." My voice cracks. "I shouldn't—I'm sorry." I turn and fly down the stairs. The door barely makes me pause. My car is at the end of the block, and bitter wind whips at my eyes, stinging with censure.

I'm almost to the Jeep when feet slap the pavement behind me. "Hey," says Owen, nearly breathless.

I don't look at him. "I already gave you a chance to punch me."

"Rob. Stop. Look—wait, are you *crying*?"

"No." I swipe at my face and turn away. I am. Great; this can be doubly humiliating.

"Stop." He grabs my sleeve. "Stop. I'm sorry. I shouldn't have gone off on you like that."

I give half a laugh. "*You're* sorry? Owen, I ruined your life."

He doesn't let go of me. "No. You didn't. Your father didn't, either."

"Come on."

"I mean, not directly. She'd finally built up a little savings, and a friend told her your dad could help—" I grimace, and he breaks off. "We weren't living on it. It was just . . ." He frowns. "For a minute I forgot you're not you anymore."

What a loaded statement. I sniff and look away from him. "Oh good."

"I hate when people ask things like that. It's not you. It's—it's everything."

"I'm sorry." His hand is still fixed on my sleeve. "I'll go. Okay? Just let me go."

"You don't have to go."

I glance back at his house. The curtain is pulled partially to the side, though I can't see Mrs. Goettler. "I'm pretty sure your mom hates me."

"Mom doesn't hate anyone."

"I saw her face."

"She was surprised. I was going to tell her. I didn't want to hurt her—"

Hurt her. "I get it. Just let me go, okay?"

His grip on my sleeve doesn't loosen. "Rob. What I said. That wasn't—that wasn't about you."

"It was about who I used to be."

Owen's face goes still, and I wonder if he's realizing I'm right. I expect him to let me go and turn away.

Instead, he screws up his expression and says, "Maybe? Not really? You can't be *so* different."

I think of my father, probably sitting in his chair in the family room, drooling all over himself while the television blares *Sesame Street*. I think of my mother and the sudden appearance of wine bottles.

I think of myself adjusting the feeding pump under Connor's judgmental eyes. "I'm different, Owen."

"Yeah, well, I like who you are now."

It's more than I can take. Especially after everything with Maegan, with Connor, with Owen's mom just now. My throat closes up and my eyes burn. I press my free hand to my face.

Owen lets out a breath. "Dude."

His hand releases my sweatshirt, and I swipe at my eyes, ready to bolt.

Instead, he wraps me up in a hug. It's so unexpected that I can't even get it together to pull away. I don't *want* to pull away. I lean against him and try to steady my breathing.

"Still friends?" he says.

"You deserve a better friend than me." My voice sounds like it's coming out of a sniveling toddler.

"I'll take what I can get." His voice drops. "Though it's going to be tough to get Mom to believe you're straight if she's seeing this."

That makes me laugh, and I draw back.

Owen's eyes are repentant, lit with a touch of concern. So different from Connor's eyes last night. "I shouldn't have gotten all over your case. You just asked me a question."

"I shouldn't have asked."

"No, you should. Mom always says we shouldn't hide from questions. People who ask want to know the answer. It's different from people who judge without asking." His expression sobers. "I guess that applies to you, too. Everyone thinks you're a thief, but you're not. Not really."

It's a generous statement. Much like everything else about Owen, I'm not sure I deserve it.

Looking into his eyes, I know he would have answered my call after I found my father. No doubt about it.

"I stole earrings." The words fall out of my mouth in a rush.

"What?"

"I stole earrings."

"You *what*?"

"I stole earrings. From Connor's house. His mom had left them on the side of the hot tub. She won't even know they're gone. I don't know why I did it." I rake my hands back through my hair. "I guess—I thought—I wanted to do something to hurt them . . . but I also want to do something to help someone else. Like the girl you gave the forty dollars to. Or your mom."

His eyes are big as saucers. "You . . . you *stole*—"

"Yes. I did. They're in my glove compartment."

"How much are they worth?"

"I don't know exactly."

"Come on."

"Like, at least two thousand dollars." I grimace. "I *am* a thief."

"Wow."

"Yeah."

We're quiet again. My heart is hammering blood through my veins.

"You're not stealing for *you*, though," Owen finally says. "You didn't even keep the ten bucks you threw at me that day."

"I'm still stealing."

"Yeah, but it's different."

"How?"

"Your dad was stealing from people who couldn't afford it. He was doing it to put money in his own pocket. That makes him like . . . like the Sheriff of Nottingham."

I roll my eyes. "And what? I'm Robin Hood?"

"Yes!" He claps me on the shoulder and grins. "Because that makes me Will Scarlet."

CHAPTER TWENTY-EIGHT

Maegan

I brush eyeshadow across my lids, wishing I was as skilled at this as Samantha is.

She's still not talking to me. She hasn't left her room all weekend. Mom's been bringing her meals.

My phone lights up with a call. It's Rob.

I give a startled yip and almost knock the phone off my vanity. I slide the bar to answer, my heart in my throat. "Hello?"

"Hey."

He has the sexiest voice in the history of time. I have no idea how I've never noticed that before. I nearly melt out of my chair.

"Maegan?" he says.

So much for being cool. "Yeah! Yes. I'm here. Sorry."

"I can't go out tonight."

I freeze. His voice may be sexy, but I can't tell what this means.

"I'm sorry," he says in a rush. "I didn't think. Mom never goes anywhere, so I didn't think it would be a big deal. But she's got plans with friends from work, and we can't . . . my dad can't be left here alone."

"It's okay."

"I wanted to catch you before you left. I really had no idea."

An edge hides under his voice, but I can't figure it out. "You sound upset."

"It's been a long day." He takes a breath. "I was hoping to get out of here for a little while."

I inhale—but my answer stalls.

"What?" he says. His voice is flat, as if he expects something bad, and he's resigned to it.

"I could come there," I say.

Absolute silence in response.

"I don't have to," I continue. "I don't want to invite myself over. I don't—I don't want to put you in a weird position."

"My whole life is a weird position."

"Yeah. Well." I fidget. He says nothing. "It's fine. I shouldn't have invited myself—"

"He might freak you out." Rob speaks in a rush. "I don't— sometimes he's fine, but sometimes he's a mess, or he'll get upset, or it's—"

"Rob. Rob, stop. It's okay. It's fine."

He takes a long breath. "Okay."

"I mean, all of that is okay with me." I hesitate. "You don't have to hide your dad."

He gives a low, humorless laugh. "You're wrong about that."

"Do you want me to come over?"

He's so quiet. I wish I knew what happened between last night and this morning.

"Rob?" I whisper.

"I feel like I shouldn't be allowed to say yes," he says quietly.

I swallow. "Then don't. Text me your address. I'll break in."

I hang up the phone.

For the longest time, the screen is blank. I don't think he's going to text me anything at all.

Finally, after an eternity, the phone chimes.

Rob's house is massive. His driveway curves through half an acre of trees that give way to a large clearing where a tall blue Craftsman-style home sits. His front porch runs the length of the house, with narrow square pillars supporting an overhang, gas lamps glowing on each one. The gabled roofs would be amazing with Christmas lights. The three-car garage looks like it must have once been detached, but a short, blue-sided section connects it to the main building now.

When I step out of the car, I can't stop staring. I expected a McMansion like Connor's, but even in the dark, it's gorgeous. A house from a magazine or a catalog.

The front door swings open, and Rob steps out, completing the photoshoot image. He's wearing a blue cable-knit sweater and jeans. His feet are bare.

"Hey," he says. His voice gives away nothing, and it's too dark to read any emotion in his eyes.

I stop at the porch steps. He's framed by warm light from the interior.

"I was about to break in," I say. To my surprise, my voice is a little breathy.

"Go ahead," he says. "Take me down."

My pulse steps up. Standing there, a hint of innuendo in his voice, he's hotter than the day is long. I'm tempted to tackle him.

I don't have the confidence for all that, though. I hesitate.

"I was kidding," he says, as if he wasn't clear.

"I know." My brain clicks, and for an instant, he's not Rob Lachlan now, he's Rob Lachlan from a year ago. We were from two different worlds once: popular boy and nerdy girl. We're still from two different worlds: cop's daughter and criminal's son.

Either way, I'm never going to be a girl like Callie, and Rob's never going to stop being Rob Lachlan, regardless of what his dad did. Last night, I was a little loopy from the beer. Tonight, I'm completely sober—and I'm not entirely sure what I'm doing here.

"It's cold out," Rob says. He pushes the door open a little wider. "Want to come inside?"

"I don't . . . I don't know if I can," I say in a rush.

He goes still. "Oh. Okay. It's fine."

"No! Wait." He's getting the complete wrong idea. "Not because of your father."

Now he looks wary. "Then because of what?"

"Because you're you and I'm me." A line forms between his eyebrows, and I can tell that's not any better. "Rob. I don't— you're—you're . . ." I gesture at the house, at him, at our epically different lives.

"Maegan." He rolls his eyes, then steps back and holds the door open wide. "Shut up and come in."

Rob doesn't move as I walk past him, which is a good thing, because I was worried he'd try to kiss me. That wouldn't have been bad, but my brain needs a minute to parse this all out.

Since the outside of his house looks so grand, I expected the interior to be the same: oil paintings and mahogany furniture and crystal vases or whatever rich people have.

Instead, the inside of Rob's house is startlingly bare. No paintings. Not even pictures on the wall. The front door opens into a wide foyer with a beautiful slate floor and floor-to-ceiling shelves, but they're all empty. Beyond is a family room with one sofa and a nearby recliner. A small television sits on an end table—but at one point a massive big-screen must have hung over the fireplace, because the brackets are still there. To the left is a kitchen my mother would die for—all white marble countertops, gray ceramic tile, and brushed nickel hardware—but no appliances sit on the counter aside from a tiny plastic Mr. Coffee. Even the trash can, plain white plastic, looks out of place.

"I know it's weird," Rob says from behind me.

I turn to face him. "It's not." But it is.

He must know this, because he offers a little shrug. "It's weird to me. Like I'm living in someone else's house."

I get it. It looks like squatters live here, but I don't say that. I doubt it looked like this when Mr. Lachlan was a pillar of the community.

"You grew up here, right?" I say.

"Yeah. But . . . it wasn't like this. Even now, I feel like we're living on borrowed time. Mom says they can't take the house away from us, but . . ." He shrugs. He clearly thinks "they" can take the house away.

I glance around the mostly empty rooms and realize he probably watched "them" take away everything else. It must be awful, to have no idea what his future holds. I know what I want—or at least what I always wanted: college for sure, with a focus on math and engineering. The school counselor said that the SAT company can't report the reason my scores were invalidated, so I don't think college is entirely off the table, but along with everything else, it's a constant source of guilt. One wrong decision, and my life skidded off the path.

But I made my choice. Rob didn't. He's not responsible for what his father did.

As soon as I have the thought, I wonder where his father is.

"There's a Harry Potter marathon on," Rob says. "If you want to watch a movie."

I wonder what expression is on my face, because he winces and says, "Or not."

"We can watch Harry Potter." I can't decide if I'm making this awkward or if he is. He's not his usual stoic, confident self, and it's throwing me. "Rob?"

"Yeah?"

"Where's your dad?"

"Oh. Upstairs."

Can I see him? I don't say the words, but I want to. Not because I want to gawk at him, but because it's weird to know there's someone else in the house.

"I've never brought anyone here," Rob says quickly. "Not since . . . before." He shakes his head and rolls his eyes a little. "It's not like it was. It's . . ."

I wait, but he doesn't finish that statement.

"Don't be embarrassed," I whisper.

Color finds his cheeks, and he looks away. "It's impossible not to be. Living in this house . . . it's ridiculous."

"You can't help your family," I say to him.

He makes a face, then reaches out to take my hand. His thumb traces my knuckles, and I nearly shiver. "I'm glad you came over."

"Me too."

We stare at each other for the longest time.

"Do you want to see him?" Rob finally says. "I can take you upstairs." He grimaces. "I hate this. I feel like I'm talking about a pet."

He's not wrong: he sounds like he's got a tarantula or a pit viper. His voice is so foreboding that a chill locks my spine into place, but I don't want to take the cowardly way out. He has to live with his father. I can look the man in the eye and say hello. "Okay. If you want."

"If you want to leave—after—it's okay."

"Now you're scaring me."

Rob doesn't say anything to that, which isn't encouraging. He uses his grip on my hand to tug me toward the stairs behind the kitchen. The rest of the house is as bare as the front. We pass a dining room with a simple table and four chairs, then a completely empty room with floor-to-ceiling windows that must have once been an office. This is the only room missing meticulous paint and flooring. The walls are bare white, unlike the trendy grays and blues of the rest of the main level. Carpeting has been torn up, leaving aged hardwood floors that haven't been refinished.

I think of his story about finding his father. I wonder if it was in there.

"Mom says we'll probably sell it soon," Rob says, as if the silence has grown too heavy, "but it's tricky with all the lawsuits and stuff." Uncertainty rings in his voice. I can't imagine living with that kind of precarious future, not knowing what the next day would bring. I squeeze his hand.

He squeezes mine back and stops me at the top of the staircase. "It's stupid, but I didn't realize how lonely I was until I wasn't."

"I know exactly what you mean," I say softly.

"Come on."

He leads me down a short hallway to a closed door, which he opens without knocking. That surprises me—who doesn't knock?—until I see the man in the wheelchair next to the window.

I should have asked what to expect. I knew his father was impaired in some way, but for some reason, I was expecting something like a stroke patient, with weakness on one side, or someone with the mental capacity of a toddler, who wouldn't be able to speak well. Dad had a police officer friend who was shot in the head and survived, and while he wasn't able to return to police work, he was able to function as an adult.

Rob's father is none of those things.

I wasn't expecting a man who looks like an older version of Rob, with slightly graying hair and a dent in his skull. I wasn't expecting a blank stare or the clicking machine affixed to a pole beside him or the tube disappearing under the waist of his clothing.

I wasn't expecting the faint smell of urine mixed with something more medicinal.

"We usually park him in front of the TV at night," Rob says, "but it's hard to get him upstairs by myself, and Mom didn't want to have to deal with it when she gets back. I put him by the window because it seems better than staring at the wall. If I put him in bed, he just falls asleep, and that means he's up at four a.m."

I swallow. "That makes sense." It doesn't make sense at all. My voice sounds like it's coming from someone else.

"It doesn't seem to make a difference either way," he continues. "Sometimes I wonder if we do all that for ourselves, you know what I mean?"

No. I have no idea. I had no idea he was living with this. I turn and look at Rob. His expression is frozen somewhere between resignation and fear.

"You take care of him," I say. "I don't think—I don't think I knew that."

"Mom does most of it. We have nurses that help."

"Does he respond to anything?"

"Not the way you mean. He can feel pain, for sure. Sometimes different things will set him off or make him upset. But calling his name or something? Never." His eyes shift to his father. "Dad! Hey, Dad!"

Nothing. After a moment, the man blinks. The machine continues its rhythmic clicking.

I look back at Rob. I've been so worried about Samantha and how our family is going to continue, regardless of her decision, but that's nothing like this. I imagine my father in a chair like this, unaware of who I am or what's going on around him. Rob Lachlan Sr. committed crimes against dozens of people, but he was still a father. He was still *Rob's* father.

On impulse, I shift forward and throw my arms around Rob's neck.

"I'm so sorry," I whisper, and the words don't sound like enough. "I didn't know."

He's so withdrawn when it comes to his family that I'm surprised when he doesn't pull away and instead hugs me back. I'm even more surprised when his breathing shakes. "You're the second person to spontaneously hug me today. I must look pathetic."

"You're not pathetic." I hold on, as if I can feed him a single strand of hope just by virtue of physical contact. "You're not, Rob."

"I am."

I press my face into his shoulder. "You're not," I whisper. "You're not. You're not."

His chest expands as he inhales, a warm rush of his breath against my hair as he says my name. "Maegan."

Abruptly, he pulls back. "Come with me." He takes my hand and drags me back through the door, down the hallway a few feet, and into another darkened room.

I barely have time to identify our surroundings before he takes my face in his hands and kisses me. He's more sure of himself than last night—if that's even possible. But there's no hesitation today, no uncertainty. He's gentle and warm and his mouth is so addictive. I'm dizzy with the taste of his breath, and I'm glad for his hands at my waist when he draws back.

"Sorry," he says pragmatically. "He might not know what I'm doing, but I still don't want to kiss you in front of Dad."

I give a soft little laugh, and he catches my lips with his. The house is so quiet, and we're not exactly alone, but I've never felt more sure. It's like we've carved out a space beside reality, where we can hide from the real world for a little while. When his hands slide under the edge of my shirt, my insides seem to melt.

He leaves my mouth to kiss his way down my neck, his slender fingers tickling the bottom of my rib cage. I gasp and giggle, but he holds me in place.

"Who—who spontaneously hugged you first?" I ask him.

"Owen Goettler." He barely stops kissing my neck long enough to answer.

"Did you make out with him too?" I tease.

"No." Rob's hands go still, and he draws back far enough for moonlight to spark in his eyes. We're in a bedroom. *His* bedroom, I realize, as I spot lacrosse gear piled in a corner and school books scattered across a desk under the window. "Do you want to go back downstairs to watch a movie?"

I have no idea how to answer. "Do you?"

His mouth quirks. "I asked you first."

I blush and look down, studying the ribbed pattern of the sweater he's wearing. "I'm okay with whatever you want to do." My blush deepens as I consider what that means in his bedroom, of all places. "Mostly whatever," I amend.

"Mostly whatever." He kisses me again, more slowly this time. His body presses into mine, his hands stronger suddenly, holding me against him. He's so sure of himself that he steals my breath with every kiss.

When his hand slips under my shirt again, I pull back. "I feel like—I feel like I need to define *mostly whatever.*"

He smiles and pauses, his hands going still, his forehead resting against mine. "Go ahead."

There's no urgency in his voice, no disappointment. No expectation. Of all the things about Rob that take me by surprise, this must top the list: he's respectful. Chivalrous. Thoughtful. Patient.

There's no entitled pawing at my chest, no fumbling to get my jeans unbuttoned.

Some of that is intrinsically Rob, I'm sure. But some of it had to come from his parents. It's bizarre to think of a man stealing from half the county but also teaching his son to be respectful of women.

I've been quiet too long, because a line appears between Rob's eyebrows, and he pulls back an inch. "Maegan, we don't have to do anything. We really can go watch a movie."

I blush and look away. "No. It's not that. I was thinking about how you're very respectful."

I expect him to take that as a compliment, but he freezes—then frowns.

"What?" I say softly. "What's wrong?"

"It's stupid. It's—" He makes a disgusted noise, then turns away from me to drop onto the side of the bed and run his hands through his hair. "Sometimes I think of these things my father used to say, and it was completely the opposite of what he did. So then I wonder what's wrong with me, that I'd listen to *anything* he'd say."

I join him on the bed, sitting gingerly on the edge of the mattress. "What did he say?"

"It's not—it's not like that." He hesitates.

I wait.

Finally, he turns and looks at me. "Okay, like this. One time, we were all at a party at the club, and Connor saw a girl he wanted to talk to. His dad said something like, 'You want her, go get 'er.'" He rolls his eyes.

"That sounds about right," I say.

He looks startled. "What?"

"That sounds like the kind of thing a guy like Connor would hear from his dad." I pause. "He sits on the quad every morning and girls fawn all over him. They used to fawn all over you, too."

Rob looks abashed. "Well. I couldn't help that."

"You poor thing," I tease.

I expect it to make him smile, but he doesn't. "Go on," I say. "I interrupted. Your dad wasn't all 'Go get 'er, Tiger,' like Connor's?"

"No." His entire frame is tense. "Connor went to talk to her, and she wasn't into him. It got really awkward, because she tried to walk away, and he kept going after her. He's not usually like that, but his dad was right there, watching. When he finally gave up, his dad said something like, 'A real man would have gotten her number.' And my dad said, 'A real man has no right to take what's not offered.'"

The words drop like a rock. Rob turns and looks at me. "I'm sorry. I got too heavy. I ruined the moment."

"No, Rob—"

"How am I supposed to reconcile that?" he demands. "Am I supposed to hate him? Love him? Does he get a pass because he wasn't a womanizing asshole? Or could I turn out like him because I'm not one, either? Was he some kind of psychopath? Like, is that how he got people to trust him? I don't get it."

I take his hand, and I'm surprised to find it's trembling. "Rob," I say. "You aren't like your father. You're kind. You're smart. You're not him. You're not a thief. Do you understand me? You're *not*."

"You're wrong," he says, and his voice almost breaks.

I don't understand. "I'm what?"

"You're wrong." He pulls his hand out of mine. "I'm not a good person."

"Rob, you *are* a good person."

"No." His voice has deepened. He turns and looks at me. "I'm not. Do you understand me? I'm not."

A chill winds through my chest at the intensity of his words. "What do you mean?"

"I am a thief."

"What?"

"I'm a thief. I stole money from the cash box of a fund-raiser last week. I used a cheerleader's credit card to order shoes. And last night—" He breaks off and shoves himself off the bed, then opens a dresser drawer to swipe something out of it.

I'm frozen on the edge of his bed.

He grabs my wrist and pulls out my hand. "Here."

Two earrings drop into my palm.

I recognize them immediately. They're the earrings that were sitting on the ledge of the hot tub at the Tunstall house.

"Rob," I breathe.

"I stole them," he says. "And I was going to sell them."

I swallow. All the heat has left my body, leaving a brick of icy tension to settle in my abdomen.

Rob's a thief. He's admitting it. He's *proving* it. I've been defending him to my friends, to my *father*, when everything everyone warned me about is true.

The earrings are practically weightless, but they burn against my palm. I don't know if I should take them with me or leave them. I don't want to be a part of any of this. Much like Samantha's secrets, I don't want Rob's, too.

I stare at him. "You were going to sell them?"

"Yes." His eyes are searing mine, like he expects me to make sense of it, but I can't.

"You stole them when we were together? Were you using me to get in that room?" All the breath rushes out of my lungs as I reevaluate the whole night at the party. "Did you use me to—"

"No!" He almost shouts the word, and I flinch. "No, Maegan. It was—I don't know what it is. It was after. After Bill. After I had to listen to him accuse me."

He was so upset when we left the house. I could almost understand retaliation as a motivation, but . . . "You said you've stolen other things."

"Only what wouldn't be missed! And—"

"That's still stealing!"

"I know. I know." Rob's eyes are panicked. Anguished. "I wasn't thinking. I was so angry. It was—it was a mistake. You understand that. I know you understand that."

"*My* mistake didn't hurt anyone else," I say.

His expression hardens, a glimpse of the old Rob Lachlan peeking through. "Yeah? I heard that it hurt about a hundred people."

"That's not fair."

"Are you kidding me? None of this is *fair*."

He's angry now. Good. So am I. "Just because people treat you like crap doesn't mean you get to take whatever you want from them."

"Just because people treat *you* like crap doesn't mean you have to sit there and take it."

That's not a dig, but right now, it feels like one. "It doesn't mean I get to forget the difference between right and wrong."

"So you only get to do that when you're jealous of your sister?"

That hits me like a sucker punch. I reach out and grab his wrist, but I'm less gentle than he was with mine. His eyes are dark pools of anger and guilt and shame and sadness, but I can't figure it all out, and right this second, I don't want to. I drop the earrings into his hand and stand.

He catches my hand. "Wait. Stop. Please. Maegan. I'm sorry."

"You are a thief," I say to him.

"I don't want to be. Do you understand that? I don't—it was a mistake. I want to undo it."

I know all about mistakes you can't undo. "Then turn yourself in," I say.

Without another word, I walk out.

CHAPTER TWENTY-NINE

Rob

Monday morning, I show up at school looking like I spent the weekend on a bender. Despite what Maegan said, I kept waiting for the cops to show up and arrest me. When car tires rolled up the driveway, I thought for *sure* it was time. My heart nearly beat a path out of my chest. I actually laced up my running shoes.

It was just Mom coming home.

That was almost as bad. I was a wreck. Confessing to her would be a lot different from confessing to Maegan, so I dove into bed and turned my lights off.

She barely looked in on me before moving down the hallway to her own room.

When the police didn't show up, that was almost worse. Was Maegan waiting until morning to tell her father? Maybe he was working a late shift and she'd have to wait for him to come home.

Maybe she meant what she said.

Turn yourself in.

I have no idea how to do that. I can't take the shoes back from Mrs. Goettler, and I don't have the money to repay Lexi, even if

I had the nerve to admit what I did. I don't even have forty bucks to give back to the sports fund-raiser, if I even had a way to put it back.

Hey, Connor, I actually stole this. Here you go.

Yeah, sure. I could hand over the earrings at the same time. *Tell your mom to be more careful.*

All that is beside the point anyway. As much as I don't want to admit it, a dark, secret part of my brain is satisfied, as if I've finally fulfilled some kind of destiny. The feeling has been lingering in the back of my thoughts since the moment I wrapped my hand around that money from the cash box, and it only intensified when I told Maegan what I was doing.

It's intensifying now, as I stride across the quad to enter school through the front doors, instead of parking around back. Connor and his friends are sitting around the flagpole, and their eyes follow me like rifle scopes.

I don't care. I keep walking. I dare anyone to say anything to me. I *want* someone to start something.

A tall girl parts from the crowd to block my path. My thoughts are so cloudy that it takes me a moment to recognize her. Rachel. Maegan's friend. Fury lights her expression.

Almost immediately, a scenario clicks in my head. Maegan told her friend about me. Of course. They chased me out of Taco Taco because they thought I was a thief, and they were right. Maegan probably called her the instant she pulled out of my driveway.

"What are you doing to Maegan?" says Rachel.

The question takes me by surprise because it's nothing like I expected. "I'm not doing anything," I say, and my voice comes out like a low growl.

"She asked you a question," says a male voice behind her, and I realize I've missed her boyfriend standing there. Stellar.

"I answered it," I say.

They say nothing, but they block my path into the school. The quad is filling up with students before the first bell, and we're generating more than a little interest.

"Please move," I grind out. "I need to get to class."

"I'm looking out for my friend," says Rachel, "and I want to know what's going on."

I don't need to stand here for an interrogation. I move to push between them.

Drew moves to block me. "Look, man, you don't have to be a jerk. She's asking you about her friend."

"Let him go." Connor steps between us and shoves Drew away from me. A couple of guys from the lacrosse team have followed him over here, too.

I lose a moment to shock.

Drew does, too. He takes a step back. "Chill out," he says. "This has nothing to do with you. Rachel is trying to look out for Maegan."

I'd be impressed at the concern if it weren't all open hostility directed at me. But as much as I don't want to be hassled, Drew and Rachel didn't confront me to give me a hard time. They really do care about Maegan.

Connor looks like he's going to unleash some douchebaggery meant to chase them off, and the last thing I want is *his* help, especially that way. "Get lost, Connor. They're just looking out for a friend." I look at Drew and Rachel. "She's fine. We're doing a math project together. That's all."

Rachel doesn't look convinced. "But—"

"That's *all*," I say. "Really."

Her eyes glance from me to Connor, who's still standing there looking like he wants to start something.

I can't handle this.

"Get over yourself," I say to him. "This guy was right. None of this has to do with you."

He inhales to snap back, but I don't bother waiting. Instead, I turn and walk into the school.

Mr. London is delighted to see me. I'm practically crawling through the doorway into the library, but he smiles and says, "Mr. Lachlan! Ready to discuss book two?"

I'm ready for coffee. A shot of vodka. A baseball bat to the face.

None of those are available. I sigh and talk about the book. "I think Cook is her mother."

"Yes," he says. "I think so, too."

I want to return his enthusiasm. I want to talk books. I want to be normal. The moment on the quad has left me shaken.

Instead, I feel like I'm going to cry. My stupid throat is closing up.

The smile melts off Mr. London's face. He raises the counter. "Office?"

No. I want to turn and bolt.

Instead, my feet march me forward, into his office, where I collapse into a chair.

Fuck. I am crying.

I scrape my hands against my cheeks and try to get it together. The sleeves of my winter coat dig into my skin. Mr. London shoves a box of tissues my way.

"I don't deserve this," I say.

"I don't think anyone ever really *deserves* Kleenex," he says.

That makes me laugh, which helps. I choke back the tears before I turn into a sniveling puddle on the floor. "No. This. You being nice to me."

"It's not charity. I get paid to do it." His expression tells me he's teasing. Gently.

Even that is more than I deserve. I don't smile back.

"You want to talk about it?" he says.

He says the words so matter-of-factly. Not the kind of warm, probing question I'd get from the school counselor, or the soft, intrusive way my mother would ask. Just straightforward.

The way my father would have asked.

I press my fingers into my eyes again.

No, I want to say. *No.* The word sits in my throat, but it's blocked by emotion.

Instead, I say, "I miss my father so much."

For the longest time, the room is so silent. Or maybe I can't hear anything over my roaring heartbeat, my shaking breath.

Mr. London lets out a sigh. I can't look at him now.

I swipe at my eyes again and stare at the bottom edge of his desk. "Everyone thinks he's horrible. Maybe he was. I *know* he was. But . . . I don't—he wasn't horrible to me."

This is humiliating. I've never said this to anyone.

Now I'm saying it to the school librarian, for god's sake.

"I'm sorry." My eyes are a blur. I shove myself out of the chair. "I need to go to class."

"Rob—"

"I'm sorry. I shouldn't have—"

"Please stop."

"I need to go." I pick up my backpack and sling it over my shoulder. My breathing is a hitching mess. I need to get it together.

Mr. London steps in front of me. "Rob. *Stop*."

I stop. I breathe. My fingers are digging into the nylon strap of my backpack with so much force that my knuckles burn.

"Sit," he says. "I'll write you a pass."

I don't want to sit, but he's blocking the doorway, and I'm not a rebel. I've never been the kind of kid to get in trouble with teachers. I do what I'm told.

I sit.

Something about the command is stabilizing, though. My tears have dried up.

Mr. London eases into his chair behind the desk. "I was thinking about you this weekend," he says. "Until you hid in here last week, I don't think I really considered what this all must mean for you."

I say nothing.

"I didn't consider," he says slowly, "that you lost your father without losing your father."

His words bring on a fresh round of tears, and I try to blink them away.

It doesn't work.

I'm so sick of crying. Being lonely sucked, but it had its advantages. No one talking to me meant I didn't talk to anyone else.

I give in and take a tissue.

"When I was young," he says, "my grandmother had a stroke."

I stiffen. I don't want an anecdote.

"She lived with us," he continues. "She used to watch my sister and me after school. So we were really close. When she had the stroke, it was really . . . really *weird*. I was twelve. She was still there, but she wasn't there."

That forces me still. I meet his eyes. *Yes*, I think. *Yes*. I can't say it. But I don't think I need to.

"This kid once . . ." Mr. London takes a long breath. "This kid once said something like, 'What's wrong? Who died?' But no one had died. It was so strange. I couldn't explain it. And because no one died, it wasn't like . . . I don't know. I don't really even know how to explain it now."

I don't, either.

The words are stuck in my throat. I try to swallow past them. If I speak, I might lose it.

Mr. London looks at me. "I'm sorry about your father, Rob." He pauses, rolling a pen between his fingers.

"He was awful." My voice cracks and I swipe at my face again. Thank god this is the library and not the lacrosse coach's office.

"But he wasn't an awful father."

"No." I press shaking hands to my face.

The room falls quiet again. The first bell rings. I don't move. I *can't* move.

Mr. London picks up the phone on his desk. After a moment, he says, "Rob Lachlan is in the library with me. Will you tell his first-period teacher?" A pause. "Thank you."

The phone clicks back into place. My heart pounds against

my rib cage. My body feels like every emotion is trying to rattle free, as if I've confined too much inside my skin.

"Tell me about him," says Mr. London.

I open my mouth to refuse. He's the last person I should confide in.

Instead, I tell him everything about my father. The man I thought he was. The man I thought I wanted to be. The way my father would show up for every game. The way I could tell him anything.

I tell him every good memory. Everything I miss.

I tell him how my father's crimes felt like such a betrayal. So big that I can barely admit it to myself.

Mr. London makes for a good audience. He's quiet, and he listens. When I'm done, I'm wrung out. I want to melt out of this chair and dissolve into the carpeting.

When he finally speaks, it's not what I expect. "You know I'm gay, right?"

There's a picture of him with his husband on the wall behind him. I'm pretty sure the entire student body knows he's gay, but his question was matter-of-fact, so my answer is too. "Yes."

"Just making sure." He pauses. "When I told my parents, they didn't react well. They wanted me to go to this . . . this *camp*."

I don't know where this is going, but it's not about me sobbing in his chair, so I'm okay with it. "A camp?"

"A religious camp. A gay-reversal camp." His eyebrows go up, asking if I'm tracking.

I am. "Did you go?"

"Yes." His jaw tightens. "They told me I couldn't live with them anymore if I refused to go. So I went. And I hated it. It was . . . awful." He grimaces and holds out his hands. "It obviously didn't work."

"So, what happened?"

"When I got home, I faked it. I hated it, but I faked it."

"You faked being straight?"

"Yes." He pauses. "It put this wall between me and my parents. I used to lie in bed and think of all the ways I hated them. My father especially. He watched me, checked my computer, searched my room—" He breaks off and shakes his head. "We were close when I was young. It was such a relief to get out."

Nothing sounds like a relief about this story.

His eyes return to mine. "My sister eventually convinced them to come around. She was the only person who let me be me—and convinced them to let me be me. But it took me a long time to forgive them. To reconcile that the good memories didn't vanish just because there were bad ones in there, too. All those memories are a part of who I am. The good ones *and* the bad ones."

His eyes are full of emotion I'm sure is matched in mine.

"It's okay to miss him," he says. "It's okay to miss him even if what he did was wrong."

The words are so simple, but they seem to find a crack in my armor. The grip on my heart eases. I let out a long breath.

All of a sudden, I want to tell him everything. About the cash box. About the earrings.

Everything.

A hand knocks on the door frame, and it breaks the spell. Another teacher stands there. I don't know her at all.

"Mr. London?" she says with an apologetic glance at me. "The computers won't log on and we need to reboot the server."

"I'll be right there," he says.

"Go," I say. I grab my backpack, then duck my head to wipe my face on my shoulder. "I'm missing calculus."

I'm through the door when his voice calls me back. "Rob."

I barely pause. I can't look at him now. I almost told him everything.

Turn yourself in.

I'm too much of a coward to do that.

"What?" I croak out.

"Come back tomorrow morning," he says. "We can finish our conversation then."

I say nothing. I can't decide if I should bolt or if I should beg to hide in his office for the rest of the day.

"Will you do that?" he prompts. "Come back?"

"Yes."

"Good. I'll be here."

I'm twenty minutes late for calculus, especially since I took a few minutes to wash my face in the men's room. I ease through the door so I don't interrupt Mrs. Quick's lecture. Maegan is sitting there in the front row. Her pencil slides along her notebook, and she doesn't even look at me.

I'm encouraged by my conversation with Mr. London. Maybe I can fix this. Maybe I can undo it.

I need to apologize. I dragged her down a road she didn't deserve.

I steel my nerve and slide into the seat beside her. "Hey," I whisper. "I want—"

She closes her notebook and grabs her backpack.

Without a word, she slides out of her seat and moves to the back.

Leaving me alone.

CHAPTER THIRTY

Maegan

Rachel finds me in the cafeteria line. She sidles up beside me with a tray full of food.

"Hey," she says, and her voice is low. "Can we talk?"

I'm so burdened with secrets about my sister and Rob that I don't have the strength to fend off Rachel, especially if she's going to start criticizing my friendship choices. I reach for an apple and add it to my tray.

"Please," she says. "I really miss you. I don't want to fight over boys, of all things."

That gets my attention. I turn my head and look at her. "You think we're fighting over boys?"

"Well, we're fighting because of a boy."

"No, Rachel. We're fighting because you and Drew were being nasty to—" I break off and shuffle forward in the line. "Forget it."

"No." Her voice takes on an edge. "Finish what you were going to say."

I want to dodge. I want to hide. I don't like confrontation, and I don't like worrying I'm in the wrong.

If anything, the situations with Rob and my sister have taught me that trying to do what everyone else wants just leads to misery. I face Rachel head on. "I was going to say that you and Drew were being nasty to someone I considered my friend. I didn't think you were being very fair."

She looks gobsmacked.

I look away from her and shove my tray forward with more force than necessary.

She hovers behind me, but I refuse to look at her.

"Wait," she says after a moment. "*Considered*? Past tense? You don't consider him your friend anymore?"

"I don't want to talk about it." And I don't. Half a day later, and I still have no idea how to reconcile what Rob told me. He carried around so much anger about how people thought he was involved with his father's thefts. So much anger that he'd built steel walls around himself. He resented that. I *know* he did.

But then to start stealing anyway—it makes no sense.

"Please?" Rachel takes advantage of my silence and jumps around to get in front of me. "Maegan. I'm sorry. But he was bad news. Please talk to me. I've been so worried about you. I actually got in his face this morning, but then—"

"Wait. You got in whose face?"

"Rob Lachlan's. I thought he was pulling you away from your friends, and that's a warning sign—"

"Oh my god, Rachel. Do you live in an advice column? Rob wasn't pulling me away from my friends." I grit my teeth and glare at her. "My friends were being *jerks*."

Now she looks like I punched her. "We were looking out for you."

"Replay everything Drew said to Rob at Taco Taco and convince yourself of that. Go ahead. I'll wait."

Rachel purses her lips. "Drew wasn't wrong."

"He wasn't wrong after Rob left. He didn't need to be nasty to Rob's face. Rob didn't do anything to him." I pause, and her face twists like she's going to defend Drew further. "Just because he's right about some things doesn't mean he's right about *everything*. You can be *right* and be a jerk at the same time. You've heard Drew make little comments to me, too, so don't try to deny it."

She inhales to say something, then closes her mouth.

Exactly. I push forward with my tray.

Rachel follows me. "So, what are you saying? Rob's completely innocent and everyone is all wrong about him?"

I hesitate.

She seizes it. "He's not. If he had nothing to hide, he wouldn't lurk around the school like he's on death row, and you know it."

"You're missing the entire point." I slide my tray along.

Rachel says nothing. I say nothing.

This sucks.

"I don't want to fight with you," she finally says.

"I don't want to fight with you, either." And that's true. I miss her friendship. I appreciate that she was looking out for me, regardless of how misguided it was.

I just don't feel like dealing with Rachel+Drew.

"Do you want to sit with us?" she says as we approach the register.

Her tone implies she wants to brush everything under the rug and go back to the status quo. I can't do that.

"Not today," I say. I type my student ID number into the machine next to the cash register and walk away.

When I turn to face the cafeteria, I realize I'm left without a destination. A week ago, I would have gone slinking back to Rachel's table, or I would have found a place to eat by myself. All these secrets would have pressed into my shoulders until I finally gave in and played tattletale.

I'm not doing that today. I storm across the cafeteria and slap my tray down beside Owen.

They both look up at me in surprise. Before they can say anything, I glare at Rob and say, "What are you doing?"

He glares right back at me. I'd forgotten that he's not one to wilt from confrontation—and I was the one who ran from him in math class this morning. "Eating lunch. What are *you* doing?"

"You know that's not what I mean."

Owen clears his throat. "Should I leave?"

"Does he know?" I demand.

Rob hesitates, and some of the attitude melts out of his eyes. "Yeah. He does."

"Know what?" says Owen.

Rob looks at him, and his voice drops. "About . . . everything."

"Why are you doing it?" I say. "You made it this huge deal about how you weren't—"

"Would you keep your voice down?"

I don't lower my voice at all. "I want an answer."

"Then sit down." He casts a look around, but we haven't attracted too much attention yet. "Stop making a scene."

I sit.

Rob says nothing. Owen glances between us.

"Hi," he says after a moment. He holds out a hand. "I'm Owen."

I know, but I shake his hand anyway, like this is some kind of bizarre business meeting. "I'm Maegan."

Rob's looking at his food now. He's not getting off that easy.

"You spent all that time telling me you weren't a thief," I whisper at him. "And now you are?"

"It's not like that," he says.

"It's exactly like that."

His eyes flash up. "It's not all black and white, Officer."

"Did you take something that didn't belong to you?"

Silence falls over the table, and he pokes at his sandwich. When he finally speaks, his voice is very low. "I didn't steal for me. I don't want it. I don't want any of it."

It shouldn't make a difference. I don't want it to make a difference. But the tone of his voice plucks a chord of mercy inside me. "Fine. Who?"

"For anyone," says Rob. "Anyone who needs it." He hesitates. "It started with this ten-dollar bill that Connor dropped. He wouldn't take it back." He nods at Owen. "So, I gave it to Owen. And then the bake sale cash box fell, and I had to help Connor clean it up, so I swiped a couple of twenties, and Owen gave it to a girl who needed it. Then Owen's mom's work shoes broke, and she didn't have a hundred bucks to replace them, and—"

All the breath leaves my lungs. "You're stealing to *help* people."

He grits his teeth and looks away. He looks antsy, fidgety. That's not him at all. This is really weighing on him.

"You don't want to do this," I guess.

"I don't want *any* of this," he says. "I don't want everyone thinking I'm a thief. I don't—I don't want to have to live with what my father did. If I can give something back, then maybe—" He breaks off with a disgusted noise and starts throwing his half-finished lunch back into his sack.

"If you're not eating that, give it to me," says Owen.

Rob shoves the food across the table, then jerks at the zipper on his backpack.

"You're leaving?" I say to him.

"Yeah." To my surprise, he does. He stands up and stalks away from the table.

I don't understand anything at all.

Owen picks up the abandoned sandwich. "We weren't going to hurt anyone," he says. "You think the bake sale is going to miss forty bucks?"

"That doesn't make it *right*," I say.

"I eat a cheese sandwich every day, but the lacrosse team is getting new sticks because some kids could afford to pay three bucks for a cookie. You think *that's* right?"

I open my mouth, then close it.

Owen's eyes are piercing. "His former *best friend* beat him up for going to that party. You think *that's* right?"

"Wait, what?"

"My mom would lose her job if she didn't have uniform shoes, but you're going to get up in arms about earrings someone doesn't even know are missing?"

"I'm not—who beat up—*what*?"

"I get why you're mad," Owen says. "But to pretend it's all one side or the other is just stupid." He polishes off the last of the sandwich, and his voice drops. "You want to come storming over here to call him a thief, go ahead. But sometimes I think everyone needs to take a long look in the mirror before they go making an issue about someone else's life."

I don't know what to say to that. It's a little too close to the argument I just had with Rachel.

"He's not hurting anyone." Owen grabs his backpack and stands up. "I think he's trying to undo the harm his father caused."

I frown. He can't solve a crime by committing more—but Owen's words about a three-dollar cookie are lodged in my brain, and I can't work them loose.

"Think about it." Owen throws his backpack over his shoulder and turns away. "We weren't all raised by cops, Maegan."

Once again, I'm left alone, everyone's secrets sitting in a pile on my shoulders.

CHAPTER THIRTY-ONE

Rob

Dinner is meatloaf and mashed potatoes, which is usually a favorite of mine. Tonight, I wish I could hole up in my room so I could avoid Mom's prying questions and Dad's blank stare.

The earrings are burning a hole in my pocket. I drove to a pawn shop after school, but I couldn't find the nerve to go in. I don't know if they'd ask me where they came from, but I wasn't ready to risk it. I'm not a liar. I'm not even a very good actor.

Then again, I've got Mom convinced that I'm seeking counseling and I'm working out every day.

At least half of that is true. The cold morning air feels like a punishment. A penance.

She's not really prying at me with questions more complicated than *how was school* anyway. It's my own guilt that makes every word out of her mouth feel like an interrogation. I shovel meatloaf into my mouth and hope that's enough.

When a lull falls between us, her gaze turns piercing, and I can feel that the topic is going to turn more personal. Before she can pry, I swallow my food and say, "How's everything going at work?"

She hesitates and gives me a small smile. "Everything is fine."

"They're convinced you know the alphabet now?"

"Better than that. They've mentioned that they might like to hire me on full-time."

I glance up. "Really?"

"Yes." She hesitates. "I've developed a good rapport with Gregory."

I glance at Dad. He clearly doesn't care. "What—ah, would that change anything?"

"I don't know yet." She stabs a piece of meatloaf. "I've been thinking about a lot of things."

There's a tone in her voice I can't identify, but I don't like the way it's making me feel. "What kinds of things?"

"Just . . . things." Another stab at her meatloaf. "Like—"

A solid knock sounds at the front door.

I freeze.

Mom freezes.

Dad . . . well. He keeps on doing what he always does.

No one ever comes here for any good reason. I think about Maegan. Her father. The earrings. I didn't hear sirens, but then there wouldn't be sirens if they were coming to pick me up to take me to jail.

One of us is going to have to move. I place my napkin next to my silverware. "I'll get it."

Dread curls through my body as I approach the door. I remember answering the door for the paramedics after I found Dad, and while this is completely different, it's also similar.

I throw the lock and yank the door open.

Connor stands on my doorstep. I'd be less surprised to find Santa Claus. My thoughts twist between anger at his presence and panic that he somehow figured out that I stole his mother's earrings.

"What the hell are you doing here?" I say.

"Hi," he says in response.

Mom must pick up on my tone or my tension, because she calls from the dining room. "Who is it, Rob?"

"No one." I move to swing the door closed.

Connor catches it and all but growls at me. "Grow up."

Mom appears behind me. "Connor! It's been ages." She pauses. "Rob? Invite him in."

I want to refuse, but that will only make me look petulant, and Mom will get her way in the end. I step back and hold the door open. "Fine. Come in."

"Are you hungry?" Mom says. "There's plenty of meatloaf."

His eyes flick to me and back to her, and he says, "Yes. Thank you."

When he steps across the threshold I want to punch him in the gut. Or maybe I don't. I'm not sure. He walks past me, unzipping his jacket as he goes, and hangs it in the front closet like he's been coming for dinner every week this year.

I wait for him to be surprised by the sparse decor, the way Maegan was, but then I remember he was already in here two days ago, when he staked out my room to sucker punch me in the stomach.

Never mind. I do want to hit him.

He's already in the dining room, though, and he pauses for a second when his eyes fall on my father, his feeding pump *click-click-click*ing. Mom has hurriedly prepared a plate for Connor in the kitchen, and she slides it in front of him with a smile.

He waits for her to sit before taking his own seat. It puts him directly across from me. Hooray.

"You still haven't said what you're doing here," I say.

"Rob," Mom says.

Connor takes a forkful of meatloaf. "I was driving around. I thought I'd stop by."

I don't believe that for a minute.

"How are your parents?" says Mom.

His eyes glance at my father, who's still staring dumbly from the opposite end of the table. Connor is unnerved. He's doing a good job of hiding it, but I can tell. "They're—they're great. Dad's business has really taken off."

Mom doesn't say anything to that. Her hand tightens on her fork, and now she's the one to stab at a piece of meatloaf. Connor's father got a lot of my father's clients when everything collapsed. Mr. Tunstall was apparently a real hero to people who still had money left.

"Sorry," says Connor. "I wasn't thinking."

"No!" Mom's voice is full of false cheer. "It's wonderful. I'm glad your family is still doing well." She takes a gulp of wine from her glass. "Marjorie hadn't mentioned that."

"She probably didn't want to be insensitive," I say.

"No," Mom says. "It's—" Her cell phone rings from the kitchen, the happy chimes a direct contrast to the bizarre tension in this room.

She stands. "I'll be right back, boys."

We're left alone. Connor eats, his fork scraping against the plate in a way that probably isn't very loud but sounds like a circular saw in the quiet of the dining room. He hasn't met my eyes since I opened the front door.

He can't be here about the earrings. He would have said something by now.

All of a sudden, I'm tired. I don't want to be at war with Connor. I don't want to be hiding things from my mother. I don't want to have cried on Mr. London's desk, talking about how much I miss my father. I don't want any of this.

"Hey," he says.

I refuse to look up.

"Rob."

"What?"

"I just . . ." He hesitates. "I'm sorry."

I have no idea what he's referring to, but the list of what he could apologize for is long and winding and he's full of shit anyway. "No, you're not."

He frowns. "What do you even think I'm talking about?"

"It doesn't matter." My voice is full of acid, but I keep the volume down because I don't want to start arguing and trigger something with Dad. "You're not sorry. What do you want? Do you feel bad all of a sudden? What was the little show on the quad? You want a cookie?"

He doesn't say anything.

I look back at my food. Jab my fork into my mashed potatoes. The worst part about this conversation is that a tiny scrap of my consciousness wishes his apology were real. Like we could snap our fingers and go back to the way things were.

Mom's in the kitchen, laughing lightly. It must be one of her new friends.

I've been thinking about a lot of things.

She never said what kinds of things.

"Trevor Casternan took your attacker position," says Connor, interrupting my thoughts.

"Good for him," I say.

"He's pretty good with the stick, but he's slow—"

"What are you doing?"

"Talking." He scoops up some mashed potatoes. "Like I was saying, he's slow. We got killed by those guys at Carroll High. Coach was pissed."

I'm tense, pushing food around my plate now. I remember Trevor, and I remember the team from Carroll, so it's not tough to envision how that would go. My brain is snapping into autopilot, wanting to hear more details so we can pick apart the game.

Connor speaks into the silence. "We all had to run laps after the game. I heard him tell Trevor he wasn't going to be able to play attacker in the spring if he can't—"

"Why didn't you call me?" I say. My fork is clutched in my hand so tightly that it's all but vibrating against the plate.

Across the table, Connor goes still. His mismatched eyes are fixed on mine. He swallows, his throat working like it hurts.

He knows what I'm asking.

He clears his throat. Looks away. "Rob—"

"Forget it. Leave."

He doesn't move, so I stand up. "Fine. If you won't leave, I will."

I'm in the dining room doorway when he says, "My dad wouldn't let me call."

I go still. It doesn't undo anything, but this is a scenario I've never considered.

Connor continues, "I got your message and I didn't . . . you were . . . I don't know. It was awful. I've never—I've never heard you like that. I panicked." His voice breaks, but he catches it. "I asked Dad what to do. I thought he'd drive us over. I thought—I don't know what I thought. He wouldn't let me call you."

I turn back and look at him. "Why?"

"I don't—I don't know." His face has paled a shade.

"Bullshit."

"What do you want me to say?" he demands. "He wouldn't let me call you. He wouldn't let me come over here. And then when they all said you were in on it—"

"Go to hell, Connor." I turn around and walk out of the dining room. This is somehow worse.

He comes after me. "Rob. Stop. I'm trying to talk to you."

I don't stop.

"Please," he says, and for the first time, desperation enters his tone.

My brain flashes on that moment in the woods, when his arm was broken and his ankle was sprained and I had to drag him out. I don't want this image, not right now, but my thoughts don't care what I want. I stop on the stairs.

"He was the one to turn your dad in," says Connor, his voice coming in a rush like he expects me to cut him off again. "I thought—I thought he knew you were in on it. I thought it was all true. I thought you'd been lying to me the whole time. You and your dad were so—you were so close—"

"Stop. Connor. Stop." My throat tightens. I don't want to think about my father or how close we were. I don't want to think about Bill's turning my best friend against me on the worst night of my life.

He stops.

I draw a long breath. "It doesn't matter."

"Rob—"

"I wasn't helping him." I look at him. "I wasn't. You could have just asked me."

"I know." He swallows. "I'm sorry. I didn't—I didn't know everything was like this."

"So what?" I make a disgusted noise. "God, do you know what you sound like? *Dad wouldn't let me call you.* You're not ten."

That pops his pity balloon. He sets his jaw and glares at me.

I set mine and glare back.

"What's going on?" says Mom. I didn't even see her appear at the bottom of the staircase.

"Connor was just leaving," I say.

"No," he says. "I'm not."

Okay, whatever. I don't care. I turn and head for my room. I try to close the door in his face, but he catches it and wrestles for control.

He never used to be stronger than me, but he is now. He muscles his way inside.

I expect him to throw a punch, but he doesn't. He closes the door and sits down in front of it. "I'm not leaving until you talk to me."

"Fine. Sit there." I go into my bathroom and brush my teeth even though it's only seven o'clock. Then I lose my jeans, climb into bed, and click the light off.

Connor doesn't move.

I'm barely tired, but I stare at the ceiling, listening to his breathing.

I have an endless supply of patience. I can outlast him for sure.

At midnight, he's still sitting there. Well, he might be lying in front of the door. I'm not entirely sure, but I heard him change position.

By two a.m., I'm still awake. I don't know how to fix anything with Maegan. I have no idea whether I'm doing the right thing with Owen. I hate Connor—but I miss him, too.

His father is awful. It's never been a secret—at least not to me. He drives Connor into the ground, and nothing Connor does is ever good enough. I imagine Connor getting my panicked, hysterical call and going to his father, asking for help.

It's easy to imagine, because I know how I would react.

My father would have thrown me into the car and started calling, trying to find out what was going on.

My father would have gotten Connor out of the house and into our car. He would have played interference with the cops and rescue workers. He wouldn't have left Connor's side.

Maybe that's why I never considered this scenario. I always thought about what I would have done. What my father would have done.

I never considered that even though our lives once looked very similar from the outside, they were nothing alike on the inside.

I look over. Connor is still awake, though he's lying on the hardwood floor, his eyes on the ceiling.

I pull one of the extra pillows off my bed and fling it at him. "Fine. Tell me what happened in the game against Carroll."

CHAPTER THIRTY-TWO

Maegan

Tuesday morning brings overcast skies and a bitter cold front. The air smells like snow when I step outside, and the wind bites at my cheeks. The only people I seem to be getting along with now are my parents, and I think that's only because they're so mentally tied up in what's going on with Samantha.

She still hasn't told them who the father is.

She still hasn't seen a doctor or made a decision about what she wants to do.

She still hasn't said a word to me.

I can add her to the list of people who are irritated with me, right along with Rob, Rachel, Drew, and Owen.

It's a miracle I'm going to school at all, honestly.

Mom has a business meeting out of town today, so one of her coworkers picked her up. It's a rare day I get the car to myself for school. I click the remote to unlock the doors, when I hear Samantha's voice behind me.

"Hey." She gives a little cough. "Megs."

I stop and turn. Her hair is piled in a knot on top of her head, and she's wearing a baggy sweatshirt and jeans. Zero makeup. "I'm sorry," I say. "Do I know you?"

I'm aiming for only mildly passive aggressive, not bitchy, but Sam scowls and glances away.

Okay, whatever. I open the car door. "I'll see you later."

"Wait."

I sigh. "What?"

"I was wondering if you would go with me somewhere."

I slide my phone out and glance at the time. "I need to be at school in fifteen minutes. Where do you need to go?"

She opens her mouth, then hesitates and wraps her arms around herself. "It's fine. Never mind."

"No, Sam, it's fine. What, do you need something from the drugstore?"

She looks up and meets my eyes. "No. I want . . ." Her voice falters, but she steels her nerve and narrows her eyes. "He won't return my calls. He's blocked me everywhere. I want to confront him."

"David?" I whisper.

"Yeah. David."

I try to work this out in my head. She goes to school over two hours away. "Does he live around here?"

"No." She looks at me like I'm being an idiot. "Megs, forget it. It was stupid."

I jingle the keys in my hand. It's not stupid. I can tell. I want to offer to let her take the car if she can drop me off at school, and those words almost spill out of my mouth. But then I consider what she just said.

"I'd have to cut school," I say carefully. "I think they send out an e-mail if you don't show up."

Her eyes widen in surprise. "You want to cut school?"

"Well. I don't *want* to." I swallow. I'd get in a ton of trouble if Mom and Dad found out. We'd be right back where we were last spring. "But what are you going to do? Confront him in his classroom?"

"Yes."

I was kidding. "Whoa."

She flinches. "You think it's stupid? I mean, he's blocked me everywhere. His wife hung up on me. It's the only place I *know* he'll be."

"But your scholarship—"

"I don't care. I can't keep hiding. I can't keep *doing* this. I can't do this alone. It's not fair."

I'm not sure what to say.

Samantha's shoulders slump a little. "You think it's a terrible idea."

I don't know if it's a horrible idea—or a great one.

Somehow this conversation feels similar to the one Owen and I had over the lunch table yesterday. Owen was right. Nothing is black and white. Nothing is simple and straightforward and easy.

I do know it's not right that Samantha is miserable and alone and this guy somehow gets to decide to cut her out of his life like it's nothing, when she has no choice but to deal with the fallout.

"If you want to go, I'll go with you." I clear my throat. "I don't know how to get around the e-mail thing."

"Oh, that's easy," says Sam. "I'll call and pretend to be Mom."

"You think they'll believe you?"

She smiles, and it's somehow both hesitant and exultant. "I know they will. I used to do it all the time."

Our drive is full of loud music and road trip snacks and many—*many*—bathroom breaks for Samantha. I worried that she would be morose and silent, but if anything, she's over the top, singing bawdy songs and flicking popcorn at me. I know now from the events at Connor Tunstall's house that this is Sam's way of disguising stress: being the ultimate party girl.

With a start, I wonder if this was how she dealt with stress in high school, too. She always made the athletic pressure seem like something that would roll right off her back, like excelling in lacrosse was a gift she was born with and not a skill that was honed to a razor's edge with every hour spent on the field. To everyone else, Samantha looked vivacious and carefree, but was she really drowning inside the whole time?

I wish I'd known before. Maybe I wouldn't have felt the need to measure up without feeling any stress myself. Maybe I wouldn't have tried to cheat.

We're thirty minutes away and giggling about a prank call they played on the radio, when Sam falls silent. It's such an abrupt shift that I reach out to lower the volume.

"What's wrong?"

She bites at the edge of her thumbnail, and her voice is very quiet. "What am I doing, Megs?"

"You're going to confront David." I hope my voice sounds strong and full of conviction.

She doesn't respond.

"Do you want me to turn around?" I say.

"No."

"Do you still want to do this?"

"Yes. Maybe. Probably." She jerks her thumb out of her mouth. "Damn it. Yes."

I hesitate.

Samantha looks over. "I mean, what's the worst that can happen? He calls campus security and throws me out of his classroom?"

"Is that a possibility?" My voice is strangled.

"No. Maybe."

"Aren't you worried about school canceling your scholarship?"

"I don't know if I can go back there, Megs. Either way." She looks over, and her face starts to crumple. "You know? Knowing all this happened? Like—" Her breath hitches. "Like, how am I supposed to go to class every day, knowing he's *right there*, on campus? The baby's daddy? Or the no-more-baby's daddy? How am I supposed to do that?" She's crying full out now. "How, Megs?"

I reach out and take her hand, and she grips mine tightly. "I don't know."

As abruptly as her tears started, they stop. She sniffs hard and wipes at her face. "Enough of this. I want to do it. I want to get it done."

I glance at the navigation app on my phone. We're less than ten minutes away. "Do you know where he'll be right now?"

Her eyes are clear now, full of fury. "Absolutely."

I'm slightly familiar with the campus from driving Samantha down here to move in, but back in August, the large brick buildings were charming, trees dripping with leaves as the summer sun beamed down. Today, a bitter chill clings to everything. The barren trees and overcast sky leave the campus looking sinister instead of welcoming.

Or maybe that's the current of dread running through Mom's car.

"We don't have to do this," I offer as I pull into a parking place in front of Guilder Hall, the building Samantha indicated.

"Oh, no. I'm doing it." She's out of the car before I even have the vehicle in park.

I hustle to keep up with her. She's the old Samantha again, bold and fearless, storming into the building the way she used to storm across a lacrosse field. The hallways are hushed, doors closed, as teachers speak to smaller groups of students. We pass all those, walking until we come to a set of wooden double doors.

Sam grabs the handle without hesitation and breezes through. I can barely keep up with her.

"Wait," I hiss. Surely she must need a plan of some sort.

She doesn't wait. She doesn't stop. The doors slam shut behind us, and we round a turn—only to find ourselves looking up at a hundred students or more.

Whoa. Of course it would be a packed lecture hall and not a group of half a dozen freshmen talking about Chaucer.

I'm staring at the students, so it takes me a moment to realize Sam is staring at the professor. This must be DavidLitMan.

He looks older than he did in the Instagram photograph. His hair is slightly thinning in front, and his jaw is a bit too pudgy. He wears a button-down oxford shirt with khakis. Nothing amazing about him at all.

"I've been trying to call you," Sam grinds out. She's practically breathing fire.

I almost miss the slight paling of his cheeks, but he recovers quickly and clears his throat. "Miss Day. We're in the middle of class. If you'd like to talk about your missed work—"

"I don't want to talk about *missed work*."

"Well, then, you're welcome to make an appointment—"

"Are. You. Insane?"

A titter of laughter runs through the class. David—can I call him David?—glares at them and they fall silent.

Sam takes a step closer to him. Her hands have formed fists at her sides.

I wonder if she'll hit him. I wonder if I should stop her.

Probably best that she not commit assault in front of a hundred witnesses.

"I want to talk to you," she says, her voice quiet and vicious.

"I'm asking you to leave," he says.

"I'm not leaving."

"You're putting your grade in danger, Miss Day. I've told you before that I will not tolerate disrespect—"

"You think I care about my *grade*?"

"I'm asking you to leave. Now."

"I'm not leaving until you talk to me. You can block my calls. You can have—you can have your—your wife—" Her voice hitches. Oh no. She's going to lose it.

I stop next to her and wrap her hand up in mine.

I don't know if it's her emotion, or the rapt attention of the students behind us, but DavidLitMan seems to lose his cool. His cheeks have reddened, and he glares at us. "Go!" he snaps. "I'm not having this conversation in class."

"I'm not leaving until you talk to me," Samantha says. A tear snakes its way down her face.

He moves a step closer to us, turning his back to the class. "I could lose my job here," he hisses. "Just—just go to my office. We'll work it out, okay?"

Samantha draws a big indignant breath—but then David adds, "I still love you. I want to work it out. I just—I can't do it here."

That breath slides out of her lungs.

No, I think. *No.*

But Samantha is nodding. "Okay," she whispers. "Okay."

She takes a step back. Turns for the door.

My strong, amazing sister. It's all a front. Inside, she's as insecure and desperate as I am. As we all are, really.

I grab her arm and hold her there. "No," I say. "No."

"I'm sorry," says David. "I have a class to teach."

"No," I say again.

Samantha sniffs and looks at me. "Megs. What—"

"You don't love her," I snap, and I make sure I'm loud enough that the back row is getting a good earful. "If you loved her, you wouldn't have blocked all her calls. You wouldn't have refused to talk to her or meet with her or discuss what you did together."

His face has turned beet red. "Young lady, you are way out of line."

"No, *you* are out of line," I say. "You don't love her. You don't have any business telling her you love her." I'm so angry, I'm yelling now. "You had sex with a student. You're disgusting. And now she's pregnant, with *your* baby, and you think you can make it all go away by whispering that you still *love* her?"

He takes a fury-filled step toward me, and he looks so menacing now that I'm worried *he's* going to hit *me*.

Samantha shoves me to the side. "Don't you dare touch my sister."

"I wasn't—" He rakes a hand through his hair. Sweat has beaded up on his forehead. You could hear a pin drop in this classroom. "I didn't do anything. I don't know what you girls think you're pulling—"

"I'm pregnant," Samantha yells at him. "I'm not pulling anything. I'm *pregnant*. With *your* baby. And you need to deal with it, because I can't do this by myself."

Then she bursts into tears. I pull her against me. She sobs against my shoulder.

David stands there, and his expression is some mixture of anger and defeat and regret and fear. A lot of fear.

But no compassion. No sympathy.

"Come on," I murmur to Sam. "Let's go." I glare at David. "I'm telling my father who you are. He's a cop. So worry about more than your job."

It's not really a threat—we live out of state and whatever he did with Samantha was consensual. But David goes pale again anyway.

We're halfway down the hallway when running steps come slapping down the tile behind us. I turn, expecting David to be barreling down on us, but it's a pretty girl with waist-length dark hair. She's slender and athletic like my sister.

"Oh," says Sam. She swipes at her face. "Hey, Vic." A loud sniff. "Megs, this is Victoria. She plays midfielder."

Victoria has no time for niceties. "Is that true?" she says, her voice hushed. "Is that where you've been?"

Sam nods hard, then buries her face in my shoulder again.

"Tell Coach that I'll call her tonight," Sam says, and somehow Victoria makes that out from the muffled sobs on my shoulder, because she nods.

"It'll be okay," she says. She puts a hand on Sam's shoulder. "It'll be okay." She glances at me. "I'm glad Sam has a sister to lean on."

I hug Sam tighter. "Me too."

CHAPTER THIRTY-THREE

Rob

"You look like *crap*," says Owen.

"Tell me how you really feel." We're sitting at our usual lunch table. Connor is sitting at his. I don't feel like anything was resolved last night . . . but I don't feel like the tension between us is the same as it was yesterday. By the time my alarm went off, he was gone.

Maegan isn't in school today. I keep looking at our text messages and want to send her one, but I don't have the courage to do it.

Owen studies me. "I'm telling you how I really feel. You look like crap."

I rub at my eyes and give him half my sandwich. "I didn't get a lot of sleep last night."

"Why not?"

"I just . . . it's a long story. Can we just eat?"

"Sure."

So, we do. It's quiet. Amiable.

Despite that, my shoulders are gripped with uncomfortable tension.

The tension doubles when Owen speaks low and says, "Have you sold the earrings yet?"

I flinch. "No."

"Are you worried about your mom finding them?"

A little, but I shake my head.

"I thought you were going to check out a pawn shop in the city."

That's right. I did tell him that. I swallow. "I don't know."

"You do know." He sounds irritated.

I snap my eyes up to meet his. "Look, you're not the one on the hook for this, okay? If you need the money so bad, do it yourself."

He jerks back in surprise. Hurt flares in his eyes, followed by anger. He shoves the remaining portion of his sandwich back at me. "Look, this all wasn't my idea. I didn't tell you to steal—" He catches himself and casts a look around, then drops his voice. "I didn't tell you to do any of this. So don't act like I'm some kind of kingpin forcing you into a life of crime."

"You read too much."

"Shut up." He still looks angry.

"I'm sorry," I say. "I told you I was tired. I wasn't thinking about what I was saying." I shove the sandwich back at him.

He takes it, and we sit there in quiet silence. He's wrong, anyway: I don't know why I haven't sold them. He compared me to Robin Hood, but that doesn't quite feel right.

As soon as the thought strikes me, I realize what my problem is.

Connor's mom didn't steal from the poor to buy those earrings. Neither did Lexi Miter or her parents when she was reckless with her credit card. That money in the bake sale cash box wasn't taken from anyone.

My dad is the one who stole.

And now, so am I.

I feel hot. Angry. Guilty and uncertain. My stomach feels like it's plummeted through my body and is now in free fall.

"Are you gonna be sick?" says Owen.

"I can't do this," I whisper.

"You can't do what?"

"It's stealing," I say. I clear my throat. "I'm stealing." I look at him across the table. "I'm not a thief."

I expect Owen to offer a sage nod and say something like, "Do what you need to do, Rob," but he doesn't. He takes on a cynical expression. "Stealing. Sure. Like it even matters. They don't even know they're *gone*, Rob. You know I don't want the money, but we could do a lot better with it."

That doesn't feel right. I still can't put my finger on *why* though. I mean, he's not wrong. On all counts. I could probably pay Owen's lunch bill for a year with those earrings. And then some.

I don't want my food. I can't eat.

Owen lifts his sandwich. His voice is low, very low, when he speaks. "Prick alert," he says, "Twelve—"

"Stop." I meet his eyes.

I can't read his expression. I'm not one hundred percent sure what's on my own face. We're frozen for a heartbeat, during which Connor stops beside the table.

"Hey," says Connor. His tone is conciliatory, his body angled slightly so that it's obvious he's talking to me.

I break off the staring match with Owen and look up. "Hey."

"You don't have to keep sitting over here," he says. "I mean, we're good." He shrugs and half glances back at his usual table. Our old table. "We're all good."

My familiar defenses click into place, and I almost want to mock him, but I don't. I've been lonely too long. As much as I don't want to admit it, I've missed my friends. My old life.

Owen is sitting across the table, watching me. Waiting for me to say something.

When I don't, he sighs, shoves his food into his bag, and gets up from the table. "It was nice knowing you, Rob."

I swallow.

Connor says, not quietly, "What a frigging drama queen. I can't believe you—"

"Stop." My tone is the same as it was when I told Owen the same thing. "Leave him alone, Connor."

"Look, I'm just saying. I'm trying to tell you that you don't need to sit here like a loser—"

"I'm not a loser. Neither is Owen." I glare up at him. "I know you're trying to make up for lost time, or whatever, but I can't undo the last eight months, okay?"

He flinches, and for a moment, I see a flash of the vulnerability I saw last night, when I finally took pity on him. In a way, he's been as adrift as I was. I never realized.

Connor really *does* think he can undo the last eight months by inviting me back to his table.

I wish he could.

I wish he could undo the last eight *days*.

"Look," I say more quietly. "I can't jump right back into the old crowd. It's too much. Do you get it?"

"Yeah. Sure. I get it." He's almost dismissive, and I expect him to turn away and leave me here.

Instead, Connor swings a leg over the bench and drops down across from me.

"What are you doing?" I say.

"You said the old crowd is too much. So I'm sitting down." He hesitates. "Is that okay?"

I don't know. "Sure."

He doesn't have any food with him, and I've already put mine away. Every vertebra in my back is tight, waiting for some kind of interrogation, but none comes. Like last night, he sits, and he waits.

He's just sitting. No demands, no expectation. Just sitting.

Connor is clueless about some things, but not about *everything*. And I was once the same way. He's trying. I should be trying, too.

I stole your mom's earrings, I want to say.

There's no way that will make anything better.

After we've been quiet for a while, Connor says, "I was kind of a shit to your friend."

Owen's parting words keep ricocheting around my skull. *It was nice knowing you, Rob.*

I wish he had a phone. I wish I could text him. I wish I could fix it. I wish I could sell the earrings and give him the money and make everything better.

This is all so hard.

I look at Connor. "You think?"

"He's the one who keeps saying 'prick alert' every time I walk over here."

"Maybe he's on to something." I'm half-teasing, half-serious. There's a note in my voice that hasn't been there in a while, a note that says, *I'm giving you crap because you can take it.*

"*Is* he your friend?" says Connor. "I thought you were sitting over here to prove some kind of point."

"What kind of point?" I scoff. "You really are a pr—"

"Okay, okay." Connor rolls his eyes. "Fine. I'll find him and apologize."

I doubt that would be welcomed by Owen, but it's not necessary anyway. I'm the one who needs to find him and apologize. "Leave it," I say. "I'll find him." I jerk my backpack from under the table. "I'm going to class." I hesitate. "Thanks for explaining. Last night."

"I should have done it sooner."

I shrug. "You did it now."

"Are we okay?" he says. "Really?"

I can't say yes. Not yet. Not with his mother's stolen earrings in my pocket and Owen pissed at me for hesitating about selling them. "Almost."

Connor gives me a nod, and I shoulder my bag to walk away from the table.

I need to fix this. I can't fix both at once, but I do know I don't want to be a thief. I wish I could break into Connor's house the way he broke into mine.

Wait. He didn't break in. What did he say? *I still have a key, you asshole.*

We were best friends for years. We practically lived at each other's houses. Of course he still had a key.

I pull my key ring out of my backpack and look at it.

So do I.

CHAPTER THIRTY-FOUR

Maegan

Samantha is telling Mom and Dad everything. I asked her if she wanted me to sit with her while she did it, but she said no, that she could do it on her own. So I've been sitting in my bedroom, staring at the darkening sky outside my window.

At first, I thought this was a good idea, but as the evening drags on, I begin to wonder about my role in everything. Cutting class. Knowing the truth about David. Keeping Samantha's secret—because I'm sure it was so much bigger than Mom and Dad ever expected.

I begin to wonder about Rob, and the secrets *he's* keeping, and what he's doing.

By the time a gentle tap hits my door, my nerves are primed, and I sit bolt upright in bed.

"Come in!" I call.

Samantha pokes her head in, and then her whole body. Her cheeks are blotchy and red, and she looks . . . drained.

"Are you okay?" I ask softly.

She comes in and closes the door behind her. "Yeah. Dad's

calling the school now, even though there's not going to be anyone there." Her eyes glance at the pitch-black sky outside my window. "He and Mom are pretty furious."

"They should be." I pause, wanting to ask if she's made any decisions now that it's all out in the open, but not wanting to push. "It's not your fault, Sam."

"Well." She gives a little laugh, but there's no humor in it. "Some of it is my fault."

"He was horrible."

"Yeah." A tear rolls down her face. "I don't know how I missed that."

"Dad said . . . he said that when people are under a lot of pressure, they don't always make the right decisions."

She swipes at her cheek. "Yeah. Well."

"I think that applies to more than just this situation, Sam." I hesitate. "I don't think I ever realized that. About you."

"I don't think I ever realized that about myself." Another tear. "Isn't that stupid? I'm so stupid."

"You're not stupid."

"I am. And now I'm going to have to deal with it."

Deal with it. I sit up straighter. "Does . . . does that mean you're getting an abortion?"

She bursts into tears. Her arms fold across her abdomen.

I shift forward and wrap my arms around her. "Sam. Sam. It'll be okay. I'll go with you. Whatever you need."

She shudders against me. "No. I'm not doing it."

"What?"

"I'm not doing it. I might—I might look at an open adoption.

Maybe. But I don't want to get rid of it." She sucks up her tears and looks at me clearly. "I went to the clinic on Friday."

"You—you went by yourself?" So very Samantha.

"Yeah. I went, and I thought about it, and the nurse was just—she was so kind. I thought I'd walk through the door and it would be fast and horrible and it would be done, but—it wasn't. I thought I would have to terminate the pregnancy or my life would be ruined. She was the first person to really walk me through everything. I don't think I realized how much I needed that. You know? Someone to show me all the options."

"Yeah. I know." I hug her again, then draw back to peer at her. "And you're okay? With everything?"

"Well, I'm probably going to lose my scholarship." She sniffs. "Mom and Dad are pretty upset about that. But it's not the end of the world. I wasn't—I wasn't very happy. I loved lacrosse, but it became something I *had* to do instead of something I *wanted* to do." She looks at me. "What you did today . . . that meant a lot."

"I didn't do anything, Sam."

"No, you did. You did the right thing, when I was about to let him get away with it." She leans forward and gives me another hug. "You're always so good at that."

I give a strangled laugh, surprised. "I don't think Mom and Dad would agree."

"What?" She's surprised.

I give her a half smile. "I'm the big cheater, remember?"

She opens her mouth, then closes it. "Megs, you made a mistake. You're allowed to make a mistake."

I chew at my lip and don't say anything.

Sam rubs at her stomach. "Something else the nurse told me really sat with me."

"What's that?"

"One choice doesn't determine your whole future." She pauses. "She was talking about abortion. But I think it applies to you, too."

She's right. I offer her a watery smile. "Thanks, Sam."

As I say it, I realize, it doesn't just apply to her and me.

One choice doesn't determine your whole future.

It applies to Rob, too.

CHAPTER THIRTY-FIVE

Rob

I'm more nervous about returning these earrings than I was about committing the actual crime.

Midnight darkness cloaks the grounds surrounding the Tunstall house, though the place is lit up as brightly as it was on the night of the party. I've been sitting in my car down the street for the longest time, watching the interior lights flick on and off as Connor and his parents go about their evening. It's been months, but I still remember their family routine as easily as I remember my own.

Dinner in the dining room around six.

Then brightness in the kitchen as Mrs. Tunstall cleaned everything up. Lights in the family room as they watched television. Those went off around ten, and lights upstairs went on.

Now it's midnight, and the house is mostly dark.

I can do this. I'll go in, slip into the pool house, and leave the earrings right where I found them.

While I've been sitting here, I've toyed with the idea of doing this differently. Things between Connor and me are . . . not as bad. I could probably engineer an invite to hang out later this week. It would be easy enough to slip the earrings back into place.

Or I could keep them. I think of Owen storming away from the lunch table. Somehow this has driven a splinter into our friendship, and I'm not sure how or why.

All of my relationships are splintered, though, so what's the difference?

But every time I think about shifting my car into drive, my muscles refuse to function.

I'm not like my father. I'm not a thief. I can't hold on to these earrings for one more minute.

I have a key anyway. I'm not breaking and entering. I'm going to slip in, put the earrings away, and leave.

It's time.

The lock gives with barely a sound, and the front door eases open. I tap the alarm code into the silent panel by the door and move away. The night has grown colder than I realized, and it's almost a relief to slip into the warm darkness of the house. I'm greeted by absolute silence. The door slides back into place, and I stop and wait, listening.

My heart pounds against my rib cage, but that's it. Nothing. Absolute silence.

I slip down the hallway where I kissed Maegan, stepping carefully so my sneakers don't make a sound on the hardwood. My fingers are trembling when I find the next keypad, the dimly lit numbers barely visible in the darkness.

I tap in the code and press the pound key to make the lock release.

It doesn't. A little light flashes red and the lock goes *beep beep*.

I freeze. This one isn't silent, and I must have mis-keyed the code. I freeze with my hand on the knob, waiting to see if anyone could have heard that.

Nothing happens. I try again.

Again, the lock doesn't release. Red flash. *Beep beep.*

He changed the code. My blood freezes in my veins. This is because of me. He changed the code because of me.

My breathing has accelerated. I need to talk myself off this ledge.

It's okay. It's okay. It doesn't matter. I don't *have* to leave these earrings by the hot tub. I can leave them anywhere. In the family room, down in the cushions. In the kitchen on the windowsill. In the powder room next to the soap dish. Anywhere.

A memory comes to me. Connor and I were fifteen. We were sacked out on the sofa, talking lacrosse. His mom came home from some luncheon, telling Connor he needed to get his room ready for inspection that night. Connor hauled himself off the couch with a heavy sigh and asked me to help him—which I did, of course.

His mother took out her earrings and dropped them in a glass bowl on a table by the staircase. I remember it because she said, "Be glad you boys don't have to wear these wretched things. Nothing gives me a headache faster."

My eyes find the table by the staircase. The bowl is still there.

I want to run across the family room and fling them down, but I need to be quiet. Every step seems to take an hour. When I get to the bowl, I meticulously place the earrings against the glass so they don't rattle.

And then it's done. The earrings are no longer in my possession. I'm not a thief.

The weight that drops off my shoulders is almost tangible. I need to get out of here.

". . . is talking to Rob again," says a woman's voice.

I freeze. The voice is muffled, coming from above. Mrs. Tunstall.

"What's that about?"

Mr. Tunstall.

"He said they're making up," says Mrs. Tunstall. "That there was a misunderstanding." She pauses. "I'm glad. You know, I've said before that it was a shame for them to—"

"It wasn't a shame. That needed to end. I know you've tried to be there for Carolyn, but we need to distance ourselves from that family."

Carolyn. My mother, who lost more than anyone and deserves nothing but kindness. I bristle, frozen in place at the bottom of the stairs. "I *need* to be there," says Mrs. Tunstall. "We need to make sure she's not going to change her mind."

Change her mind. About what?

"She won't change her mind," says Bill. "Not if she knows what's good for her. She needs to ride out the lawsuits and then she can put it all behind her. We can't be seen associating with that family. It's not good for business."

He's such an asshole.

"It'll be fine," says Bill. "A few more months. You'll see. But I don't want you to encourage Connor to rekindle this friendship. We need a clean break."

A clean break from *what*?

"I do feel badly for young Rob," says Mrs. Tunstall. "He was such a good boy."

"Oh, please. He knew. He had to know. He's lucky he's walking around without an ankle bracelet. I knew it was a mistake when Robbie Senior was bringing him in to help out on the weekends. A kid could bring the whole thing down around us—and look what happened."

Wait. *Wait.*

"It's not his fault," says Mrs. Tunstall.

"I probably owe the guy a drink for pulling the trigger." A darkly amused chuckle.

My hands form fists.

A phone rings throughout the house, and I jump, bumping the table. It cracks against the wall and the bowl rattles.

"Hello?" says Bill from upstairs.

"Did you hear something?" says his wife.

"The alarm company is on the phone—a bad code was input after the front door opened."

The alarm company.

He changed the panel by the hallway. Of course he changed the front door code.

"I knew I heard something downstairs!" Panic in hers.

"Mom?" Connor's sleepy voice. "Is something going on?"

"They've sent a patrol car," says Mr. Tunstall, and now there's alarm in his voice.

A patrol car. Shit.

I tear across the living room and throw open the front door, making no effort to be quiet.

I'm instantaneously lit up with spotlights.

"Freeze!" yells a voice. "Put your hands on your head. *Put your hands on your head!*"

I put my hands on my head. Breath escapes my mouth in fast, panicked bursts. I don't know what to do. I hadn't planned for this.

Cops are screaming at me. *"Do you have any weapons? Lie down on the ground! Lie down on the ground NOW!"*

A knee lands in my back when I comply. Handcuffs slam onto my wrists, and they haul me upright. The front of the house flickers with emergency lights. Everything is spinning. I can't breathe.

My eyes find Connor, standing on the front porch with his parents. He's in boxers and a T-shirt. His father looks furious. His mother looks shocked.

Connor looks confused. "Rob? What—what are you doing?"

"He was in on it," I call to him, and my voice breaks. "Your dad. He was in on it."

Then I'm shoved into a police car, and the door is slammed.

CHAPTER THIRTY-SIX

Maegan

My father is waiting in the kitchen when I come downstairs before school. Full uniform and everything, which isn't unusual, though the dark scowl on his face is. Mom is sitting at the kitchen table in her robe, a damp towel wrapped around her head. Her expression is equally tense.

We don't usually have this much drama before six in the morning.

"What's wrong?" I realize who's missing, and I add, "Is it Samantha? What happened?"

"It's not Samantha," says my mother quietly.

My father's voice is not quiet. "Did you continue to see Rob Lachlan after I told you not to?"

The question hits me like a slap. I falter and blush and have to clear my throat. "It wasn't—not really. We're just friends."

"Did you go to a party with him?"

I'm frozen in place in the kitchen doorway, and I wish so badly that I could go back to my bedroom and start over.

"Answer me," he says.

"Yes," I whisper.

He gives a heavy sigh and exchanges a glance with my mother.

"Why?" I ask.

"What did he do at that party?"

"I don't—" I falter and have to start over. "I don't know what you mean."

My father's voice could cut steel. "I mean, what did he *do* at the *party*?"

"Jim," whispers my mother.

"It was a party." I'm all tripped up, wondering if this has to do with Samantha's drinking, though Rob had nothing to do with that, so I can't make any connections there. "Just a party. Why?"

"Bill Tunstall says you and Rob snuck into a private area of his home."

I suddenly feel light-headed. I put a hand against the door frame. "We didn't—we didn't sneak. Rob knew the code. He and Connor used to be friends, so he knew—"

"*Used to be* friends." My father's hand is tight on the edge of the table. "They *used to be* friends. So, you know they are not friends now. You know Rob would not be welcome to use a code to access a locked door."

I inhale to answer, and my dad makes a slashing motion with his hand. "Don't answer that. I know you know."

"Yes," I say softly. I feel like I'm going to vibrate apart. "I know."

"Damn, Maegan."

"Are we in trouble?"

"That depends." His eyes narrow, as if his gaze could slice me apart. Cop eyes, Samantha calls them. "What did you do after you went behind those locked doors?"

Okay, *now* I'm going to pass out. "Nothing," I mumble.

He leans forward. "You're either going to talk to me or you're going to tell an officer down at the station. Your choice."

This is humiliating. Tears form in my eyes. "Nothing! We just—we kissed! Okay? We kissed."

"Bill Tunstall says he found you without your shirt on."

"Oh, Maegan." Mom puts a hand to her eyes.

I have never wished to be Samantha so hard in my life. She'd roll her eyes and say something like, "He's lucky he didn't see me without my pants on." But I'm not, and I can't.

"It was kissing," I say. "Just kissing. I swear."

"What else did you do?"

"Nothing! He walked in on us, and Rob told me to leave, so I did."

"And that's all?"

"Yes!"

"So, you don't know that Rob Lachlan stole a pair of diamond earrings?"

I thought I had blood left in my face. I was wrong. *Now* I'm going to pass out.

Mom gets up and pulls a chair away from the table. "Sit down," she says. "Jim. This is too much."

"It's not too much!" he says fiercely. His eyes haven't left mine. "You knew," he says. "You knew what he did."

I can't even lie. My face has already given it all away.

"Did you help him?" my father demands. "Did he plan it?"

"I didn't!" My father's face is full of disbelief, so I shake my head fiercely. "I didn't! I swear! I didn't find out until later!"

"Maegan—"

"I'm telling the truth! I didn't find out until Sunday night!"

Those cop eyes are back. "Three days ago. You've known for three days." He pounds a fist against the table. "I told you to stay away from that boy, and not only did you disobey me, you've been covering for him."

"Did he turn himself in?" I whisper.

"No! He was caught! He says he was returning the earrings, but at this point who knows the truth?"

He was returning the earrings. "He was!" I exclaim. "I know he was. I know—"

"Enough." Dad sighs. He smooths his hand over the spot on the table that he just struck. "I expected more from you, Maegan. Again, you're letting us down."

Again.

I swallow. Tears sit heavy behind my eyes, and I take a breath. "I made a mistake, okay?"

"This is more than a mistake, Maegan. This is—"

"Just like last spring. I know." I burst out of my chair and head for the stairs.

"Get back here!" my father thunders.

He's never yelled at me like that. Not even last spring. Tears are in a free fall on my face now. I sprint up the stairs.

I'm about to go into my room, but Samantha is in her doorway.

"Megs," she whispers. She steps back and holds her arms wide.

I don't hesitate. I fly into her arms and hold on, as my sister closes the door behind me, locking our parents out.

CHAPTER THIRTY-SEVEN

Rob

When Dad tried to kill himself, I was questioned by the police, but it happened in my living room, and it was done with an air of sympathy.

Today, there's no sympathy. I'm in a jail cell, sitting on a metal bench, staring at a gray wall. I'm not alone, but the other guy is pushing fifty, and he looks less eager to talk than I am.

We've been in here for hours. The room smells like a combination of vomit and urine and bleach. I'm tired and cold and starving. They took my picture, asked me some questions, and locked me in here.

I wonder if they called Mom. I expected to be taken to some kind of juvenile detention center, but one of the cops laughed and said, "When you do big-boy crimes, you do big-boy time." I don't know exactly what that means, but I'm guessing it means I'm being treated as an adult.

None of this seems fair. I was putting the earrings *back*. I wasn't even going to admit the theft, but I stupidly thought somehow that would excuse me from breaking into their house.

I was wrong.

On top of it all, I can't shake what I overheard. They can lock me up forever, but it won't change the truth.

Connor's father is just as guilty as mine was.

I tried to tell the cops what I overheard, but they exchanged glances and sighed and ignored me.

I'd ignore me, too. I have no proof. Nothing. A conversation I barely overheard bits and pieces of. It means nothing.

To them. It definitely means something to *me*.

The man across the cell shifts his weight and sighs. I understand the feeling. Fear and adrenaline and fury battled for space in my brain when they locked me in here, but they've long since settled into my bones. A sleeping lion, waiting to consume me.

There are no windows in here, and they took my phone. Nothing but a row of bars separating us from a narrow hallway, with a locked door at the end. I don't even know how much time has passed.

I wonder if that's deliberate. A torture method.

I wait.

I wait.

I wait.

The worst part is that I don't really know what I'm waiting for. If I'm an adult, will I be allowed to see my mother? I get an attorney at some point, right? Will I have to go to prison? How does bail work? Where would Mom get money for that?

I swipe suddenly sweaty palms across my thighs.

Eventually—an hour later? A minute?—a loud buzzing sound echoes through the cell, and the door at the end of the hallway opens. We both turn to look as an officer comes through.

He looks at me and makes a *come here* gesture with his hand. "You're out, kid. The family isn't pressing charges."

I almost choke on my breath. "I'm what? I'm out?"

"Yep. Let's go."

"Take me with you," says the middle-aged man. It's the first thing he's said to me since we were locked in together.

I don't say anything to him. I spring off the bench and make a beeline for the officer. Relief has bled through all the anxiety, and I practically want to give the guy a hug. I'm jittery with adrenaline again, but this time for an entirely different reason. I wonder if Mom is here to take me home.

The police officer leads me back through the doorway and into the main part of the police station. My eyes find a wall clock, which tells me that it's ten o'clock in the morning. I've been here almost twelve hours. I expect everyone's eyes to be on me, like they were after my father put a gun to his head, but they're not. Maybe breaking and entering isn't as exciting as white-collar crime.

The officer stops at the front desk and hands me an envelope that holds my cell phone and my keys and my wallet. My cell phone has gone dead. Fantastic.

"That's it?" I say.

"That's it," he says. "You're free to go."

I stand there dumbly. Do I ask them to call me a cab? I don't have any money. I can't exactly walk home from here.

A man in the waiting room stands and approaches the desk. I'm so wrapped up in my own drama that I don't pay him any attention until he stops in front of me and says, "I've talked to your mother. I told her I'd give you a ride home so she doesn't have to leave your dad."

Bill Tunstall. He looks smug and well rested.

Every muscle fiber in my body freezes in place.

The officer behind me chuckles and claps me on the shoulder. "You're a lucky kid. If I broke into a friend's house when I was a teenager, I think they all would have let me sweat it out a little longer."

Lucky. My tongue won't work.

I want to bypass theft and commit a murder right here. A flicker of thought makes me wonder if I can grab the cop's gun.

Bill's eyes are fixed on mine. There's no love lost there. This isn't a kind gesture.

He knows I know.

"Come on, Rob," he says casually. "We can talk it out on the way home."

I don't want to. My heart hammers away at my rib cage.

When I don't move, his eyes narrow a fraction. "Your mother is worried. I know she's waiting for us."

Nothing in his words are a threat, but somehow I hear one anyway. He can do whatever he wants to me, but my mother is the last innocent person in this whole thing. She doesn't deserve this.

I swallow. "Fine." It's impossible to keep fury out of my voice. "Thanks a bunch for the ride, Bill."

Bill drives a Tesla. The door handles pop out as we approach. I've been inside it, but before now I never realized how pretentious it makes him seem. The doors seal shut, locking me inside with him.

He can't really lock me in here, and I know that, but the cool silence of the interior makes this feel like a cage all the same.

I'd rather be back in the jail cell.

I don't trust myself to speak. I don't have enough details, but I know this man was in on it with my father. I know he should be paying, too.

He says nothing as we pull out of the police station parking lot. As the car accelerates, I'm tempted to grab the wheel and jerk the vehicle into a telephone pole.

Then again, this car cost over $100,000, and I'm sure it's loaded to the gills with safety features. Bill would probably walk away without a scratch. Hell, it would probably brake automatically.

"I'm waiting," he says eventually. He delivers these words like I'm a toddler and he's ordered me to issue an apology.

I turn my head and glare at him. I never liked him much, but right now, I hate every fiber of his being. "For what."

"For you to explain yourself."

"Why don't you go first?"

We've come to a traffic light, and he glances away from the road. "Watch the attitude."

"Fuck you."

His hand comes out of nowhere and backhands me square across the face.

He's driving, so it's not a forceful blow, but he's bigger than me and stronger than I expect. I feel it in my nose. My lips. Blood is in my mouth, along with a sharp pain between my eyes that draws tears against my will. My breathing hitches more from surprise than anything else.

He's pointing a finger at me. "I told you to watch the attitude."

I press fingers against my face. I can't help it. I feel like I ran face-first into a wall. My nose is bleeding.

"You can hit me all you want," I say. My voice is nasally. Great. "I know what you did. What you've done."

"You don't know anything."

"I know what I heard."

"Like that matters. You think anyone is going to believe you?" We're going fast now, but he looks over at me and snorts disgustedly. "Seriously. You think anyone is going to believe you?"

I wipe at my nose, then scrape my hand along the side of my seat. I hope I'm leaving streaks of blood and snot on the tan leather. "Maybe no one. But I'll figure out a way to make sure—"

"To make sure what? To make sure I'm caught?" He chuckles. "Rob, if the feds didn't find anything when they came after your dad, they're not going to find anything now."

"I don't care." I shake my head and spots flare across my vision. "I'll do whatever I have to do—"

"No. You won't." He glances over. "Unless you want your mother to go down, too."

Those words stop time. I turn my head to look at him, and it's as if I'm underwater. "What are you talking about?"

"You think she didn't know? You think she didn't help? How naive are you?"

This is worse than everyone thinking I knew. At least people leave my mother alone. "She doesn't! She doesn't know anything—"

"Come on."

"You leave my mother alone. Do you understand me? You leave her—"

He reaches out a hand, and I flinch.

He chuckles again, as if that's amusing. He's pointing at the glove box.

I hate him. I hate him so much.

"Look in there," he says. "Look."

I don't want to look.

"Look!" he snaps.

I open the glove box. A folded piece of paper sits there. It's a printed e-mail.

From: Marjorie Tunstall
To: Carolyn Lachlan
Connor said Robbie is working with his dad on weekends. Bill doesn't think that's a good idea.

From: Carolyn Lachlan
To: Marjorie Tunstall
Robbie is only handling clerical tasks. He won't know.

They don't say anything. It's not conclusive—at all.

But in a way, it is. That last line is searing my eyeballs.

He won't know.

I can't breathe. I feel like I'm burning to ash right here in the passenger seat.

"So, you see," says Bill. "If you bring me down, I'm bringing your mom down."

I force myself to swallow.

I can't speak. I don't know what to say. I barely register that we've turned down the road that leads to my house. I want to get out and sprint through the woods. I want to run until my lungs explode or I catch fire or I rot into nothingness. I'm choking on air. Dry heaving in the front seat of Bill's stupid, awful car.

"If you vomit in here, you're going to clean it up," he says.

"Let me out," I grind out.

He pulls to a stop right there. Unlocks the doors.

"Remember what I said," he says. "That's not the only proof I have."

"Connor knows," I say.

"Connor doesn't know anything. He knows how to respect his father. He won't believe you over me."

I didn't call because my father wouldn't let me.

He's right. Connor always obeys his father.

I think of the way Bill's hand smacked into my face and realize Connor has good reason to.

I open the door and put a foot on the ground. The wind whips at the paper, and I'm careful to keep a grip on it.

"And even if he does, Connor has seen what has happened to you," Bill says. "I don't think I could teach a lesson any better, do you?"

"Go away." I slam the door and glare at the darkened glass. "*Go away.*"

He goes.

I walk. I think. I seethe.

When I get home, my mother is waiting in the dining room. My father is beside her in his chair.

She looks like she's been up all night, but she flies across the room and wraps me up in her arms.

"Oh, Robbie," she says. "I've been so worried."

"Me too." I don't hug her back.

She hears the tone in my voice and draws back, studying my face.

I shove the paper in her direction. "Did you know what Dad was doing?"

She takes the paper from my hand, and her expression goes still. After a moment, she takes a deep breath and looks up. "Robbie. I'm sorry."

My heart stops. I'm sure of it. I can't move.

I don't think I realized how much I needed her to deny it until she didn't.

She must finally get a good look at me, because she touches a hand to my lip. "What—what happened?"

"Bill happened." I brush her hand away. I don't want her touch right now. I don't want any of it. Behind her, my father sits silently. I've hated him for a long time.

This is the first time I've hated her, too.

"What does that mean?" she whispers. She glances down at the paper in her hands again. Her face pales a shade. Her face crumples. "I can—I need to tell you—"

"Don't bother." I brush her aside and head for the stairs. When I reach my room, I slam the door.

The noise or the tension must affect my father. He starts making panicked sounds.

I don't want to care. I don't.

Mom yells, "Oh, *shut up!*"

The front door slams.

He doesn't stop.

A car starts in the driveway.

After a long moment, I take a breath. I open my door and go downstairs to take care of my father.

CHAPTER THIRTY-EIGHT

Maegan

Rob hasn't shown up for school. Obviously.

Samantha tried to convince me to skip classes and stay holed up in her room, but I don't have the strength to avoid my parents all day long. At least school offers a break from them, from Rob, from all of it. I've been keeping to myself, hiding in plain sight. My nerves have been a jangly mess, as if I'm waiting for some other shoe to drop. Will cops show up to arrest me, too? Am I an accomplice? All I did was . . . do nothing. Does that make me guilty?

Sometime midmorning, I get a text from my father.

DAD: All charges have been dropped. You're off the hook.

Relief should be the natural reaction, but it's not. I feel like I've cheated again or gotten a free pass.

MAEGAN: Thanks. Does that mean Rob is free?

He doesn't write back. Of course. Knowing my father, he's mad that I even asked.

The day drags, but I'm dreading the end of it, so I don't mind. When the final bell rings, I can barely convince myself to head to the parking lot. To my surprise, Owen Goettler is waiting by the side of the building, right at the edge of the lot. I doubt he has a car, and I've never seen him over here. When he spots me, he peels away from the wall and approaches.

I'm still stung from his comments yesterday, when he lectured me that Rob wasn't hurting anyone. Was he right? Is that why I didn't turn him in?

Is Owen going to yell at me some more?

But no, as he gets closer, I see that his expression is tense with worry. "Have you seen Rob?" he says.

I'm surprised by the question, and I'm sure my expression shows it. "No, you don't know?"

"Know what?"

Of course he wouldn't. Why would he?

"Rob was arrested," I say. "He was breaking into the Tunstall house."

Owen swears. "I told him not to do that."

"You *knew*?"

"Yeah, I knew. He wanted to return those stupid earrings that no one was missing."

I can't tell if he's upset that Rob was arrested or upset that he was returning the earrings or what.

Owen drops his voice. "Is Rob going to be okay?"

"Yeah. My dad said the Tunstalls dropped the charges."

"Why?"

I inhale to answer—but I have no idea. "Maybe they figured he's been through enough."

"Do they strike you as those kind of people?"

I remember what Rob said about Connor not answering when he really needed him. "No," I admit. "They don't." I look across at Owen. "Not that it matters."

He hesitates. I hesitate. We're both the unlikely friends of Rob Lachlan, but that doesn't make *us* friends. I feel like we're different planets orbiting the same sun.

The thought adds another weight to the pile of guilt sitting on my shoulders.

Owen raises his eyebrows. "Want to come over and talk about it?"

I take a long breath. Dad probably wouldn't like me going over to a strange boy's house any more than he'd like me hanging out with Rob.

"Don't worry about it," says Owen, misinterpreting my silence. He begins to turn away.

"No." I find my keys in my pocket. "Let's go."

Owen's mother is sleeping because she worked the night shift, so we have to tiptoe into the house. I don't know where I expected him to live, but I'm surprised that it's clean and bright inside, though the kitchen appliances look old and the carpeting is worn thin in places. Owen offers me a diet soda from his refrigerator.

"It's all we have," he says. "Unless you want water."

"This is great, thanks."

We take seats at the kitchen table and stare at each other.

One of us needs to speak, so I take a sip and smooth a hand across the table. "Did you really tell him not to return the earrings?"

"Yeah," he says. "I thought we could have done something better with the money." He pauses. "It doesn't seem fair that they have them and they don't care, and it doesn't seem fair that Rob got arrested for returning something they weren't missing anyway."

"Well." I clear my throat. "Technically he was arrested for breaking and entering."

"We had a good plan," Owen says, and even in a low whisper, I can hear his passion. "We weren't going to hurt anyone. We weren't really *stealing*. We were just taking what people weren't going to miss and giving it to people who needed it."

"Owen." A stern voice makes us both jump. "*What* did you just say?"

His mother stands in the kitchen doorway, in leggings and a T-shirt and a threadbare robe. Her face is clean-scrubbed and her hair is in a messy ponytail. "I'm waiting," she says when Owen doesn't say anything. Despite the pajamas, her stance is fierce. "What do you mean, you were taking what people weren't going to miss?"

"Mom, it's nothing—"

"Don't you dare tell me it's nothing." Her eyes flick to me. "And who is this? Another *friend*?"

I scrape out of my chair. "Mrs. Goettler," I say hurriedly. "I'm—I'm a friend of . . . um . . ."

"She's Rob's girlfriend," says Owen, his voice resigned. "Mom—"

"Don't you *Mom* me. I'm still waiting for you to explain what you're talking about. Were you and Rob *stealing*? Is that why you were hanging out with him? Did he force you to help—"

"No. It's not like that." Owen puts up his hands, as if she needs to be placated. "It's not a big deal."

She comes farther into the kitchen. "You'd better start talking. Right now."

I back away. "Maybe I should go."

"No." She points at the chair I just vacated. "Sit. I want an explanation."

I sit.

Owen talks.

While he's talking, I realize how little I knew about what Rob was doing. Through it all, I want to go back to the Rob Lachlan I first talked to about our math project. I want to shake him and say, *No, don't do this. Don't get tangled up in this. You can't make up for what your father did.*

Owen's mother listens as he spills it all out, and she's better at that than my father. When he gets to the part about Lexi Miter's credit card being used to buy shoes, her eyes grow wide and angry, which makes Owen duck his head, but he keeps talking.

At the end, her voice is deathly quiet. "And you think you were helping people?"

Owen straightens in his chair. "Well . . . yeah," he says earnestly.

She takes a long breath, then looks at me. "Do you think they were helping people?"

"I don't know," I admit. "I mean, he's right. No one was hurt. No one was missing those things."

"Owen. I don't even know what to say."

"You were so mad about the guy who stole from us!" Owen explodes. "All I ever hear about is how hard you've had to struggle. How Rob Lachlan was the only one who got caught, how they're all crooks." He's glaring at her. "I go to school with kids who have everything—and I don't complain. You know I don't complain. But it's not fair that they get it all, and we get . . . we get *this*." He gestures around the tiny kitchen.

She leans forward. "Owen," she says evenly. "Just because we don't have something doesn't mean we *take* it."

"But they don't even need it!"

"Says who?"

He opens his mouth. Closes it.

"You don't get to decide who deserves to have what," she says. "Or who doesn't, for that matter." She pauses, then pulls a pendant out from under her shirt. It's a heart twisted into the shape of a mother and a baby, with diamonds mounted onto the setting. "Your father gave this to me the Christmas before he died. Do you think I should sell it for money?"

Owen swallows. "Of course not."

"You don't really *need* that Xbox upstairs. Should we sell that for money?"

He flinches and doesn't answer that.

She puts her hand on Owen's forearm. "You said they wouldn't miss it. But how do you know? How do you know those earrings weren't special to that woman?" Her voice has softened. "What puts you in the position to determine the best use of what you were planning to steal?"

He looks down. "You don't understand."

"Of *course* I understand. Of course I do. Just like I know there are people out there judging me for this necklace or judging you for getting a free lunch. Other people don't have the challenges we have, Owen. *But that doesn't mean they don't have their own.*"

Owen is quiet, very still in his chair. I wonder if he's even breathing.

Finally, he looks up. "I'm still not sorry." He pulls his arm out from under her hand. "Maybe that makes me a bad person, but I'm still not sorry."

She stares at him. "Owen."

"I'm not," he says, backing away. "No one got hurt. It might not have been right, but it still doesn't feel wrong."

"Come back here," she says.

Owen doesn't. He heads up the stairs.

She turns her gaze on me. "Were you a part of this little crime ring, too?"

"No!" I want to flee, too, but the part of my brain that controls my good-girl tendencies keeps me pinned in this chair. "I didn't know until they'd done everything."

"And that Rob boy was arrested?"

I swallow. "The Tunstalls decided not to press charges."

She takes a long breath and lets it out. "I regret the day I trusted that man with one cent of my money."

And "that man's" son apparently wasn't much better. I bite my lip and look down. I do not like this feeling.

She puts a hand over mine, and I look up in surprise. "Owen can make his own decisions. I don't blame Rob for all of it." She pauses. "He seemed like a very lost boy."

"He is," I whisper.

"Are you a lost girl?"

As soon as she asks the question, I realize I was. I was a lost girl. Lost in everyone's impressions of me. Lost by letting their impressions replace the ones I have of myself. I force myself to hold her gaze. "I'm not lost. I want to do the right thing."

"Most of us do," she says ruefully. "The problem is that it doesn't always look the same for all of us."

CHAPTER THIRTY-NINE

Rob

It's well after dark, and Mom still hasn't come home. I don't know where she's been all day, and I really don't care. Maybe she's over at the Tunstalls' house, and they've all been laughing it up about how clueless I am.

The nurse never came today. Maybe Mom canceled her because she was home, or maybe the woman didn't show up. Either way, there's a part of me that was glad to be left alone, even if it required taking care of Dad. I can't get him upstairs by myself, but spending one night in his chair won't kill him. We had dinner, and now we're bingeing *Doctor Who* on Netflix.

As the hours wear on, though, resentment builds in my chest. It's not the first time Mom has walked out on me and Dad. Always before, I've had some sympathy.

Tonight, I do not.

Her key slides into the lock just before ten. Dad has fallen asleep in his chair. I pause the television and wait.

She sneaks into the house as if she expects us all to be asleep, then jumps when she meets my eyes from the hallway.

"You're still here," she says.

"Where else do I have to go?"

She winces, then looks past me, to Dad. "Do you want some help getting him upstairs?"

Like I'm in charge. "He's already asleep."

"Oh." She hasn't moved from the doorway.

She says nothing.

I say nothing.

Finally, I turn back to the television and press play.

My shoulders are tense, wondering what she's going to do. As the minutes tick by, I think she's slipped out of the room and gone to bed.

The resentment grows, threatening to crowd my organs out of my rib cage until there's nothing left but anger.

Then she steps into my field of vision and presses the button to turn off the television.

"I need to talk to you," she says quietly.

I'm frozen in place, my eyes locked on the black mirror of the screen. I don't want to hear this, but I do.

She eases onto the couch beside me, her face a shadow in the darkness of the room.

"Yes, I knew," she says.

No kidding. I do not thaw.

"Bill Tunstall had a plan," she continues. "It started—it started very small. And I truly think, at the time, he believed he was doing something good for his clients. He was taking on risky invest-ments in his own name and allowing them to buy in to share the profits."

I hold very still.

She glances at Dad. "Bill invited Dad to do the same thing. With our money. For a while, it worked out great." She swallows. "When the markets turned a few years ago, Bill couldn't maintain the returns he'd promised his clients. He was in a sticky position. He could have lost his license. He and Dad were best friends, so when he asked your dad to help, of course he said yes. It was supposed to be a tiny loan. A little fibbing with numbers. It was supposed to be a month and then he'd put it all back." A tear sneaks out of her eye and she swipes it away. "He told me what he was doing, and I couldn't sleep for weeks. I was so worried they would get caught." Another tear. "But they didn't. It was easy. Because they were moving money between two different firms and a separate bank, there was no paper trail. The market started going up again, and everyone was making money. The clients *and* us. It seemed too easy." She has to swipe at her eyes. "It *was* too easy. When we had that market correction last January—you remember?"

I nod. I remember everything in Dad's office turned hectic. Clients were losing money, and the phones were ringing off the hook.

Mom glances at Dad again. "Bill wanted Dad to cover again. To double down. Dad refused. I think the pressure was getting to be too much for him. People thought their accounts were down ten percent, but he knew they were down more than that. Most were down to nothing, but he was faking it. He cared about those people, Rob. He wanted us all to make money. With Bill in his ear promising good returns, bringing their friendship into it—I don't think Dad considered the risk when it would all start falling apart."

"So, what?" I say, my voice dark. "Dad was such a great guy?"

She begins crying in earnest, and to my surprise, she's nodding. "Yes. He made some mistakes, but yes. He was a great guy, Robbie."

I swallow hard.

"He wanted to pull the plug," she says. "He told Bill he wanted to come clean. Your father wasn't a dishonest man, but it got away from him. Do you understand that?"

"No." I don't understand any of this.

She shakes her head and puts her hand on the sofa between us. "He was going to replace all the money we'd taken. We were going to borrow against my trust. He was going to put it back, and we'd absorb the hit. He wanted Bill to do the same thing." Another tear, but this time she swipes it away angrily. "Bill didn't want to stop. He wanted Dad to put that trust money into their scheme. They argued, but Dad refused. He thought it was done. He told Bill he was replacing the money and getting out."

I stare at her. "But Bill turned him in."

"Yes. He turned him in. And Rob, he was crafty." Her voice turns hushed. "So very crafty. He'd planned for it. He'd been *ready* for it. He made sure everything pointed at your father. Everything."

I don't know what to say.

"Rob, he couldn't take it," she says. "Your father—he couldn't take it. Bill was coming out looking like the savior, while your dad was the thief. And the worst part was that I had to play along. Bill said he would keep me out of it. Otherwise we'd lose everything. I would have lost *you*, Rob." She puts her hand against my cheek, and I jerk away.

That wounds her, and I don't want to care, but I do. She presses her hand to her stomach. "I didn't know what to do. There was no right path, Rob. Your father was going to turn on Bill, but Marjorie came here, sobbing that she would lose Connor, that we'd all be in prison. We didn't know what to do. It was all a mess, and the press was going crazy. Everyone hated us—you remember."

I do remember. I don't need to remember.

Everyone still hates us.

"Your father couldn't take it," she says. She's stumbling over her words now. "The night—the night he tried—the night he tried—"

"I know what night you're talking about," I say.

"I didn't realize how bad it had gotten for him," she says. "I didn't—I didn't know. I wish I hadn't stormed out. I wish I hadn't left him. I wish I hadn't—"

She dissolves into tears again.

I sit and I wait. I wish all of those things, too. I feel no pity for her.

I'm lying to myself. I feel nothing but pity.

My throat is tight. I put a hand on her shoulder. "Mom."

She reaches out and pulls me against her. She's shaking with the force of her tears. "I never wanted to hurt you, Robbie. I love you. I couldn't lose you. Not with everything else. I couldn't lose you. I never would have left you alone to find that. Please know that. Please. Please don't hate me."

"I don't hate you." I almost choke on the words.

I hate Bill Tunstall. Now more than ever.

She speaks into my shoulder. "Bill came the day after that. He said he would make sure I was kept out of it if I could play the role of clueless wife. If I could be devastated at my husband's actions. If I could be—be *grateful* to him for being such a savior to the community."

"That's why you stayed friendly with them," I murmur. "That's why you kept asking about Connor."

"Yes." Her voice breaks. "It was so hard. You have no idea how hard. And now I've got this job, and every time I leave here, I see how it could be. I could have a life. I could have friends. But I can't. I'm stuck here, because otherwise I lose what little I have left."

"Is that why you've been drinking so much?"

"I wouldn't classify it as *so much*."

I give her a look.

She sighs. "I mentioned to my boss how much I liked the first bottle, so he brought me another, and then we went out to dinner—"

"You went out to *dinner*?"

"As friends! Just as friends." She sniffs hard and mops at her face. "I've been so lonely, Rob. Do you have any idea what it's like to be so lonely?"

"Yes!" I snap. Dad jerks in his sleep, and I lower my voice. "Yes, I do." I grit my teeth and glare at her. "Do you have any idea what my life is like?" She doesn't answer that, and I power on. "You get to run out of here when Dad is too much for you, but I'm the one left behind. Do you know what *that* is like?"

She flinches, but I keep going. "Do you have any idea how much I hate that Bill was in on this, and there's nothing I can do about it? He's probably *still* doing it, but if I turn him in, I'm turning in my own mother. Do you have *any idea*?" I yell.

Dad jerks and moans. He's waking up. He's reacting to the yelling.

I don't care.

Mom looks at him and then back at me. "Please," she says. "Please stop. Please understand."

Dad's moaning is rising in volume.

I ignore him. It takes everything I have, but I ignore him.

"You didn't want to lose me, Mom? Well, too bad. You've lost me."

"Rob—"

I don't listen to what she says.

For once, I'm the one who gets to walk out.

It's after ten, but I know Wegmans will be open. I dig for change in the center console of my car and buy a cup of coffee, then dump a ton of cream and sugar into it.

When I turn from the counter to head for the shadowed alcove under the stairs, I discover one chair is occupied.

Maegan stares up at me in surprise. "Rob."

I'm so thrown that I stand there like an idiot, holding my coffee. "Maegan."

We're trapped in this space, staring at each other. She looks small and hidden, all curled up in the chair in jeans and a green sweater, her hair in a loose braid down over her shoulder.

I shake myself and look away. "Sorry. I'll go sit somewhere else."

"No!" She half rises from her chair. "No. Wait."

I turn back, ready to sit, and I'm surprised when she wraps her arms around me. "I've been so worried about you."

The words are more surprising than the hug, and it takes me a moment to figure out why: I'm not used to anyone worrying about me.

I wrap my arms around her, careful of the coffee, glad to have someone to hold on to. We stand there for a minute or an hour or an eternity.

"I'm sorry I've been such a mess," I say quietly.

"Me too," she says.

"You aren't a mess."

"I have been." She looks up at me, and tears are sparkling on her lashes.

I didn't expect that. "You're crying?" I lift a hand to brush them away.

She makes a sound that's half laugh, half sob. "Yeah. I guess. I haven't been home."

"You snuck out to Wegmans again?"

"Yeah."

"Me too."

Now her eyes widen in surprise. "Want to sit?"

We do. I drop into an armchair, and just like Saturday night, she drops into the microscopic space beside me, half sitting in my lap.

I don't know what's happened to erase all the tension between us, but after the day I've had, I don't mind at all.

"I'm sorry," she says. "I didn't understand what you and Owen were doing. I thought—"

"I know what you thought," I say. "And we were wrong."

"Owen doesn't think so."

I turn my head to look at her. Her eyes are so close. We could share breath. "You talked to Owen?"

She blushes. "I couldn't talk to you. He was worried when you didn't show up for school, so I told him what happened. I went to his house, and his mom overheard us talking."

Great. "So, I guess I'm not going to be best friends with Mrs. Goettler anytime soon."

"She's not your biggest fan. But I think she feels sorry for you."

Double great. I grimace, then frown.

"She's going to make Owen figure out a way to pay for another pair of shoes, and she's going to return them to replace the ones you guys ordered." She hesitates. "She spent a lot of time talking about how stealing is wrong, but she doesn't want to turn Owen in. Or you."

This is all so complicated. Just like the story Mom told me about Dad. Does it make him better in my eyes? Or worse? He was still stealing. He just didn't get the chance to pull the plug.

"Dad said you were arrested." Maegan's eyes are warm and intent on mine. "Are you okay?"

"Yeah." I'm nodding, but this feels like the last few months, when I kept my head down and faked living.

I remember how it felt to finally let loose in Mr. London's office, and I take a deep breath.

"No," I say to Maegan. "No, I'm not okay."

"Do you want to talk about it?" she says.

I'm so sick of secrets and drama and everyone hating me.

She finds my hand and squeezes it. "It's okay," she says. "You don't have to."

"No." I squeeze her hand back. "I want to. I want to tell you everything."

So I do.

CHAPTER FORTY

Maegan

As usual, I have more secrets in my head than I know what to do with.

Somehow, it's different this time. Owen's mother was right—doing the right thing really does mean different things to different people. Nothing is clear-cut, and maybe that's okay.

Rob says he has no proof about what Mr. Tunstall is doing, but even if he did, he doesn't want to turn him in. He doesn't want to destroy his mother. He doesn't want to destroy Connor.

I've been turning it over in my head all night, and I still don't know.

I do know that Rob shouldn't be the one paying the price for all of it. But if I tell someone everything he told me, am I throwing Connor under the bus? What would happen to Rob if his mother went to prison? What would happen to his *father*? Would his life be better than it is now? Or would it be worse?

There's a soft knock at my door before I've turned off my light. It must be Samantha, because my parents' door was closed when I came in, no light shining from under it.

"Come in," I call softly.

The door swings open silently. My father.

I sit bolt upright in bed. "Dad."

"I wanted to talk to you," he says.

I can't read anything from his voice, but I'd rather face him like this, in an old T-shirt and a pair of sweatpants, than how he was this morning.

He seems to be waiting for some kind of response, instead of barreling in here, which I appreciate. I clear my throat. "Come in."

He sits on the edge of my bed and smooths his hand over the coverlet. "I shouldn't have yelled at you this morning. You didn't steal anything. You still should have said something." He stares at me, and his voice takes on a firm note. "But I shouldn't have yelled at you. I didn't want you to be caught up in something else that could damage your future." He pauses. "You're old enough to pick your friends, too. Though I hope you've learned the truth about Rob Lachlan."

I've learned that Rob is loyal and kind. That his moral compass works better than most.

I don't know what to say to my father. This doesn't quite feel like an apology. Then again, maybe it's not supposed to be. Maybe I don't need one.

Dad looks at me. "Sometimes when we're trying to protect the people closest to us, doing the right thing doesn't always look so clear."

I swallow and think about how I kept Samantha's secret. How I'm keeping Rob's.

I consider how Rachel and Drew acted at the dinner table

when Rob was there. They were wrong, for sure, but at the same time, was Rachel trying to protect me from someone she saw as a danger? Did that make her behavior more acceptable?

"I know," I say softly.

"Well, maybe you know," Dad says, "but I'm still learning." He pauses. "Samantha told us how you stood up for her in front of that . . . that . . ." His voice tightens. "That horrible man."

It sounds like he wants to call DavidLitMan something entirely different. "Someone had to," I say.

"I know. I'm glad it was you. He's lucky it wasn't *me*." He gives my shoulder a squeeze. "I'm proud of you."

The words bring a swell of tears to my eyes. "Thanks, Daddy."

He looks at me with a kind of wonder. "Why the tears?"

I sniff and swipe at my face. "I've always thought you were disappointed in me."

"Never," he says, and pulls me into his arms. "Never."

CHAPTER FORTY-ONE

Rob

Wegmans closed at midnight, but I've been sitting in my car for a while. I can't go home. Not yet.

Eventually, I realize I'm going to burn through a tank of gas trying to stay warm. I don't have a heavy coat with me, and it's dropped well below freezing. I can sit here in judgment of my mother and the role she played, but it's not going to keep me warm.

Or fed, now that I think about it. I drive home.

It's after two a.m., but she's still awake. I want to blow past her and storm up to my room, but it's clear she's been crying for a while, and I can't turn off my heart.

I stop in the doorway to the family room. Dad is asleep in his chair. She couldn't get him upstairs alone, either.

"You came back," she says.

"I came back."

"I was worried."

"Yeah. Well." I look away. "I have nowhere to go."

"Rob, please know that none of this was easy for me. Everything I did—after—was to keep you safe. Please know that."

It's tempting to shrug off this statement, but I can hear the emotion in her voice. We've been trapped here together. None of this has been easy for her. I should hate her, but I can't.

"I know," I say quietly.

"Please don't hate me," she whispers.

"I don't hate you." I glance at my father and wish again that I could rewind time. "I don't hate him."

I drop onto the couch beside her and put my face in my hands. "I hate that Bill started it all, and he's the one who's getting away with it."

She rubs my shoulder. "I never wanted this, Rob."

I don't pull away. "I know."

My cell phone vibrates in my pocket, making me jump. No one ever calls me, especially not in the middle of the night, so I jerk it free.

The display is lit up with *Connor Tunstall.*

I stare at the screen for a moment too long, then swipe the bar to answer.

The phone nearly explodes with noise, and I have to hold it away from my ear.

"Connor?" I say.

"Rob." He sounds like someone is choking him. A man is speaking in the background. There's a lot of yelling. "Rob."

"Connor? What—what's going on?"

"Rob, I'm sorry. I'm sorry. I didn't—I had to—"

"Slow down." I'm standing now. I put a hand over my other ear as if that will somehow block all the background noise. "What's going on?"

"I turned him in." He makes another choking sound. "I

didn't—I didn't believe you. When the cops arrested you. But when he was gone this morning, I went through his office. I found the proof. I confronted him about it, and he—he—I can't. I called—I called—I don't know—they're arresting them both. I don't know what to do."

Holy shit.

A man says, "You're going to need to hang up that phone, son."

"Please come, Rob. I know I don't deserve it. But please—"

The line goes dead.

Mom is staring at me, her hands over her mouth. Her fingers are trembling. She must have heard most of what he said.

"It'll be okay," I say, though I have no idea whether that's true. "It'll be okay." My heart is rocketing along so fast that I'm almost dizzy.

Please come. I know I don't deserve it.

My keys are still in my pocket. I thread my fingers through the loop and stand up.

Mom catches my arm. "What are you doing?"

I'm doing what Connor should have done last February. I give Mom's hand a squeeze and then pull free. "I'm going over there."

Half a dozen cop cars line the Tunstall driveway, along with a few unmarked vehicles that I know from experience are probably FBI. All the lights in the house are on.

I don't have to go far to find Connor. He's sitting on the front step, wearing an unzipped parka, his arms wrapped around his midsection.

He barely looks up when I approach.

"I'm so stupid," he says. His voice is rough and dull. A shaky hand pushes the hair back from his face.

He's either shivering from cold or shock or both. I reach out and give the lapel of his jacket a tug. "Zip up," I say, like he's five years old. "How long have you been sitting out here?"

He doesn't obey. "Since they started searching the house."

I sit down next to him. I don't know what to say, but he doesn't seem to mind. We sit in silence, until his breathing slows.

Eventually he shivers, and I punch him in the arm. "Zip up your coat, you idiot."

He sniffs and does it.

"I didn't know," he says. "I realize how stupid that sounds now, but I know you get it."

"Yeah. I get it."

"I should have known."

"So should I." I shrug. "Hell, I was *working* for my dad, and I didn't know."

He lifts a shaking hand to his face, and I realize he's crying.

I don't say anything. I get that, too.

A tight band has a grip on my chest. I don't know what this is going to mean for my mother.

"I thought he was going to kill me," says Connor.

He drops this statement without any preamble, and my head whips around. "What?"

"I thought he was going to kill me." Another sniff. "My father. I found—I found his files. I don't know what I was going to do with them, but he started—he started fighting me for them, and then he was choking me, and Mom was fighting to get him off me . . ." He presses his hands to his eyes.

I hate his father.

"What's going to happen?" I say softly.

The question seems to stabilize him. "They called my aunt. Mom's sister. She's flying in from Portland."

That's not quite what I meant, but he doesn't have the answers I need anyway.

I shift my weight, and Connor looks up in alarm.

"I'm not leaving," I say.

The panic bleeds out of his eyes. "Thanks."

I sigh and look up at the night. "That's what friends are for."

Connor's aunt arrives around sunrise. I'm half-asleep on his front step, but he's in good hands, so I take it as my cue to go home and take a shower.

When I get out, Mom is waiting with red-rimmed eyes and a wilting frame.

"You should go to bed," I tell her.

"You too."

I have to take a deep breath. "I'm worried Bill is going to turn you in, too."

She swallows. Her voice is barely audible. "I know."

I step forward and give her a hug, holding on for a long time.

When I let go, she takes a good look at me. "You're dressed. Where are you going?"

"School," I say.

"Rob, you've been up for twenty-four hours."

"I need another hour."

"But why?"

"I need to talk to someone."

"Mr. Lachlan!" says Mr. London. "I expected you yesterday."

"Sorry," I say back. "I was arrested."

The words have the effect I expected. The good nature slips off his face, replaced with concern. "Are you okay?"

The fact that he cares almost makes me collapse from exhaustion. "Yeah." I take a breath. "Can I talk to you about it?"

"Of course." He raises the counter.

When we're in his office and the door is closed, I tell him everything.

Everything everything.

When I'm done, he's staring at me, his fingers steepled in front of his face.

I feel both lighter and heavier after sharing it all, and his silence is killing me. "Would you please say something?"

He sighs. "I think I need to process all this." He leans back in his chair. "I'm proud of you for realizing that playing Robin Hood isn't the answer."

I blush and look away. "Yeah. Well. Everything else is still a mess." I scrub my hands over my face. "I'm really worried about my mom."

"I can see why."

I swallow hard. "Is there a way she can get out of this? Is there a way I can protect her somehow?"

His eyes darken with pity. "I don't know, Rob."

Of course he doesn't. He's a high school librarian. Why would he have any idea? I was so foolish to come here.

He leans in against the desk. "But," he says, "if there's one thing librarians are good at, it's finding answers." He pulls a note-pad out of his desk. "I'm going to write you a pass for first period. Take it to your teacher and come right back, okay?"

I stare at him in surprise. "Okay."

"Don't worry." He pats my hand. "We'll figure it out."

CHAPTER FORTY-TWO

Maegan

When Rob walks into first period with a yellow pass slip, I nearly fall out of my chair. I didn't expect him to show up for class this morning. He looks rough, pale and unshaven, and his eyes are a little wild. He hands the pass to Mrs. Quick, who glances at it and nods.

Rob looks so scattered that I don't expect him to look my way, but he does.

He slides a note onto my calculus book. "I can't stay," he whispers. His fingers brush across mine, and then he's gone.

I carefully unfold the note.

Connor turned in his parents. Mom might be arrested, too. I'm with Mr. London. I'll tell you everything at lunch.

I almost gasp out loud.

Lunch. I glance at the clock. Lunch is three hours away.

I start counting the minutes.

Whether by coincidence or accident, I run into Rachel in the cafeteria. I'm still in line, but she's walking away from the register with a soda. She flinches from my gaze and turns away without saying a word.

I step into her path. "Hey," I say. "Rachel." I hold my breath. "I'm sorry."

That gets her attention. "You're sorry?"

"Yes. Kind of. I didn't consider that you were looking out for me."

"Yes. I was." I can't read her expression.

"Drew was really mean to Rob. He didn't deserve that. I know you were trying to protect me, but that doesn't mean it's okay to be mean to him."

She says nothing, so I keep going. In for a penny, in for a pound, I guess. "And I don't like the way you stand by and let Drew say mean things to me, too."

She frowns. "I—I've felt bad about that for a long time." She takes a breath. "That's kind of my fault."

"Your fault!"

She looks away and fidgets. "Yeah. I don't—I don't know how to explain."

"Try." My voice comes out too sharp, so I soften it with, "Please, Rachel. I miss you."

She takes a deep breath and meets my eyes. "I was so mad at you when you cheated."

It's literally the last thing I expected her to say. "*What*? Why?"

"Because you're so smart!" she explodes. "You practically had straight A's last year. You're in five AP classes. I can barely handle *one* honors class."

I jerk back.

She's not done. "I struggle for every single grade I get. You sail through AP classes with no effort—"

"It takes effort, Rach."

"Fine." Her voice cracks. "Fine. It takes effort. But I can't do it. You would have sailed right into college, probably with a ton of scholarships."

"Yeah, maybe. But I don't play any sports. I barely have any extracurriculars. I mean—"

"Would you listen to yourself?"

The rushed passion in her voice stops me short.

She swipes at her eyes. "This is so stupid. You're completely missing the point."

She's so clearly upset about this that I can't decide whether to be angry or compassionate. "What *is* the point? What does this have to do with Drew?"

"How do you think I felt when a girl like you thought she had to cheat on the SATs? I mean, you're right. Drew makes asshole comments, but he's trying to make *me* feel better." She sniffs. "Look at your perfect sister. Look at your perfect *family*."

And then I get it. I think about Samantha and all the pressure she was under—and how I compared myself to her. Just like Rachel was apparently comparing herself to me.

I stare at her. "Rachel. We're not perfect."

"You kind of *are*," she says. "You have everything you want, and you almost threw it all away. I'm not even going to be able to go to college."

"You're going to go to college, too!" I say to her. "Your dad used to brag about how he'd been smart enough to save for his little girl to—"

"Not anymore." She sniffs again. "It's gone."

"What do you mean, it's gone?" But as soon as I ask the question, I know. "Rob's dad?" I whisper.

She nods and ducks her head to swipe her cheek on the shoulder of her sweater. "No one knows, okay? Well, Drew knows. Dad's still really upset about it. He doesn't want the other cops to think he was stupid enough to be taken in."

Now I understand her attitude about Rob. I understand the vitriol behind Drew's comments.

She looks down at me. "I'm sorry, though," she says. "I know this is about me. I shouldn't have been taking it out on you."

"I should have been a better friend," I say. "I didn't know you were feeling this way."

"*I* should have been a better friend," she says. "What happened wasn't your fault."

I step forward and wrap my arms around her. "No more secrets," I say.

She nods against my hair. "No more secrets." She hesitates. "So, are we going to have lunch together again?"

"Not today. I promised Rob I would eat with him."

She draws back. Her expression has evened out.

I wince. "He didn't do it, Rachel. His dad did."

She frowns. "I know."

There's still some trust to be earned back there. At least I understand it better now. I bite the edge of my lip. "Maybe we can get coffee after school?" I hesitate. "I have a lot to tell you."

Her expression softens. "I can't wait."

She heads off to her usual table, where Drew is waiting.

"Soup, dear?" says the cafeteria lady.

"Yes, please." It's broccoli and cheese, my favorite. They sprinkle shredded cheese on top and serve it with a biscuit. It's amazing.

Owen Goettler comes to mind. I can see him from here, a lone cheese sandwich in front of him.

I clear my throat and catch the cafeteria lady's eye. "I'll have two," I say.

By the time I get to the table, Rob and Owen are sitting there. Without a word, I slide the soup off my tray and give it to Owen. Then I sit down beside Rob. He takes my hand and holds it between us.

Owen is staring at me in surprise.

"Nothing was missed," I say, feeding his own words back to him. "No one was hurt."

"You stole this?" he says in surprise.

"What?" I say. "No! I just mean it's fine. I can afford an extra soup without hurting anyone."

His face softens. "Thanks." He picks up the spoon.

I look at Rob. "Are you okay?"

He doesn't look it, but he nods anyway. "Mr. London's sister is an attorney with Legal Aid. We had a long call this morning.

She's going to help Mom arrange a 'surrender,' in the hopes that by testifying against Connor's parents, she can avoid jail time."

I squeeze his hand. "Rob. Are *you* okay?"

"Yeah." He rubs his eyes with his free hand. "But I'm exhausted. Ms. London says Dad will have to go to a state care facility for a while." His voice breaks, but he catches it and steadies it. "Because I can't do all that by myself. Am I a bad person that it's kind of a relief?"

It's such a crazy question that I'm shocked he seems completely sincere. "No. Rob. No. You're the most decent person I know."

"No," he says. "Not by a long shot."

"You are," Owen says. He hesitates. "You're more decent than I am, and I never expected to say that."

Rob looks at him. "I'm still not introducing you to Zach Poco."

Owen doesn't smile. "If they take your mom, what happens to you?"

"I turn eighteen in six weeks. Ms. London says they can appoint a temporary guardian to make sure I stay alive, but I can stay in my house." He pauses and takes a heavy breath. "Until I can't."

I squeeze his hand again. "Who's going to be the temporary guardian?"

"I don't know yet." His voice cracks again. "But Mr. London said he would do it. He asked his sister to get the necessary papers." He presses his fingers into his eyes. "I didn't know what to say. I don't deserve that."

"You do," I whisper, putting my forehead against his. "You do."

EPILOGUE

SIX WEEKS LATER

Maegan

I've never really thought about teachers living in normal houses, but of course they do. Mr. London and his husband live in a townhouse in the southern part of the county. The garage door is open, as Rob promised, and I slide past a small Honda to get to the door at the back. When I knock, Rob throws open the door.

I haven't seen him in weeks, though we've been able to text. Right now, he looks ready to burst, like a kid on Christmas morning, so I smile. "So, are you all moved i—"

He stops me with a kiss, catching my elbows in his hands. "Yes. Come in."

It's a basement apartment, sort of. He's got a bedroom and a private bathroom, along with a tiny refrigerator and the small television that must have come from his house.

His mother has to serve ninety days.

His house has to be sold.

His father has to remain in state care.

But Rob is okay. He had to move out of his house so it could be put on the market. I expected the decision to upset him, but it actually seemed to be a relief. He said he felt like a ghost, living there alone with all the bad memories.

This moment, right now, when he's inviting me into his temporary living arrangement, is the lightest I've ever seen him.

"I love it," I say, looking around.

"Owen came over yesterday."

"He told me he was going to." Once Rob's attendance grew scarce, I invited Owen to join me and Rachel and Drew at lunch. I was worried they wouldn't get along, but to my surprise, Drew likes Owen's quirky honesty—and Owen takes none of Drew's crap. Drew helped get Owen a job in his parents' restaurant, and they work the same shifts, so Drew's been giving him a ride. "What did he think?"

"He thinks I need an Xbox."

I glance at the ceiling and tease, "The landlords don't hassle you?"

"They're great. They have books everywhere." He smiles, but for the first time, a bit of sadness sneaks into his expression. "They've been helping me keep up with schoolwork while everything else has been going on."

"Nothing like living with two teachers to make sure your GPA doesn't slip."

"You're not kidding. How's Samantha?"

Duke is allowing her to defer her scholarship until next year, which shocked my sister. Despite everything that happened with David, I think this news was more than she expected, especially since David lost his job. Mom is telling Sam to keep her options open, so right this very instant, my sister is enrolling to take her spring courses online, so she can go back as a sophomore if she can find a balance between motherhood and school and lacrosse. "She's finally wearing maternity clothes, but she wants me to tell you that she could still kick your ass on the lacrosse field."

He laughs. "I believe it."

"Also . . . Craig finally asked her out, and she said yes."

His eyebrows go way up. "The Taco Taco guy?"

I nod.

"Wow."

"She's been going over there a few nights a week, and she kept telling me that the guacamole was the only thing that settled her stomach." I roll my eyes, but my voice softens. "Apparently they've been talking a lot."

"Good for her."

I smile. "Have you heard from Connor lately?"

Rob sobers. I know from our texting that Connor had to move to Oregon to live with his aunt. "He's having a hard time with it." Rob pauses. "We talk a lot."

I wonder if it's easier that Connor got the chance to start over somewhere new, instead of having to endure school the way Rob did. Then again, he moved across the country in the middle of his senior year. He lost both parents at once.

"I'm glad he has you," I say.

"Alex says maybe I could fly out over spring break."

Alex is Mr. London. Rob's casual use of his first name makes me smile. "It's so good to see you like this," I say.

He blushes. "Like the old Rob Lachlan?"

"No." I lean in to kiss him. "The new one."

ACKNOWLEDGMENTS

Call It What You Want is my tenth published novel, and I've gotten to the point in my writing career where I just want to weep and thank everyone for helping me get this far. The UPS man. The grocery store cashier. The guy two doors down for letting me know the siding was coming loose on my house. But I realize I have to narrow it down a *little*, so here we go.

My husband, Michael, comes first. Always. Yesterday I was at Starbucks writing for five hours, and I texted him in the evening and said, "How's everything going?" He wrote back that he'd cleaned the house, given the kids baths, ordered pizza, and SAVED ME BREADSTICKS. He's amazing. You can't have him. Thank you, Michael, for everything.

My mother, as always, is a constant inspiration. You would not be reading these words if not for her unwavering encouragement when I was growing up—and even now. She doesn't read many of my books, and she might not even be aware of what I write in the acknowledgments section, but she knows I love her, and I hope she knows what a profound influence her positivity has been in my life. (I literally copied this paragraph from the acknowledgments in *A Curse So Dark and Lonely*. *Shh*. Let's see if she notices.)

Bobbie Goettler is my BFFOAT (Best Friend Forever of All Time) and has read almost every word I've ever written, since the beginning, when I was writing about silly vampires running around the suburbs. Thank you, Bobbie, for being such an amazing friend. Your support over the years has meant everything to me. I love that my kids call you Aunt Bobbie, and when they refer to their "cousins," they include your kids. For a friendship that started on a message board about writing, I think that's pretty powerful.

My amazing agent, Mandy Hubbard, has been a wonderful source of guidance for my writing and my career. From supportive text messages to amazing email GIFs to listening to me sob over Google chat—plus all the actual agent businessy-type stuff—Mandy is beyond compare.

Mary Kate Castellani is my fearless editor at Bloomsbury, and I cannot thank her enough for every moment she spends working with me. Whenever I think something is good enough, she pushes me to make it better. When it's better, she pushes me to make it the best. Mary Kate has a brilliant vision and always finds the story I didn't know I was looking for. Thank you, Mary Kate, for everything.

Speaking of Bloomsbury, tremendous thanks to Cindy Loh, Claire Stetzer, Lizzy Mason, Courtney Griffin, Erica Barmash, Cristina Gilbert, Anna Bernard, Brittany Mitchell, Phoebe Dyer, Beth Eller, Melissa Kavonic, Jeanette Levy, as well as

Diane Aronson and the copyediting team, along with everyone else at Bloomsbury who played a role in putting this book into your hands. I wish I knew everyone's name, so I could thank you all individually. Please know that my gratitude is endless, and I can't tell you how much I appreciate your efforts on my behalf.

It takes a village to make a book come together, and this book is no exception. Many people read this manuscript, offered support, or gave me feedback and input and insights. Special thanks to Michelle MacWhirter, Diana Peterfreund, Lee Bross, Shyla Stokes, Steph Messa, Emile Horne, and Joy George. I couldn't have gotten to this point without you all. Thank you.

A lot of research went into this book. Many thanks to Special Agent Tom Simmons of the FBI for insights into how Rob's dad's crimes would be handled (and the aftermath). Also, tremendous thanks to my friend Maegan Chaney-Bouis, MD, for insight into both Rob's father's medical condition and Owen's TBI effects. (You all need an FBI agent and a doctor in your text list. I swear it makes me feel like such a badass.)

Tremendous thanks to book bloggers, bookstagrammers, and book vloggers. I appreciate everyone who takes time to talk about my books on social media. I still remember the first bloggers who spread the word about my debut novel in 2012, and I won't forget anyone since. Your support means everything to me. Thank you.

Before I "quit the day job" to write full time, I worked in finance for almost twenty years. That background gave me the experience and insight to write a story about some truly shady people. (I knew all those learning modules about how to spot criminal activity would come in handy one day!) I had the privilege of working with many fine financial advisers and support staff who truly do care about their clients, none of whom were like Rob Lachlan Sr. or Bill Tunstall. Special shout-out to all my old CSA friends from MindAlign, especially Rhonda Barth, Stephanie Martin, Rachel Pinner Lobdell, Laura Kurtz, Amy Kerr, Jenny Krejci Dimmitt, Carla Tyner, Emily Reed, and Jaime Rogers. I love and miss you all. Thank goodness for Facebook.

Finally, huge thanks to the Kemmerer boys, Jonathan, Nick, Sam, and not-such-a-baby Zach. Thank you for being such wonderful boys, and for letting Mommy follow her dreams. I can't wait to watch you soar as you follow your own.